MINE
to crave

New York Times & *USA Today* Bestselling Author

CYNTHIA
EDEN

Copy-editing by: J. R. T. Editing

PROLOGUE

"Going to shoot me?" The woman before him taunted. A woman who should have been a ghost. *"Going to leave me to die alone? Again?"*

Drake Archer circled her. They were in a small apartment, and the scent of death already filled the air around them.

The beautiful woman before him—Anna Jean—she had a knife. He had to get that knife away from her.

She's already hurt too many people. I have to stop her. He opened his hand. Held it out to her. "Give me the knife."

She laughed at him.

Her laugh was so familiar. Once that laughter had seemed to warm him, now it made ice grow around his heart because he saw her for exactly what she was.

Her beauty only went skin deep. Evil was at her core.

Drake started to shake his head. How had he been so wrong about her? How?

And in that one moment, Anna Jean attacked. She lunged forward and drove her knife into Drake's stomach, and then she yanked, jerking the blade to the right. He fell back, stunned, as his blood pumped from him and a chill seemed to consume his whole body.

"This time, you get to die," Anna Jean told him and she was smiling.

His knees sagged. Drake hit the floor.

No, no, he wasn't supposed to go out like this. And...it was all his fucking fault. He'd trusted the wrong woman. Fell for lying eyes.

Anna Jean wasn't going to stop. She was a killer, straight to her soul. There were others in the apartment. Others that she would take out with a cold, calculated brutality. He had to stop her.

His blood soaked his shirt. He tried to look up, to move, but his whole body trembled.

Anna Jean drew closer to him. He could feel her gaze, even though he couldn't see her face. "Maybe he did love me," she mused. "Because if he'd been smart, he would've shot me when he had the chance. Instead, I had the pleasure of gutting him." Her voice dropped. "That's what you get for leaving me in the cold."

I never loved you. When Anna Jean moved to step around him, his hand flew out. His fingers locked around her ankle. "No..." Drake growled.

"Oh, darling, relax, I'll slit your throat and end things soon."

And she would. Without any hesitation. When *he'd* been the one to foolishly hesitate.

He would never hesitate again. Drake tried to heave his body up. *I have to stop her.*

He would do anything...*anything*...to stop her.

Drake pushed through the pain even as more of his blood pumped from his body. He managed to grab the knife that Anna Jean had used on him. She wasn't expecting another attack from him, not then. She thought he was too weak.

Her mistake. Drake lunged up, and he drove the knife into her heart. Anna Jean gasped. Her eyes widened. She turned her head to look at him.

"I didn't...miss this time," he managed to tell her. No, he'd ended Anna Jean.

She died in his arms.

And his blood kept flowing out...

***

Drake jerked upright in bed, his body soaked in sweat and the memories still twisting in his head. Because that hadn't been a dream. No nightmare to mess with his head.

That had been his sick reality.

His hand slid over the newest scar on his stomach. A wound that had come far too close to taking him out.

Only he'd survived.

His ex-lover hadn't.

Anna Jean...

She wasn't his first kill. Not even close. But she was the one who haunted him. Because of her, he'd learned an important lesson.

Drake would never again fall for another woman's lies.

Not-fucking-ever.

CHAPTER ONE

Drake Archer wasn't looking for trouble. He didn't want complications. He didn't want questions.

He wanted to fuck. Wanted to sink into the arms of a sweet-smelling woman and pretend the nightmares that chased him every time he closed his eyes weren't real.

Even though he knew they were.

The club was packed. *His* club. He owned the casino and the club that was attached to it. So he stood on the top floor of his domain, behind the tinted glass, and he watched the crowd. Bodies gyrated down there. Women and men heaved against each other. Music was pounding, but he didn't hear the beat or any of the voices that must be rising down there. He'd soundproofed this room. He liked to watch the others, but he sure as hell didn't want anyone seeing—or hearing—him.

Some women wore glittering dresses. Some wore scraps that were designed to tempt and tease.

His gaze swept over the crowd, moving a few more feet, as his attention slowly shifted toward the bar.

Then his eyes narrowed.

The woman standing at the bar—her fingers curled around the slender stem of a martini glass—she wasn't like the others.

Her hair was a dark red, glinting under the lights. It skimmed her shoulders, moving slightly as she turned her head and gazed—*right up at me.*

She wore all black. Not some seductive dress. But pants and a form fitting turtle-neck. She reminded him of a sexy jewel thief for a moment, and his lips quirked at the image.

He put his hand to the glass when another man approached her. A slickly dressed guy, oozing pompous confidence and cash. The jerk put his hand on her shoulder.

She shrugged him away.

Then she kept staring right up at Drake.

His jewel thief truly acted as if she saw him. Impossible, of course. There was no way that she could see through that tinted glass.

She crooked her finger at him.

Hell, no.

A wide smile flashed across her face, and the redhead crooked her finger one more time. A dare. A taunt.

She *did* know he was there. Maybe she'd gotten chatty with the wait staff. Maybe the bartender had told her that Drake would occasionally invite women up to his private lounge.

But the redhead was dead wrong about the way this scene was played. He didn't dance to anyone else's tune. A pretty face and a sexy body wasn't about to get to him.

He needed, he wanted, but *he* was the one always in control.

In business and in the bedroom, Drake knew how to dominate.

He wouldn't be going to the little redhead.

He dropped his hand.

That just wasn't the way he worked.

***

Jasmine Bennett's heart was about to burst right out of her chest. And, thanks to the ever pounding music, she was pretty sure that her ear drums might be about to burst, too.

"Let me buy you a drink," the guy next to her said, and the fellow's lips brushed over her ear as he leaned in real close to make that offer.

She shoved him back. He was in the way. The last thing she wanted was for Drake Archer to think that she was involved with this bozo. She'd planned too hard for this moment. There was no way some drunk playboy was going to wreck her night.

"Not interested," Jasmine gritted out. Talk about not taking a hint. The guy just couldn't get it to save his life. This was the third time. The *third time* that she'd told him to back off. But he wasn't backing anywhere.

He was crowding even closer to her. The guy seemed to have bathed in cologne, too—the cloying scent was about to choke her.

"I've got other plans for the night," she told him, keeping her voice firm. Plans that involved her getting invited for a personal meet and greet with Drake Archer. Failure wasn't an option for her. She *had* to get up there. Access to that private lounge of his was her end-goal for the night.

A desperate woman would do some very, very desperate things.

"No, love, you don't have other plans." His hand locked around her wrist. "You're coming with me."

That was the moment when Jasmine realized that the guy wasn't quite as drunk as he'd appeared to be. Swallowing, Jasmine glanced down at her wrist. His fingers had closed around her in a too tight grip. An unbreakable one.

Oh, hell. Had her past just caught up with her?

"Now you don't want to start a scene here, do you?" he murmured. "Because that could just get embarrassing for you."

She'd thought her heartbeat was racing before. The frantic beat now shook her whole chest.

"We're gonna walk out of here," he said, his mouth right against her ear. "We'll head to the parking garage, and then you're gonna play things nice and easy."

She was? Since when?

But he kept talking. The guy told her, "You're gonna get in my car, and I'll be taking you back home."

Since he was being all chatty, Jasmine could hear the Texas drawl in his words.

That drawl had her muscles locking. Home was the last place she wanted to be, and she sure as heck wasn't going to play the good girl and just march along with the man.

"You have me confused with someone else," Jasmine said. She tugged on her wrist. No give at all. "Before this goes too far, you need to let me go. Then you need to walk out of this club. Just—go."

He grinned. He was a fairly handsome guy, but he creeped her out. "No," he told her, "I know exactly who you are—and you're worth way too much money for me to walk away."

She'd tried to warn the guy. He should have listened to her. Did the fool really think she cared about making a scene? Like embarrassment was an issue for her.

The way Jasmine figured it, she had two options. She could scream her head off, but with the music pounding, it was highly doubtful that anyone would hear her or try to intervene.

So that left option two. Throw the jerk off-guard. He was stronger than her physically—hence the unbreakable grip—but...all attacks didn't have to involve physical strength. There were lots of other areas in which she excelled.

She'd always been told that she was one hell of a kisser.

Instead of trying to pull away from him, she turned toward him and Jasmine put her mouth right on his. She felt the ripple of surprise that went through him. Obviously, the guy had expected her to fight for her freedom.

He should have read her file more thoroughly. She was all about doing the unexpected. She leaned into him, arching slightly and, sure enough, she felt his grip on her wrist start to ease.

Your mistake, buddy.

***

The redhead was kissing the jerk.

What kind of game was she playing? Drake had been about to turn away from the glass when he saw her rise onto her toes and push her mouth against the man's.

Drake's hands clenched at his sides. He didn't know the woman. Didn't care who she kissed. No, he *shouldn't* care.

But I want her.

And if Drake wanted her...

I'll take her.

He pulled out his phone. "Get the redhead at the bar," he barked the order. "And—"

She yanked away from the dark-haired stranger's embrace. Turned on her heel and *ran.*

Drake's brows shot up.

The crowd swallowed her almost instantly and Drake saw the fury harden the other man's face as he surged after her.

"Stop the redhead and the asshole who is following her." She'd been the only redhead at the bar, and Drake knew his security team would already have her image in front of them.

He couldn't see her in that crowd. Not even a glimpse of her hair.

But he did notice that the STAFF door to the right of the bar was swinging closed. That door led to the stock room—and to a flight of back stairs that his employees used. He knew exactly where those stairs would take the redhead.

The night had just gotten a little more interesting.

He turned on his heel and decided to give chase.

It wasn't like he had to even work hard at the chase. Just a few feet outside of his lounge, a private elevator waited for him. That elevator was the only way to access his lounge. Drake pushed a button on the wall, and his elevator immediately opened. When he stepped inside, the mirrored walls tossed his reflection right back at him.

A flick of his hand and a quick press of his fingers had the elevator heading straight down to the parking garage.

At this rate, he just might beat her before she had a chance to escape.

In seconds, the elevator doors were opening again. He took his time strolling down the hallway, and when he reached the end of that small space, he typed in his security code on the keypad. The door opened and Drake found himself in the cavernous parking garage.

It was close to three a.m., and the folks in his club and casino weren't about to pull it in for the night. Vegas didn't sleep, and he knew this town was going strong.

He stilled for a moment and heard the fast and frantic pounding of footsteps as someone rushed down the stairs to the right. Leaning back against the stone wall of the garage, Drake crossed his arms over his chest and he waited.

Five...

Four...

Three...

Two...

She flew down the stairs. Her hair swirled around her face as she ran out of that stairwell and—

The dark-haired man was right behind her. He grabbed her arm and yanked her back.

The man snarled, "You're not getting away, Jasmine!"

Drake was in the shadows, and he knew they hadn't seen him, but he could see the woman's face clearly—and he didn't like the fear that flashed across her delicate features.

Women were to be fucked. They were to be enjoyed. They weren't to be afraid.

They also weren't to be trusted, but that was another rule he'd learned...

The man's hands were locked tightly around the woman's arms, and she was struggling against him.

She fired at the guy, "You're making a mistake! Just *stop*—"

"Let her go." Drake stepped from the shadows as his arms fell back to his sides. He hadn't raised his voice. Just kept it low. A few ladies from his past had told him that he had a low and lethal voice.

What the hell ever.

All Drake knew was that his voice usually got action.

It got action right then, too. The woman gave a yelp, and the man swore.

But the fool didn't let the lady go.

Jasmine.

Drake liked that name.

"This is personal, buddy," the man snapped at him. "You just need to mind your own business."

"Oh, but it is my business." Drake waved a hand toward the parking garage. "My casino, my club, my parking garage. All very much *my* business." He cocked his head as he studied his prey. "So when a lady gets accosted at my place, well, you can imagine that tends to piss me off." He kept his eyes on the man. The guy had dark hair, thinning a bit, a broad forehead, and a too perfect tan. Drake pretty much hated the fool on sight. "Let her go," Drake ordered, "then get the hell off my property."

More footsteps pounded in that stairwell. Drake's gaze lifted just a bit, moving over the man's shoulder. The security team was right on time.

Swallowing, the guy dropped his hold. "This is a huge mistake," he began.

Nodding, Drake said, "Yes, it is."

The redhead quickly made her way to Drake's side. As she neared, Drake caught the sweet rush of her vanilla scent.

"No!" The man's face had flushed a dark red. "You don't know who she is! She's—"

"Some men just can't take no for an answer," the redhead murmured. "You would think when a woman ran away that would be enough of a clue."

The guy growled and lunged toward her.

The security team locked their arms around him and jerked the idiot right back.

And the redhead sidled even closer to Drake. That vanilla scent was tempting. The lady smelled good enough to eat.

Drake had a very big appetite.

"Get him off my property," Drake ordered. He pointed at the struggling SOB. "If I ever see you at *any* of my casinos or clubs again," and *Archer Entertainment* was becoming huge, "then you're going to be sorry." Because Drake knew too many ways to make a man pay.

He had his own law. His own rules.

The redhead's hand curled around Drake's arm. "I-I...thank you."

The guards hauled away the jerk. But he kept shouting. Dumbass. The man didn't know when to shut up.

"You're the one who'll be sorry!" The words thundered from the dumbass in question. "I'm Wayne Hardin. I'm a bounty—"

Heavy, metal doors swung shut behind him, finally stopping the guy's snarling words.

The woman stepped in front of Drake. She was about five foot eight, maybe five nine so she had to tilt her head back to stare up at him. This close, he could see that her skin was a light gold, and a faint dusting of freckles scattered across her nose. Her eyes were dark—deep. He hadn't expected that darkness. Her lips were red and full.

A beauty, no doubt, with her heart-shaped face, sharp cheekbones, and kiss-me lips. Plump, full, and red, those lips begged him to have a bite.

Her body was slender, but curved in all the right places. And her scent...

"Maybe you shouldn't kiss strangers..." His words came out as a growl. "That's a real bad habit, princess."

She nodded, but then said, "Desperate times can call for desperate actions."

Those sure weren't the words he'd expected. He leaned toward her.

"You're Drake Archer."

"Guilty." He'd confessed to owning the casino, so her knowing his identity wasn't exactly a huge surprise. He'd made headlines in the Vegas press when he opened the Archer's Arrow Casino a month before. He owned four other casinos, but three of them were in Biloxi, Mississippi, and his biggest place was in New Orleans.

He was already jonesing for a trip back to the Big Easy. That place had become home for him.

And I'll be heading home very soon.

She smiled up at him. Her smile took him off-guard because he hadn't anticipated the woman's dimples. Cute, curving dimples that winked on either side of her mouth.

She was sexy. She had deep, dark, bedroom eyes. Curves that made him hard.

And...a damn cute smile.

"Thanks for being my hero tonight, Drake Archer."

He had to laugh. "Trust me, I'm not exactly hero material." He was more used to playing the villain of the piece.

She was still touching him. He was far too aware of her touch. He could actually feel the warmth of her hand through his suit coat. What was up with that?

"Why did you kiss him?" Wait, shit, had he just asked that question?

Her head tilted a little to the right as she studied him. "You were watching me."

He didn't reply. She already knew he'd been watching from upstairs. She'd crooked that finger, after all.

And here I am.

His shoulders stiffened as he stepped away from her.

She blinked a few times, appearing a bit lost.

"If you'd wanted to get fucked..." he said, and it wasn't hard to make his voice cold and unemotional. Plenty of folks said that ice water ran through his veins, not blood. "Then all you had to do was ask."

Her lips parted in surprise, but she didn't speak.

Fair enough. Drake gave a little nod. He'd never been the sort to ask twice. He also wasn't the romancing kind. "You'll be safe for the rest of the night. My men won't let that guy get within fifty feet of the Arrow." But now it was time for him to leave. He'd thought that getting close to her would satisfy his curiosity. He'd been wrong.

Instead of being satisfied, he wanted to learn more about her.

Drake knew that was a definite sign he needed to back off. He eased to the side. Straightened his coat. And took a step forward.

"You're just...going to leave me now?"

She had a faint accent in her voice. There one second, gone the next. Definitely something from the West. Maybe Texas? There were times when Drake's voice slipped, too, and he let his southern accent roll out with a hard rumble.

That usually happened when he was angry. Or aroused.

"Head back into the club," he told her and he didn't look back as he began to make his way toward the elevator that would take him to his private lounge. "I'll send orders for the bartender to give you whatever you want—"

"I know what I want." Her voice was soft. Seductive.

Drake stopped.

"I-I have to ask, though...is that the way it works?"

His back teeth clenched.

"The ladies you take upstairs to your private room...they all *ask*?"

Those women knew the rules going in. Sex. Hot. Fast. Hard. No promises. No ties.

Ties were the last thing he wanted.

He turned back to look at her. "You came to this place looking for me."

She backed up a bit.

He let his lips curl and knew his smile wasn't going to be reassuring. "Be very careful. You don't want to play with me."

He expected her to scurry away.

But her chin notched into the air. "Maybe I do," she said and her voice made his cock jerk. Sex and sin—that was what she sounded like. Taking her time, she walked toward him. He noticed her shoes then. High, black heels. So she wasn't as tall as he'd thought.

And those heels were definitely fuck-me shoes. *She can keep them on for me, but I don't want her wearing anything else.*

The vanilla scent teased his nose once more. "I came here looking for you."

Ah, a confession.

"I know you watch from up above, like a king surveying his land."

He shrugged. "Maybe I just don't like crowds." A car horn echoed through the garage.

Why was he still standing there? Why hadn't he left her already?

Her hand touched his chest.

The heat hit him again, rushing right from her hand to his heart.

And his dick.

Ah, yes, that would be the reason I haven't left.

"I want to go upstairs with you." She licked her lips, a sensual glide of her little pink tongue. "I need to go up there."

He cocked a brow.

"So I'm asking, all right?" Her voice was breathy, and he hesitated. Was that quiver from excitement—like he sure wanted to think?

Or fear?

Unfortunately, Drake was too well-acquainted with fear.

But he offered his arm to her. He saw the quick exhale that she gave. That smile of hers flashed again.

Drake had to reassess. The smile was disarming with its flashing dimples. But it wasn't cute, as he'd first thought.

Her smile was killer.

***

"You're making a mistake!" Wayne Hardin snapped as the two goons dragged him out of the casino's parking garage.

"No, it's your mistake buddy." Goon Number One shoved him so hard that Wayne stumbled out onto the street. A taxi missed him by about five inches, and the angry horn had him jerking.

The guards glared at him as Wayne staggered to his feet.

"You heard the boss," Goon One said. "Stay away from his business."

And the guy's business was now Jasmine? This was a headache he didn't need.

He reached inside his coat.

"Don't!" The sharp bark came from both guards.

Wayne stilled. "I wasn't reaching for a weapon. You two already patted me down. You *know* I'm not armed. I was getting my ID!"

They turned away.

"I'm a bounty hunter! That little redhead who just sucked in your boss—she's wanted in Texas!"

The door slammed shut behind them.

"Sonofabitch." Wayne huffed out a hard breath as the lights of Vegas blazed down on him. Bright, blinking lights. So far away from the darkness of his Texas nights. "I hate this town," he muttered.

He tilted back his head and stared up at the Arrow. Jasmine was in there. Thinking she was all nice and snug. Safe for the night. Safely away from him.

She was dead wrong.

He intended to collect on the bounty that was being offered for her. Giving up wasn't part of his personality.

Soon enough, she'd be the one tossed into the street. Maybe she thought cuddling close to Drake Archer would offer her some kind of protection.

Think again, sweetheart.

He'd be waiting for her ass to hit the street. And when it did...

You're mine, Jasmine. He'd take her back to Texas, bound and gagged if necessary.

CHAPTER TWO

The door shut behind her with a faint click. Jasmine absolutely didn't flinch, but she wanted to, and her muscles ached from stiffness. Her whole body was locked down because she didn't want to show any weakness in front of Drake.

I'm here. I just have to take this whole business one step at a time.

"What's your name?"

His voice rolled over her. Low and hard, a sexy, deep growl that had caught her off-guard when she'd heard him speak in the garage.

He had caught her off-guard. The shadows had surrounded him. Made Drake appear dark and dangerous. Well, he *was* dark and dangerous. Tanned skin. Tall and muscled, with broad shoulders that just stretched and stretched.

Yum.

"Your name."

Crap. She'd just been standing there, staring into his green eyes. Talk about not playing it cool. "Jasmine."

Wait, she probably should have given him a fake name, but no...that jerk downstairs had called her Jasmine, hadn't he? It was better to just stick to the truth. A bit, anyway. She forced herself to smile. "Last names aren't important, are they?"

Hers was, and she planned to keep her mouth closed about it.

"You don't look like the type." He headed toward the bar on the right side of the room. There were at least four giant bars downstairs, but the guy had his own stash up there in his private lounge area.

Someone was overindulged a bit.

He popped open a champagne bottle. Poured the bubbly into a slender flute, then brought it back to her.

She took the flute quickly. Gulped down the champagne.

His brows rose. "Not the type," he said again, voice musing.

She was so messing this up. "What type is that?"

His gaze swept over her. Lingered on her breasts. Her hips. Her legs. The green of his eyes seemed to heat, and Jasmine found herself clutching the champagne flute in a too tight grip. So tightly that she was afraid she might just shatter the thing.

"You aren't dressed for seduction."

Mostly because she didn't have tons of clothing options at that moment. But, jeez, hadn't he seen her shoes? Those were kick-ass sexy. She shifted her feet a bit, hoping to draw his attention there.

His gaze came back to her face. "Thief."

It was a good thing she'd gulped the champagne. If she'd been lightly sipping right then, Jasmine would've choked. "Wh-what?"

He smiled. His smile made her nervous. It was too knowing. And it seemed to hold a threat. Smiles weren't supposed to be threatening. They were supposed to be warm and reassuring. Apparently Drake had missed the memo on that one.

He took the empty champagne glass from her hand. His fingers brushed hers. Okay, now the guy was just making it hard for her to breathe. He put the flute down on a nearby table and then his hand came back. Those fingers of his—warm, strong, and slightly callused at the tips—curled under her chin. "You're dressed like a jewel thief or a cat burglar."

She felt heat sting her cheeks. "Know a lot about burglars, do you?"

"I know you aren't what you seem, not at all. This isn't about sex, is it?"

Jasmine inched closer to him. "Kiss me, and find out."

"Is that what you said to the jerk downstairs?" Anger hummed in those words.

Jasmine shook her head. "You shouldn't just watch..." And wasn't that exactly what he was doing? Shutting himself away up there and watching the world below?

She pushed higher onto her toes.

But she didn't need to press upward. He was already bending over her. His mouth pressed to hers.

This wasn't anything like the kiss downstairs. His mouth was hard, but sensual. He explored her lips. Stroked her, and when she gasped against him, his tongue thrust into her mouth.

Wow. The guy definitely knew how to kiss. *He's better than I am.* A whimper built in her throat. She'd thought—mistakenly, obviously—that she was skilled. Drake was in a whole new category. The make-you-weak-in-the-knees category. Her knees were already jiggling.

Her lips parted even more for him—because Jasmine wanted to make sure that she savored this experience. The man's taste was incredible. Enough to make her feel a little drunk, and, as a rule, Jasmine *never* got drunk.

Her hands grasped his shoulders. Her short nails sank into his coat. Her breasts were aching, the nipples tight...just from his kiss.

He was controlled. Deliberate. He seemed to take his time caressing her, and she liked that. She liked far too much about him.

A pity, since she'd been sent to betray him.

His head lifted, and their lips broke apart. She sucked in a breath, gasping for that last taste of him. A girl had to enjoy her moments when she could. Then she forced her eyes to open.

There was desire on the hard planes of his face. In the glint of his green eyes. He wanted her, as much as she wanted him. She could certainly feel that proof in the hard thrust of his cock against her.

She didn't speak for a moment. Jasmine normally had plenty to say, but she found that she didn't want to speak at all in that moment. Maybe because she didn't want to lie to Drake.

Maybe because she wished that things were different.

"Unexpected..." His voice came out as a deep rumble.

Yes, he certainly was unexpected. Not an easy mark. Not a man to use and forget. More like a man who would haunt her long after she'd slipped from his life.

She was too conscious then of the watch around her wrist. Jasmine knew she should be monitoring the time. Oh, so carefully, especially because of that little detour she'd been forced to take to the parking garage.

But she didn't move. She kept her body against his and kept pretending that she was just a woman who wanted the man before her.

"I like the way you taste," Drake told her.

She could've given the same words right back to him, only "like" seemed to be far too tame of a word. She wanted to drink him in, to take more...to take everything that the guy had to give.

A faint vibration shook her wrist. Her alarm. Quickly, Jasmine pulled her left hand away from Drake, hoping that he hadn't felt that slight movement of her watch. But he was still staring at her with the gaze that had gone hard and dark with lust.

She had a role to play. Jasmine was supposed to smile up at him, give some flirtatious line, and keep him distracted for a few more minutes. She *should* have done that, but instead, she heard herself say, "I have a problem. I tend to want what I can never have."

Holy hell. Those words had *not* been on her agenda.

A faint furrow appeared between his brows. "What is it that you want?"

Right then...*you.* Jasmine pulled in a deep breath. One more. She tried to steady her racing heartbeat. No luck there. "I'll be gone in the morning."

She didn't even have a hotel room in Vegas. It wasn't a pleasure trip. Just business.

She was there to destroy Drake.

The man had no idea just how many enemies he'd made. Or maybe he *did* know, and he didn't care.

"We can have tonight," she said, lifting her chin before she realized what she was doing. Jasmine could've cursed herself for that little "give." She'd been warned about it before. She notched her chin when she was scared, and she was never, ever supposed to show fear—not *real* fear, anyway.

But Drake's big, warm hand curled around her waist. "Damn straight," he said, voice thick with his own hunger. "Let's enjoy the night."

His head lowered toward hers once more.

His lips were an inch away from hers. A breath of space. Jasmine wanted that space gone.

A shrill alarm cut through the room. *Right on time.*

Drake jerked away from her. "What in the hell?"

Jasmine let surprise flash across her face. "Wh-what's happening?" She rather thought that the tremble in her voice was a lovely touch. "Is that a fire alarm?" Hurrying now, she rushed toward the tinted glass so that she could look down at the crowd. "No one is moving." The alarm kept beeping—the sound was making her ears ache. That noise was worse than the music had been. "They have to hear it—"

"It's not a fire alarm." Now he was grim. "Those people down there don't hear anything. It's a private alarm—a signal just for me and my security team."

She whirled toward him and gasped dramatically. "Are you being robbed?"

Drake's jaw had locked down as he checked his phone. *Got the system linked in there, do you?* "The warning alert is coming from the casino's vault," he said. Um, his expression was *deadly.* "Someone's tampering with it." He rushed for the door.

Jasmine hurried after him. Now he had his phone to his ear, and Drake was barking orders like mad to whoever was on the other end of the line.

"*No one* screws with my business," she heard him snap.

She gulped at that. He had the door open. She was just a step behind him.

Drake whirled around. The phone was still at his ear, but now he seemed to be focused on her. "Where are you going?"

"Uh, with you?" Wasn't that obvious?

He shook his head. "Stay here. We're not done. Not even close."

A vault break-in hadn't stopped the guy from wanting sex?

His eyes gleamed. "Not even close." Then he shut the door and vanished.

Jasmine didn't move. The alarm stopped after a few more tense seconds, and then she heard nothing. Nothing but her own drumming heartbeat, anyway.

How long would Drake be gone? And he truly expected her to just sit and wait for him like a good little girl?

Poor guy. He didn't realize that she'd never been good. Not really.

Turning, she let her gaze sweep over the room. Leather couch. Bar. And...

His desk. His computer.

Because this place wasn't just a private lounge. It was his inner sanctuary at the Arrow.

Jasmine sidled toward the desk. Her avid stare skimmed over its surface. Then she reached down and opened the top drawer. Business papers were inside. Spreadsheets. Profit projections.

The second drawer contained some mail. One big, brown package had already been opened. She lifted that package. Let the contents spill into her hands.

But the only thing inside that package was a picture. Black and white. Drake was there...so were two other men. Men she recognized because they were both famous and *infamous*.

Trace Weston, the man behind Weston Securities. Weston Securities was the biggest private security firm in the U.S. From the rumors she'd heard, Weston had plans to make his firm the biggest in the world.

The other man she recognized was Noah York, a hotel magnate who'd made headlines because he and his fiancée had both barely escaped death a few months before.

Only he wasn't engaged any longer. Noah York was married now. She was staring at his wedding picture. Noah was in his tux, and his bride beamed at his side. A woman stood with Trace, too—a delicate ballerina type. Well, that fit since Jasmine knew that Skye Sullivan-Weston *was* a ballerina.

In that picture, there was no woman on Drake's arm. He had a faint smile on his lips, not the wide grin that Noah sported.

A note was attached to the pic.

Thanks for being my best man. —N.

Her hand trembled a bit.

She pushed the photo back into the package. Shut the desk drawers. Then Jasmine sat behind Drake's desk. She slipped her equipment from the little case she'd strapped to her ankle.

Drake had been wrong about her. Well, partially wrong. She wasn't a jewel thief. Her business was information.

She stared at the computer. Getting *to* his computer had been the trick. The rest...it would be easy.

Jasmine knew that she just had to work fast.

Her gaze strayed to that second drawer once more.

Thanks for being my best man. —N.

Straightening her shoulders, Jasmine went to work.

***

"Smoke bombs?" Drake demanded in disgust as he watched the pink flumes—seriously, *pink*—drift just outside of the vault door. No one had breached the casino's vault. The guards there had panicked when they saw the smoke. They'd been the ones to pull the alarm and get the whole security team mobilized.

"Looks like they were on a timer," Chad Thatcher, Drake's chief of security said as he lifted one of the little, pink smoke bombs. It wasn't smoking anymore. "Real clever device...looks handmade." The guy's tone was admiring.

Drake didn't exactly feel *admiration.* "Someone tried to break into my vault."

Chad's lips twisted as he eyed the three nervous guards who'd pulled the alarm. "Not with this thing. This is a prank. Not a threat." Chad would know threats. Drake had recruited the man because of his diverse background. Swat Team leader. Undercover police officer. Bomb squad technician.

Yeah, Chad knew his bombs. Very well.

Chad tossed the little device lightly in his hands. "Someone was messing with you guys," he told the flushing guards.

Drake looked around the room. The other security team members were all starting to relax. The core team had been called in—his strongest men and women, but other guards were still positioned throughout the casino. Just not as many as he normally had at the Arrow. "A distraction," Drake realized as his gaze turned back to Chad.

Chad's fingers closed around the device. The smile left his face. "No one is stealing your money," Chad said. "We're right here. No one is getting past us."

Drake whirled away from him. *Sexy jewel thief.* "That's because she's busy stealing something else." Dammit, he should have *known* better. A pretty face could hide the best lies.

He ran for the elevator. "Get a lockdown in place!" Drake shouted over his shoulder. "The redhead I took upstairs earlier—Jasmine—*she doesn't leave the premises.*"

There was no way that woman was going to escape from him.

***

Jasmine backed away from the computer. She knew time was running out and she had to make her exit.

The thick carpeting swallowed the sounds of her footsteps. She reached for the door handle.

Only it didn't turn beneath her hand.

Jasmine jerked it harder. No give at all. *He locked me in?* She hadn't exactly counted on that part. And she was sure looking at a primo lock, too, not the easy pick-me-in-a-moment variety.

Hell.

Drake's image flashed before her mind. *Stay here. We're not done. Not even close.*

The only window in that place overlooked the club. It wasn't like she could jump through it.

Her fingers skimmed over the lock once more. She'd wrangled the invitation up to this room because she knew that guards watched the entrance to this private lounge. The only way up to the area was Drake's elevator and once *up* there, she would've had to contend with the lock. If she'd stopped to work her wiles on the lock in order to gain entrance, a guard would've seen her.

But the guards are distracted, and I'm not on the outside. So she should be able to finesse this lock, no problem.

It was an electronic lock after all. She'd always had a knack for working electronics.

A few seconds later, the lock slid open. "Piece of cake," Jasmine murmured as she slid her little packet of tools back into place on her ankle once more. Her fingers slipped around the door knob. The door opened with a soft click.

Jasmine grinned. She pulled open the door—and found herself staring right up into a pair of glinting green eyes. Very, very, angry green eyes.

"Going somewhere?" Drake drawled. Ah, there it was. The hint of the south, Mississippi if she wasn't mistaken, rolled beneath those two words.

Her heartbeat sounded like a drum in her ears. "I was coming to find you."

He smiled at her. She did *not* like that smile. Goosebumps rose onto her arms.

He stepped forward.

Jasmine fell back.

"There's something you should know about me," Drake said as he took another stalking step toward her.

Jasmine found herself retreating again even as her chin notched up.

Stupid move. She had to learn how to control that chin move.

He shut the door behind him. "I don't like liars, Jasmine."

I am so screwed. "Neither do I."

"I fucking hate betrayal."

Oh, crap.

His hands lifted. His hold was hard and tight as he grasped her shoulders and pulled her up against him. "Who the hell are you?"

"You're scaring me." Total truth there. A lot of Drake's past had been shrouded in secrecy, and when she started searching online in order to learn more about him, she'd come across some strong government security measures. She could've hacked past the red tape, of course, but she hadn't wanted to raise too many flags with Uncle Sam—or anyone else who might have been watching.

With his hold still tight on her, he pushed her back against the nearby wall. "Your name," he gritted.

"Jasmine!" She gave it willingly enough, just as she had before. Her first name would mean nothing to him.

"Last name."

"Bennett." He had no reaction to her name. Awesome. Fantastic. Now to get out...Jasmine shook her head. "What is happening here?" She huffed out a hard breath and tried to look properly insulted. "Because if this is your idea of seduction then we are totally not compatible. I was thinking we'd enjoy a few hot hours..."

His hold loosened and she yanked away from him. Since her back was against the wall, though, there wasn't exactly any place for her to go.

"But I never thought I'd have to deal with a psychotic episode." Jasmine drew herself up, straightening her spine but not, *not* notching up her chin. "I want to leave now."

One golden brow rose. "The cameras caught you."

Liar. When she'd set her timers earlier, she'd made sure no cameras were close by. This wasn't amateur hour. "Caught me doing what? Having a drink at the bar?" She lifted her hands before her, trying to appear innocent and confused. "Good for the cameras." She tried to sidle around him.

But Drake's hand flew out and he grabbed her wrist. "The cameras in here, princess."

Her heart sank. She'd done a quick sweep for cameras in this room. There hadn't exactly been time for a thorough search. She hadn't seen any, so she'd hoped... Jasmine cleared her throat. "I don't know what kind of joke you're trying to pull, but it's not funny." Maybe he was bluffing about the cameras, just to see her reaction. She'd keep playing the injured party a bit longer and see how that worked for her. If she could just get to the door...

Wait, does he have his security team waiting in the hallway? And if they weren't in the narrow hallway, would they be waiting for her at the elevator?

It was just not her night.

She tried to break away from him again, but he moved in a flash. He twisted his body, twisted her, and in the next moment, Jasmine found herself pinned to the wall. He was in front of her, solid, unmovable, furious. He'd pushed her wrists back against the wall, and he glared down at her.

"I thought you might like things a little rough," she tossed that out, hoping to distract him.

His pupils seemed to swallow the green of his eyes. "You have no idea."

That response got right past her guard. Her mouth dropped open and—and his hands flew over her body.

"Stop!" Jasmine shouted at him. "You have no right to—"

Search her? Yes, dammit, that was exactly what he was doing. She recognized a pat-down when she felt one. She'd had her share of brushes with the law over the years. When you were on your own at fifteen, staying on the right side of the law wasn't always an option.

She tried to shove his hands away.

It was like shoving away steel.

"So I poked around your desk," she told him, getting a little desperate now. "I was curious about you, okay? I'm not curious anymore. Not even a little bit. I've learned from my mistakes. I am not—"

His hand stilled near her left ankle.

Hell.

He lifted the leg of her pants. She felt the pull of the strap that held her gear set in place.

Then he rose to his feet.

She tried to grab his hand.

Too late. He'd opened his prize. He stared down at the lock picking set.

She never left home without one of those.

There was a flash drive nestled beside the lock set, too. Make that three flash drives. Some wires. A very small screw driver.

Tools of her trade.

"Jasmine..." He sighed out her name as his gaze came back to her. "I think we have a problem."

A muscle flexed in his jaw.

I fucking hate betrayal.

Her body trembled. He was a businessman, despite those somewhat shady governmental ties. He wasn't just going to—to—

"You came to steal from me, and now you're going to have to pay the price."

"I didn't steal from you!"

He laughed. His laugh was rough and angry and it sure didn't alleviate any of the tension that she felt.

His face was locked in hard, furious lines. Rage glowed in his eyes. He looked scary as hell and—

Sexy, still.

What was with her and her stupid attraction to bad boys? Would she never learn that bad boys were considered "bad" for a reason?

"I didn't steal," Jasmine repeated. "Check the flash drives. Nothing is on them. I came up here to be with you, not to—"

"You're saying you still want to fuck me?"

Jasmine licked her lips.

His gaze immediately fell to her mouth.

"Tempting..." And his head lowered. Before she could speak again, his mouth was on hers. Hot and hard. Not as controlled as before. Actually, there *was* no control now. The kiss was wild and rough, and if she'd thought her toes curled before, well—she nearly lost her shoes then.

Liquid heat spilled through her body. She *wasn't* supposed to react to him this way. She wasn't—

His head lifted. "Cause I can always fuck you before I call in the cops."

Her eyes turned to slits.

"Now I'm wondering about the guy I tossed outside," he nearly growled those words. "Maybe I was too hasty. Maybe I should've listened to just what the fellow had to say."

Then the cops would already be here.

"Check the flash drives," Jasmine said. Her voice was husky, but steady. "You'll see the truth."

His eyes held hers. "How do I know you haven't hidden more drives...?" His gaze dropped to her body once more.

"Because you already searched me, jerk." She shoved against him. Hard. Hard enough to send him stumbling back a step. Not because she'd gotten some super strength, but mostly because she was pretty sure the move had caught him by surprise.

How do I get out of here...how do I get...

He turned away from her. Stalked toward his desk. She didn't move as he searched through the flash drives. Jasmine was too busy trying to figure out what story to give him.

She even considered the truth. Like he'd believe that.

His fingers tapped over the keys. "They're empty. All of them." He straightened.

She gave a firm nod. "Like I said. Now, as *un*-fun as this little night has been, it's time for me to leave."

His head tilted as he studied her. "You think I'm going to let you get away?"

"I haven't done anything to you. So I carry a lock picking set. Big deal." She shrugged. "I don't like to get locked out—"

He laughed again. It wasn't the hard laugh from before. It was more surprised, more real.

"I've taken nothing from you," Jasmine said, knowing that she sounded like a broken record. He had no idea how much that non-theft was going to cost her. But she was trying to be good. It was a fairly new thing for her. "And I won't steal anything, but I am leaving." She turned, took some fast steps, and reached for the doorknob.

"You planted the smoke bombs."

"I don't know what you're talking about." She didn't look back.

"You're a thief..."

"I took *nothing* from you." She had the door open and a quick peek showed her that—thank goodness—there wasn't a whole security team waiting to drag her away in that little hallway.

She stepped over the threshold.

"I'm not just going to let you slip away."

Try to stop me. "It's better this way. Meeting you...it certainly was interesting." Scary, too.

She marched forward. Her heels sank into the carpet. She thought he'd grab her again. He didn't.

She didn't break and run, though she sure wanted to do that. She walked away, real nice and slow, totally *not* like a thief running in the night.

Even though he was right. That was exactly what she was.

Probably all she'd ever be.

But I didn't steal from him.

And she wasn't even sure why she hadn't.

Jasmine's fingers reached out for the elevator. She'd memorized his security code when he typed it in earlier, so getting those doors to open wasn't hard.

Now to just get out of here...

***

Even before Jasmine had left the room, Drake had a security team trailing her. "Watch her," he barked into his phone. A few clicks of his computer had given him access to the club's security footage. Her image was currently on his screen. He was following her, without stepping a single foot outside of his sanctuary.

Did the woman really think he'd just let her vanish? No, not happening.

But he *had* wanted privacy to view the video footage...and he'd also wanted to see just where her grand exit would take the lovely Jasmine. Maybe she would lead him straight to a partner that she had waiting in the wings...

"Keep a tail on her until I say otherwise," Drake added. This wasn't over. But he was willing to give the woman a false sense of security...the better to make her vulnerable for his attack.

Betrayal.

It burned like acid within him. He'd been betrayed too many times in the past. Another pretty face, another woman ready to wreck him.

Jasmine wasn't running away. No blind flight for freedom from her. Instead, she was strolling slowly, appearing to take her sweet time as she left him.

He tapped on his keyboard again, accessing the security footage for *this* room. He rewound the images, determined to see exactly what Jasmine had been doing in his office. He wasn't a fool—he'd deliberately started the recording as soon as he'd left his office. A quick tap on his phone had triggered the hidden camera.

Jasmine filled his computer screen. In that video, she walked toward his desk. She opened the drawers. Pulled out the package that his buddy Noah had sent to him. Stared at the photograph.

Her expression tightened as she stared at that image, and longing flashed in her eyes.

What the hell?

Jasmine put the photo and the package back in the drawer. She pulled out one of her flash drives. She pushed it into the computer.

She glanced back at the shut drawer.

She pulled the photo out for a *second* time.

Then she gave a hard, negative shake of her head.

She yanked out her flash drive. Didn't access any of his files.

She didn't steal from me.

In the video, Jasmine rose quickly. She hurried toward the door—and when she realized he'd locked her in, the woman used her lock-picking set and had that door open in seconds.

But she hadn't been able to flee. He'd been there.

Frowning now, Drake opened his desk and pulled out the package Noah had sent to him.

Both of his best friends were married now. Both claimed to be deliriously happy.

Both were fools, of course. And they were too obsessed with their women. They'd risked their lives for their ladies, and Drake had seen their desperation.

Noah York and Trace Weston. His friends in battle. His friends through blood and death.

They were smiling in the picture. He was, too, and for once, the smile hadn't been forced.

His gaze swept the image. Just what had Jasmine seen in that picture? Whatever the hell it was, she'd changed her plans because of it.

He had no doubt that she'd come to the Arrow in order to steal secrets from him. Intel. But she'd left with nothing.

The phone on his desk began to vibrate. Drake grabbed it and put it to his ear. "Where is she?" Drake asked because he'd recognized Chad's number on the screen.

He heard the head of security inhale sharply. Oh, the hell, no.

"Sir, I, um, the team on her—"

"Tell me that she's in their sights right now."

"They thought she was just heading to the bar, but in the crowd, she slipped away from them and—"

"*Find her.*"

"Do we need to call in the authorities? Did she—"

"No authorities. She's mine." His hand was too tight around the phone. "Now get out there...*find her.*"

He rewound the image on his screen. Froze it at the moment when Jasmine first stared down at the photograph.

The longing on her face was so strong. Longing. Sadness.

The woman was a mystery. He headed for the door. She only had a few moments lead on him.

And he *never* let his prey escape.

***

The Arrow's goons had no idea how to deal with a woman like Jasmine Bennett.

But Wayne did. So he wasn't waiting for her near the hotel's main entrance. He was in the back. In the alley. And when Jasmine slipped out, joining with the shadows, he was right on her trail.

The woman was good, he'd give her that.

But he was better.

He reached into his pocket. While he'd been waiting, he'd taken the liberty of getting a few things from his car. The handcuffs would definitely come in handy. And if she fought, he'd have to use the knife, too.

He smiled as he followed Jasmine into the darkness.

CHAPTER THREE

Jasmine knew she was being followed. Unfortunately, her list of enemies just kept growing and growing, so she wasn't exactly sure who might be shadowing her through Vegas.

The city had too many lights. Way too many. She stuck to the shadows as best as she could, and she hunched her shoulders each time she heard a voice floating on the wind.

She'd made it at least a mile from the Arrow. In her heels. Damn impressive—especially considering the path she'd taken.

Jasmine wanted to jump toward the main strip, hail a taxi, and get out of there but—

Someone is following me.

At this point in her life, she knew better than to ignore her instincts. And the tenseness at the base of her neck, that too-aware intensity, it told her that she was being followed through those Vegas alleyways.

Was it that bozo who claimed to be a bounty hunter? Like she believed that BS.

Was it Drake's security guards? *Drake?*

No, she discarded that idea almost immediately. Drake wouldn't bother coming after her himself. If he'd had cameras in that room, like the guy claimed, then he would've watched them by now and seen that she hadn't taken anything.

So that left her with option three...the man who'd put her on Drake's trail...he could be the one in the shadows. She did not want to come face to face with him. Especially since she had to let him know that she hadn't managed to get the information he wanted.

Her back brushed against a brick wall. She strained, trying to listen desperately for a sign of her pursuer. But the fellow was good. She'd give him that. No rustles. No heaving breaths. No—

"Got you, sweetheart."

The rough words came from her left. Jasmine rushed forward as the dark form of a man pulled away from the shadows.

The bounty hunter. Something was glinting in his right hand. She didn't know if that glint was from handcuffs or from a knife, and Jasmine wasn't in the mood to find out.

She kicked off her shoes and sprinted for safety.

The pavement bit into the bottom of her feet, and she heard the bounty hunter huffing behind her. Ah, now there was the huffing breath. If only he'd given away that sound earlier!

Jasmine jumped from the shadows and ran for the brightly lit street. Horns honked. Cars whizzed past. She only had a few seconds lead on the guy. She raised her hand. "Taxi—"

He grabbed her hand and whirled her around in his arms. Jasmine was pretty sure that she felt the sharp tip of a knife shove into her side.

"You're not getting away this time."

Her head turned, and her eyes met his. Even in the darkness, she could see the evil twist of his lips.

"No one's gonna save you now, sweetheart."

That was the story of her life. Good thing she'd learned to save herself.

The knife pricked her side. Jasmine gasped.

"This time, you'll pay."

***

Jasmine.

Drake saw her, on the side of the street. A taxi was pulling away from the curb, as if she'd just tried to hail it.

She was in a man's arms. It was too dark for Drake to see the man's face, but a nearby street lamp spilled light right onto Jasmine's dark red hair. He saw the back of her head, but he *knew* it was her. Same dark clothes. Same tempting thief.

He jerked his steering wheel to the side, parking as quickly as he could.

Jasmine and the man were rushing away. The guy glanced back, and Drake caught a glimpse of his face.

The jerk from my club.

Had he been working with Jasmine all along? Were the two running a scam together?

Only...Jasmine was fighting with the guy. Struggling against him.

"Stop!" Drake shouted as he hurried after them.

Jasmine's head whipped back. The man didn't stop, though. He started rushing forward even harder, nearly dragging Jasmine with him.

Jasmine drove her fist into the fellow's face.

He still didn't let her go.

They were heading for the alley, and Drake raced into that darkness too. He wasn't just—

"Man, you need to back off."

Drake stilled. He couldn't see the guy clearly, but he *had* caught sight of the weapon. A knife. The SOB had a knife pressed to Jasmine's side.

Fury pumped through Drake. "Let the woman go."

"I told you before..." The man inched forward a bit, and the blade of the knife glinted. What had been the jerk's name? Hardin. Wayne Hardin. "I'm not letting her just get away again. She's a wanted woman."

"And you have a knife to her side. Drop it." Or Drake would drop that bastard.

But Hardin just shook his head. "It's her eyes, isn't it? You aren't the first dumbass to get pulled in by them. She looks all innocent, then you blink, and that innocence is gone. If you gave her the chance, she'd rob you blind, just like she did to the others."

"Help me..." Jasmine's voice was so low that Drake had to strain in order to hear it. "Please."

"I wanted to explain before," Hardin said, his words rolling right over her soft plea, "but you didn't give me a chance. I'm a bounty hunter. She's wanted in Texas—"

"No, I'm not," Jasmine said, sounding desperate.

"—and I'm taking her back. I'm gonna collect on everything that's owed to me."

A bounty hunter? Interesting. Drake braced his legs apart. He kept his hands loose at his sides. "The first thing you're going to do is drop the knife."

Hardin laughed. "Seriously? Dumbass, we're not in your casino anymore..." He pushed forward, coming more into the light, but carefully staying away from the street. *So no one else will see you're a bastard with a knife against a woman's side.* "Your goons aren't here, and a useless playboy like you sure doesn't scare me."

Drake almost smiled. He was far, far from useless, especially in a fight. He'd seen more blood and death than Hardin could imagine.

"First, you drop the knife," Drake ordered. "Then you let her go."

"I'm *never* letting her get away—she's gonna be my payday!"

"Then..." Drake said, because he wanted to be clear, "I'm going to hurt you. Because I think you hurt her." That knife was far too close to Jasmine's side. He *knew* the fool had cut her. "And *you're* going to pay for that."

"You fucked her," Hardin said with certainty. "You fell for the eyes, you fucked her, and now you want more just like—"

Jasmine drove her elbow back into Hardin's stomach. He grunted and his hold eased on her. When his hold eased, Jasmine shot forward, rushing right toward Drake.

She ran straight into his arms.

And she seemed to...fit.

"*Sonofabitch...*" Hardin snarled as he leapt after her.

Drake pushed Jasmine behind his back. He kept his focus on Hardin. "I told you what to do...I gave you a chance..." Now he'd just take care of things. His way.

Hardin lunged at Drake. Hardin still had the knife in his hand. A quick chop and Drake sent the knife falling from what he knew were Hardin's now numb fingers.

First order...drop the knife.

Drake kicked the knife aside. "Bounty hunters don't drive a knife into women. That's not the way their business works."

Jasmine was silent behind him.

"Did he cut you?" Drake demanded without taking his gaze off his current prey.

Hardin swung at him then, a left hook that Drake easily caught—and held—in his fist.

"J-just a little..." Jasmine whispered back.

"A little is too much." Drake slammed his forehead into Hardin's. Hardin stumbled back, and Drake let loose. His hits made instant contact, they were brutal in their intensity, and in seconds, Hardin was on the ground. He was—

"Stop!" Jasmine was in front of Drake. His fist was up, ready to strike again.

But he'd never hit her.

And no one else will, either.

He shook his head as that thought snaked through his mind.

"This isn't your fight. You need to get out of here." Jasmine looked back down at Hardin. He was trying to rise to his feet. "Just leave him here."

What? "He attacked you with a knife!"

"And you just beat the shit out of him." Her voice lowered and he was pretty sure he heard her mutter, "Scary. So didn't see that coming."

He didn't want her scared of him. Wait...*what the fuck is happening here?*

Her hand went to her side. He grabbed that hand and felt the warmth of her blood on his fingertips. Fury spiked through him. "That beating is just getting started." She'd lied to him. It wasn't a little cut. The guy had sliced her.

"Let's go," Jasmine urged. Her fingers tangled with his. "Just get me out of here, okay?"

Hardin was on his feet. Not advancing. But backing up.

Drake pulled Jasmine closer to his body. "You're no bounty hunter."

"Check my ID, check—"

"I don't need to see your fake ID. No bounty hunter in his right mind would use a knife on a woman. I'll call the cops and then—"

Hardin laughed. "Hero, you don't even know the game that's being played."

Game. "I know that in any game, I win."

Hardin backed deeper into the shadows.

"I warned you before to stay away from her. You didn't listen." Drake was pretty sure he'd broken Hardin's nose. Good. "I'm not warning you again." And he also wasn't done. He was going to—

"I'm not the only one who'll be coming for you." Hardin was still retreating and still making threats. "Get ready, hero. *Get. Ready.*"

Then Hardin turned and fled into the darkness. Drake heard the sound of his pounding footsteps and he wanted to rush after the guy, but he knew that the second he gave chase, Jasmine would vanish.

His hand still held hers. That was probably the only reason she hadn't already run from him.

He stared into the darkness, listening to those fleeing footsteps.

"I'm sorry," Jasmine said, her voice as soft as a breath.

He gazed down at her. Her head was bent.

"I-I got blood on you."

He caught her chin with his left hand. Forced her head to rise, but in the darkness, he couldn't read her expression.

"I'm sorry," she said again, then even softer, "for everything."

"Don't lie, princess."

Then he was pulling her from that alley. The light of the strip seemed even brighter as he hustled her into his car.

"No, I'm bleeding—"

"And if I don't get you some help, you're gonna keep bleeding." She would need stitches. He'd take her to a doctor. Then he'd get his answers. Drake hurried around the car. It was a sleek, sexy ride. A black Porsche that could cut right through the night. The seats were leather and—

And now the car smelled of vanilla.

"I-I can't go to a hospital. They'll ask questions. Questions that I can't answer."

His hands tightened around the steering wheel. "Are you wanted in Texas?" Had that part been true?

"Not by the cops."

That wasn't quite a full answer, now, was it?

"It's just a scratch," Jasmine said, her voice a little stronger. "I can slap some bandages on it and be fine."

Doubtful. "You're still bleeding." That bastard had wanted to hurt her. He had.

And I want to destroy him.

He sucked in a deep breath. Another. What in the hell was happening to him? Sure, control was never actually his strong suit, but wanting to pound a man into the ground?

Not...me.

Drake turned his head and stared at Jasmine. She wasn't looking at him. Her eyes were on the alley.

"Jasmine." He liked her name. Sexy. Feminine. Drake liked the way her name rolled off his tongue.

Her head turned. Her hair slid over her cheek. "If the cops aren't after you, who is?"

She bit her lip.

He wanted to be the one doing that biting.

You fucked her. You fell for the eyes, you fucked her, and now you want more just like—

"Thank you," Jasmine told him.

"For what?"

"Saving me. That doesn't happen a lot for me."

He cranked the car. The engine immediately purred to life.

"Please." The word seemed to be a bit hard for her to say. Interesting. "Don't...don't take me to a hospital. I'm staying in a motel just outside of town. Just drop me off there, and I'll vanish from your life. I promise."

He pulled into traffic. He was far too aware of her next to him.

"If you turn right at the next intersection, you'll be able to get back to my motel."

Drake stared at the road ahead of him.

"The turn is here," Jasmine said, her voice breaking a bit. From pain? From fear? "You should go right—"

He didn't go right.

"Drake?"

"You've got a lot of secrets."

"Why didn't you turn? I told you, I'd vanish. I won't bother you again."

She was already bothering him plenty. He should drop her off at the nearest hospital. Get on a plane and head down to New Orleans. Find another woman and forget about her. But he heard himself say, "You're not vanishing."

The Porsche accelerated.

He wasn't done with Jasmine yet. She wasn't going any place, not until he'd figured out just who had sent her into his life...and why the sight of a wedding picture had made her nearly crumble.

***

Dammit. Wayne slammed his car door shut. He turned the key, but the old engine didn't spark to life. Not on try number two or three. On the fourth try, the thing finally sputtered to life.

Good.

He had a meeting, one that he was way overdue for, and the boss sure wasn't going to like the news that Wayne had to share.

He didn't have Jasmine.

And Drake Archer did.

Wayne swiped his hand over his face. His nose throbbed like a bitch. He'd be sure to pay Archer back for those blows. So he'd cut Jasmine a bit. Wasn't like it was the first time she'd been roughed up. He'd read her file. The woman spent most of her nights on the wrong side of town and with the wrong people.

Archer had enemies. Plenty of them. Did the fool even realize how intimately connected Jasmine was with those who wanted the casino mogul taken down?

"The bigger they are..." Wayne muttered. *The more they should suffer when they fall.*

***

Drake drove through the heavy gates that led to his estate. A new acquisition, much like the Arrow. Drake didn't like staying in hotels. That was his buddy Noah's bit. Hell, hotels were Noah's life. Drake needed privacy. A sanctuary away from the rest of the world.

Guards waved to him from their post at the gate.

"Uh, want to tell me what's happening?" Jasmine's voice was low.

He pulled up near the front of the house.

"Drake." Now anger vibrated in her voice. "Answer me. You've been dead silent the whole drive. *Talk to me.*"

He killed the ignition and slowly turned to face her. "You said no hospitals, so I brought you here." He paused. "And you know it's my house. The way I figure it, you must have conducted some research on me. So I'm sure you recognize this place."

She didn't deny the charge. Instead, Jasmine asked, "Why would you bring me to your house?"

"You mean...why would I trust you enough to let you inside? Princess, it's not about trust. Because I don't trust anyone."

He caught the faint flicker of her eyelashes.

"You know I made a phone call on the way here." She'd asked who he called, but he hadn't told her. He'd been too pissed for much talking. Pissed at her, at Wayne, at himself. *Why am I keeping her so close?* "A friend of mine is waiting inside for you."

He slid from the car. She didn't move. He hurried around to her side of the vehicle. When he opened her door, the Porsche's interior light came on, and as the illumination poured down onto Jasmine, he realized that she'd turned pale. The gold of her skin was a pallor that he didn't like.

Drake reached for her.

She pulled back. "Is this...friend...a cop?"

"You sure have some cop issues."

"Yeah, I do."

She rose from the car. Swayed a bit. He grabbed her, and she just felt so slight in his arms.

He'd noticed it before. A delicacy that he didn't expect. Back at the Arrow, she'd seemed full of energy and life, but when he'd touched her, Drake had thought...*I have to be careful.*

"Is the friend a cop or not?"

Then her knees buckled.

He held her easily. Lifted her into his arms. "Dammit, you're worse than you said! You need—"

"Don't let...anyone take me away."

He hurried up the steps. The front door opened as if on cue for him.

"That's something I didn't expect to see..." An amused voice drawled from the doorway.

Drake's hold tightened around Jasmine. "He's not a cop. He's a doctor."

"A doctor who had other plans for the night," Carson Thorn muttered as he stepped out of the doorway. "I left one very hot blonde in the lurch, and you so *owe* me for that."

Drake grunted. Carson could be an ass, but he was one useful commodity. Drake had discovered early on that it paid to have connections—legal, social, and medical. In Drake's world, there were plenty of times when a doctor's services were needed.

Jasmine isn't the only one who doesn't always trust the cops.

He had an agreement with Carson. Carson took care of Drake's employees and any...unusual situations that might occur. And Carson kept a fat bank account.

"I've got your bedroom set up for her." Carson waved his hand down the hallway. "Standard rate will apply, of course."

Drake carried Jasmine down the hallway. He carefully arranged her on the bed, and when he pulled back, he saw her blinking groggily. Hell, had the woman passed out for a few moments? Just how much blood had she lost? His hand went to the hem of her shirt. Blood was thick on her side, soaking the material.

She tried to bat his hands away.

"Do I need to sedate her?" Carson asked. He already had a syringe in his hand.

Jasmine's head turned at his voice. Her eyes widened. Sounding utterly horrified, she demanded, "Why is a GQ model coming at me with a needle?"

Carson flushed a dark red.

Drake laughed. "He's the doctor, and he's coming at you because he's worried you won't stay calm while he sews you up."

"I'll stay calm." She shook her head. "Not my first time...to be stitched."

His eyes narrowed. "You get sliced up a lot?"

Carson put down the syringe. He arranged his instruments, and then his gloved hands reached for Jasmine's shirt. He cut the shirt away when it stuck to her.

Drake's teeth clenched as he got a look at the damage. That was sure no *little* scrape. "He wanted to hurt you."

"He didn't like being out—outsmarted at the Arrow." She hissed out a breath when Carson started probing her wound, but her eyes didn't leave Drake's face. "It was his payback."

Carson was carefully cleaning the wound. "She's gonna need about five, maybe six stitches. Not nearly as bad as I thought it would be. I've seen a lot worse."

"So have I," Drake said. Back when he'd been in the military, he'd seen images so brutal and bloody that they still chased him into his nightmares. And after he'd left duty, well, his business dealings hadn't exactly gotten any prettier.

His gaze slid over Jasmine's wound, then up...almost helplessly. She still had on a bra, a black, lacy thing that pushed up her breasts. Fabulous breasts. She was hurt and weak and he shouldn't be noticing them but he did and—

"At least this side will match the other," Carson said, voice droll. "Guess someone likes to play with knives, huh?"

Drake's attention immediately shifted to her left side. Sure-damn-enough, there was a faint white scar there.

"I'm not the one who plays." Her voice was quiet. "I'm the one who has the bad luck to get hurt."

His gaze came back to rest on her face.

Her eyes were waiting for him. So dark and deep.

"Turn more onto your left side," Carson instructed her. "I need a good angle for the needle."

She started to turn. Drake quickly leaned forward. His hands eased her over and, once she was positioned for Carson, he didn't let her go. Her skin was so soft and warm.

He didn't let her go.

"You sure that you don't want something for the pain?" Carson asked her.

"I hate drugs." Her stare still held Drake's. "Never touch them. Alcohol is as far as I will go."

"Uh, you want some booze to help—"

"Do it," Jasmine said, cutting through Carson's words. "Or else I might be passing out again soon. I hate the sight of blood. Especially when it's my own."

Carson went to work. Jasmine sucked in a sharp breath and her hand flew out.

Her fingers, still marked by her blood, locked around Drake's. She held him tightly. Tighter than anyone had ever held him before. As if he were her lifeline.

When he wasn't. He was more like her destruction.

"How'd she get sliced?" Carson asked as he leaned over.

Drake shook his head. "You know the drill. You don't get to ask questions." Mostly because the guy was better off not knowing the answers.

A tear slid down Jasmine's cheek. But she didn't make a sound, and her expression never altered. She just kept staring up at Drake. Kept holding his hand. "I love your eyes," she whispered.

He blinked. Uh, was the lady getting delirious?

"I've never seen quite that shade of green before. Your eyes...they tell me that you can't be as bad as the stories say."

Drake knew there were plenty of stories circulating about him.

His right hand kept holding hers. His left rose and wiped away the tear tracks on her cheek. Then he leaned in close to her. "You're wrong. I'm even worse than they say."

If she knew the full truth about him...but then, only Noah and Trace were aware of all he'd done. The deaths. The lies.

They knew because their pasts were as twisted as his own.

"Why did the picture matter?" The question slipped from him.

A furrow appeared between her brows.

"Two more," Carson said, voice strangely chipper.

She flinched. Held Drake even tighter.

"You were going to steal my files, but you saw the picture in my desk, and you changed your mind."

Her lips trembled. "So you did have a camera up there." He heard the faint click of her swallow. "Were you going to record us having sex?"

Carson coughed. "Wow. I don't think I need to hear—"

"No," Drake ignored him. "When we have sex, that's for us. You and me, and no one else. Not ever."

"*When*?" She licked her lips. "Sounds like someone still has plans."

"I do."

She wasn't crying anymore. Not those silent tears that had made his chest ache. She was staring at him with a sharp gleam in her eye.

"Done," Carson said, sounding exceedingly relieved. "Now I can get the hell out of here, but I do think I need to give some doctorly advice...no rough sex for a bit, okay? Hold off on that chandelier swinging a while because I just patched the girl up."

Drake looked over and saw that Carson had put a bandage over Jasmine's wound. The tightness in his chest eased. No more pain for her.

Ever.

He shook his head. His thoughts were screwed up tonight. Probably because he'd been up for nearly twenty-four hours straight. He should crash but...

He had some business to take care of first.

He was also still holding Jasmine's hand. She seemed to realize that fact at the same instant he did because she tried to pull away from him.

He let her go. She was in his house. In his bed. The woman wasn't going far. "I'll be right back. Don't move."

Her lips lifted in the faintest of smiles. "Since it looked like this place was surrounded by miles of desert and I just got stitches in my side, I was planning to stay right here for a bit. Not because you ordered me to, but because I don't feel like falling on my face right now."

Carson laughed. "She's got some fire, doesn't she? That's what I've heard about redheads. Once they—"

Drake grabbed his arm and hauled the doc out of the room.

When they were near the front door of his estate, Drake glared at Carson. "This never happened."

"It never does," Carson agreed as he rolled back his shoulders. "But that money sure looks nice when it appears in my bank account."

"It's already on the way."

Carson turned to leave. Then he hesitated. "Is she...safe?"

He sure hadn't expected that question.

"I mean..." Carson cleared his throat. "She's not one of your employees—"

"How do you know that?"

Carson gave a rough bark of laughter as he glanced back over his shoulder. "Because even though the woman was bleeding all over your bed, you still stared at her as if you could eat her alive. And you don't exactly get all touchy and hold hands with my usual patients."

"She's not your concern anymore."

"But she's yours."

Carson was annoying him.

"I'm just saying be careful, okay? She might not be up to your usual games. Hell, I'm not up to them, and I'm the guy who has to patch up all the players."

Then Carson was gone. Drake locked the door behind him.

You don't know her, Carson.

And neither did Drake, but he needed to learn more about her. In general, he had a rule about secrets. He didn't want to hear them. He didn't want to share his own past, and he didn't want to dig into the hell that could be someone else's sordid history.

But he wanted to know more about Jasmine.

He pulled out his phone. Called the man that he knew could give him the information he wanted.

The phone rang once, twice, then a groggy Trace Weston picked up. "Are you dying?" Trace wanted to know. "Because, seriously, it's—"

"You and Noah have woken me plenty of nights. And it's too freaking early for you to be sleeping any way. It's barely—"

"Four a.m.," Trace growled.

Drake's lips twisted.

"You don't sound like you're dying," Trace pointed out. "So I'm about to hang up—"

"I need background intel."

And Trace was the best in the business at gathering intel. Investigation *was* Trace's business. Weston Securities was the most respected security firm in the U.S., thanks to Trace.

Drake, Trace and Noah had formed a private company of their own after they'd left the military. They knew how to get in and out of every hotspot on earth, and they'd used their special talents to their advantage. They'd retrieved wealthy businessmen and women who'd found themselves in some very serious and deadly situations...for a hefty fee.

After a while of earning as much cash as they could, Trace had decided to expand the business— he'd hired new teams. Developed Weston

Securities. Noah had turned his attention to growing a hotel empire, and Drake...

Life's a gamble. His philosophy, and the reason he'd opened his first casino with his share of the security profits.

"Drake...who do you want me to investigate? What dumb bastard has pissed you off now?"

Drake's gaze slid toward the dark hallway. He didn't hear a sound coming from the bedroom. Was Jasmine awake?

"It's not like that," he heard himself say. "I just need...I need background on a woman with the name of Jasmine Bennett. She's from Texas, about twenty-eight years old. Red hair, brown eyes. Her eyes have a little gold in them and—"

It sounded like Trace was choking. "Her eyes have *what* in them?"

Asshole. Drake growled, "She's five foot six," without those sexy shoes to bump her up. "And the woman probably weighs about one thirty-five. She's got a knife scar above her left hip," and now one above her right. "I want to know everything you can find on her."

"This business or is this personal?"

"It's both," he said as he turned to type in his security code on the control panel.

Silence, then... "Where is Ms. Bennett right now?"

"My bed."

"Ah...then you probably should've gone for the background check first."

He had to unclench his jaw. "Just get me the intel."

"I'll work it personally," Trace promised him. "But man, just...be careful okay. Last time—"

"I know exactly what happened last time, and I'm not ever going to make that mistake again."

"I just don't want you hurt." Trace's voice was lower now.

Drake laughed. "Don't worry about that. She doesn't matter enough to hurt me. None of them do."

The floor creaked, and he looked up—and right into Jasmine's dark eyes. She stood in the hallway, her hand pressed to the wall.

"Get me that information as soon as you can." Drake ended the call and marched toward Jasmine. "You should still be in bed."

She gave a little shrug. "I...um, I figured since I was all stitched up, I should probably get out of your way now."

Bullshit. She was trying to run again. "I told you to stay in my bed."

Her brows rose. "*Your* bed? That was your room?" She shook her head. "I didn't see any pictures or—"

"Because I don't put fucking pictures all over my room. I sleep there. I screw there. And I move on."

She backed up a step.

"You don't leave until you tell me everything I need to know." Actually, she didn't leave until Trace gave him the intel he wanted. Drake didn't trust her not to lie. He didn't trust her at all.

His gaze slid over her. She'd put her bloody shirt back on. That wasn't going to do. And there were dark shadows under her eyes.

"Come on..." He took her arm.

She didn't move. "Why are you doing this?"

"Because you wanted to take something from me." He stared into her eyes. They did have fucking flecks of gold. He'd just been stating a fact when he told Trace that detail. *Asshole.* Drake had wanted to be thorough. How was that wrong? "No one takes from me."

"Are you going to hand me over to the cops?"

No, he wasn't handing her over to anyone. He shook his head as she began to walk down the hallway with him.

When they were back in his room, she hesitated near the bed.

"Take off the shirt," Drake told her flatly. The woman couldn't sleep in a blood-soaked shirt.

He caught the fast sound of her indrawn breath. "But...that GQ doctor said—"

"I'm not fucking you tonight, Jasmine." *Tomorrow night?* Maybe. He went to this closet. Came back out with one of his shirts. "Put this on."

Her fingers reached for the offered shirt. Brushed against his. An electric current seemed to shoot right through his hand.

He'd felt attraction before. Plenty of times. After all, the world was full of beautiful women, and he could certainly appreciate beauty. But this was different.

He looked at her, and he ached.

He touched her, and he craved.

"Turn around," Jasmine told him.

He didn't. He did raise his brows. "I've seen you without a shirt before."

Her lips thinned. "Turn. Around."

Pity. He turned. Heard the soft rustle of clothing behind him.

"Okay." Her voice was hesitant.

He looked back. She had on his shirt, and it swallowed her. It also made her look delicate, vulnerable. Sexy. "You still have on the pants."

Her eyes widened as she glanced down at herself.

"You can't sleep in them. Finish stripping, then get in bed." He motioned to said bed.

"You expect me to sleep with you?"

He folded his arms over his chest. This shouldn't be so hard to explain. The woman obviously had issues following orders. "I expect you to get in bed before you collapse."

She bit her lower lip.

Shit. Shit, *shit*. He wanted a bite.

"I don't understand you," Jasmine murmured. "If you want answers..."

"I don't want a fainting woman on my floor, and princess, I'm dead on my feet, too. We're crashing. Everything else can just wait until the sun comes up."

Her gaze slid to the king-sized bed. "I'm just supposed to trust that I can sleep here, safely?"

"No."

Her dark stare snapped right back to him.

"You shouldn't trust me, because I sure don't trust you." But he'd give her tonight—or what was left of the night. Because he could still see the image of a needle sliding into her delicate flesh. "Rest." The order came out hard and gruff as he headed for the door.

"Thank you."

Her soft words stopped him at the threshold. "What was I supposed to do? Walk away and just let you keep bleeding out in the alley?"

"It's not like that hasn't happened before."

He grabbed the door frame. Held it too tightly. *It won't happen again.*

"I'll find a way to repay you," Jasmine promised. "I always repay my debts."

He spared her a brief glance. "Good...because I always collect on the debts owed to me." He figured that she deserved that warning.

Then, because the bed behind her looked too good—no, *she* looked too good, wearing his shirt, waiting by his bed, Drake left her. He shut the door firmly, and headed down the hallway. Even though he was bone weary, Drake knew sleep wasn't going to come easily for him.

It never did. The dead haunted him too much.

***

"You seem to be missing someone..."

Wayne tensed when he saw his boss stride toward him. The dawn Vegas sky was streaked with lines of red and gold. They were meeting in the middle of nowhere, and Wayne was nervous as all hell.

This place is too much like a body dump site.

No one would find remains out here in the desert. If the animals *left* any remains.

"Jasmine Bennett was supposed to be with you."

Wayne didn't try to hide the truth. He knew better than to lie to this man. "She's with Drake Archer."

He expected fury. He expected the boss to take out a gun and shoot him right there. According to the stories he'd heard, the guy had done that before. Wayne tried to brace for impact.

Instead, the man smiled. "Is she now?"

Wayne nodded. Sweat drenched his forehead.

"Good. Then keep an eye on her until she leaves him, and when she does...bring her in to me."

What?

The guy turned on his heel and headed back toward the limo that waited for him.

"That's it?" Wayne called after the man. "You're not—you're not angry?"

The boss stopped. "Why would I be angry? I told Jasmine to get close to Archer. Seems like she's done her job very well."

He was so lost. "But...but my job was to bring her in. You hired me—"

"Your job was to make sure she didn't run from me. She's not running...not yet. She's doing exactly as I ordered." He turned his head. The sky was on fire behind him. "You're my security, in case Jasmine tries to go soft on this one."

Soft? The report he'd read on the woman sure didn't indicate any "soft" tendencies.

"Jasmine is important to me. I don't want to lose her talents."

Oh, damn. Talk about misreading a situation. When he was hired to tail someone, it was usually because that *someone* had screwed up.

Only I'm the one who screwed up this one. He should've asked more questions, instead of just taking the money.

But he liked money.

"You don't want Jasmine hurt?" Wayne asked carefully. There was, ahem, no need to mention that she'd already been hurt. The boss didn't need to know about the little knife incident. He hadn't *meant* to slice her.

Okay, he had.

"I don't want to lose her," the boss said again, but then his face hardened. "But I would see her dead before I'd let her betray me."

And that's where I come in. "That's why you hired me. In case she turns on you." It would have been helpful to know this earlier.

"You're a hunter. She's your prey...the instant she runs."

He realized the truth. "You thought she'd run last night!" No wonder he'd gotten the call to close in. He'd thought the order meant he needed to detain Jasmine, but—

"Jasmine has a...special connection with Archer. I was worried it might prove to be a weakness for her. I sent you after her because if she wasn't doing her part, I wanted her brought to me." The boss waved his hand. "She's not here...so she's still in play."

Wayne had no clue what was going on. *Above my pay grade.*

"Jasmine had her orders. She'll make contact with me in twenty-four hours, and if she doesn't, then...well, everything will change for her. She won't have my protection any longer—and she will feel the force of my fury."

Wayne edged back a bit. He sure didn't want any of the boss's fury to be turned on him. *I'm not telling him about the knife. What he doesn't know...*

"Better see about that nose," the boss ordered with a wave of his hand. "I've heard Archer can throw a killer punch."

The man truly had eyes and ears everywhere. *But he doesn't know I sliced, Jasmine. Not yet.* Talk about a lucky break.

Wayne stood there, at that body dump site, frozen, until the boss vanished in his fancy limo.

If I'm the security to make sure Jasmine doesn't screw him over...then who the hell is watching me?

Because the twist in his gut told Wayne that the boss was all about contingency plans. Screw him over...*and you die.*

Wayne hurried back to his car. He knew better than to screw over that man.

CHAPTER FOUR

"Rise and shine, princess..."

Jasmine's eyes flew open and she jerked upright, a gasp shaking from her as her hands immediately flew out toward the rickety nightstand and the weapon that had *better* be there—

This isn't my motel room.

Her hand slammed into a lamp and it went crashing to the floor.

"Interesting wake-up method you have there," that deep, rumbling, very male voice told her.

Her gaze shot toward the doorway. Drake stood there, one sardonic blond brow lifted, a faint smirk quirking those sexy lips of his.

No, not sexy. They were hard. They were cruel. They were—

She focused on his eyes even as her hands snatched up the covers. "Did you ever think of knocking politely?"

"My house. My bedroom." He shrugged. "Besides, it's getting close to noon. I was afraid you were dead in here."

Noon? She *never* slept to noon. Not ever.

"I've got some clothes for you." He glanced down at the bag in his right hand. Wait, that was—

"My bag." She scrambled from the bed, pulling the covers with her. She kept them around her, toga style, and Jasmine ignored the ache in her side.

"I had one of my men collect your things from that little motel."

Did she look stupid? "You mean you told the guy to rifle through my stuff."

He lifted the bag toward her. "I thought you might like some non-bloodstained clothes to wear. And some shoes. Guess I was wrong."

She hurried across the room and grabbed the small duffel bag.

But he reached out before she could retreat from him, and his fingers wrapped around her wrist. "You keep a gun in your nightstand drawer."

And she was betting that gun wasn't tucked securely in her bag. "A lady traveling alone has to protect herself." Especially when she was dodging trouble.

"It's time," Drake told her.

Did he realize that his thumb was slowly rubbing against her inner wrist? Because she did, and that teasing contact was making her all kinds of nervous. "Time for what?"

"The truth. You put on your clothes, then you come to the den and you tell me everything I want to know."

Not going to happen. "Or what?" He'd already said he wasn't planning to call the cops on her. So as far as she was concerned, he had zero leverage.

The smirk was gone from his face. He looked...cold then. Hard. Dangerous.

Don't fall for the bad boys, don't!

"You don't want me for an enemy, Jasmine."

"I thought that you already were my enemy. Didn't realize I had a choice in the matter."

"I don't want to hurt you."

Okay, now that scared her. Her chin started to lift.

"But one way or another, you *will* be answering my questions, and if you lie to me...that will be a mistake I punish you for."

Then he freed her wrist. Only she felt like he was still touching her. Her skin was hot and sensitive.

"You've got five minutes to dress."

"And you sure like giving orders."

He flashed her a wide grin. Wow. The man had a really nice, *sexy* smile.

"Time's ticking..."

He shut the door.

Her gaze darted around the room. There had to be a way out of there. A way to escape Drake...

Because he wouldn't like her secrets. She knew because Jasmine hated them, too.

***

Drake was waiting in the garage. He stood in the back, keeping his body hidden as Jasmine snuck inside. He almost smiled. Did she even realize how predictable she was? She'd ducked out the back of the house, circumventing his security—a nice touch—but he knew the woman would need a ride for her escape off his property.

His garage had, of course, been her most likely destination. So he hadn't bothered waiting inside the house for her.

He'd just made himself comfortable out there.

Her shoulders were hunched as she made her way to the line of cars. Which one would she pick? The Corvette? The Lincoln?

His lips firmed. Oh, hell, no, the woman was *not* planning to take his Porsche.

She *was*.

She slipped inside the car, then disappeared beneath the dash. He stalked toward her as anger pumped in his blood. "If you mess up those wires, I'll—"

Her head shot up, and she screamed.

He took that opportunity to haul her out of his Porsche. That car was his favorite, his favorite in Vegas, anyway.

"I didn't plan on us talking out here," he murmured as he held her. "Princess, you missed the den by about fifty feet."

She jerked against his hold. He didn't let her go.

She still smelled like vanilla.

He still wanted a taste.

"I didn't miss your dang den. It took me five minutes to get out of that house." She sounded disgruntled enough that he wanted to smile. *Again.*

Then he remembered that she'd been intent on wrecking his baby. "You don't touch the wires, got it? You don't damage the Porsche."

Jasmine rolled her eyes at him. "I've been hot wiring rides since I was fifteen. Your precious little baby wasn't in any danger from me." Her eyes narrowed and she appeared insulted. "I'm a professional."

"Are you now?" Ah, so there was secret number one. "A...professional."

Her cheeks flushed a dark red but her eyes— they seemed to darken even more with...pain? "I'm not a whore." She pulled away from him and started heading back toward the house.

He stared after her a moment, aware that he felt...*shame.* "I didn't think you were a whore. I'm...sorry." His words hadn't come out right. He'd meant to taunt her, not accuse her of—*shit.*

She glanced back at him, frowning. The light hit her hair. Rolled over her skin. Made the woman seem to glow. "Did you almost choke as you just said those words? Because it sounded like that apology got stuck in your throat."

It had, a little bit.

She sighed. "You like trouble, don't you?"

"No, I don't."

Jasmine gave a slow shake of her head. "Then you need to just take me out of this place. Let me get away from you, and then we can both never look back."

He took his time closing the distance between them. Mostly because he was enjoying the view of her in the sunlight. "You made a mistake, you know."

"Seems like I've made a few of those," she groused.

Dammit, she kept making him want to *smile*. What in the hell was up with that? "You interest me."

Surprise rippled across her face. "You make me sound like some kind of weird science project. You know, when it comes to talking with ladies, you rather suck at it. How, *how* do you have so many chicks throwing themselves at you?"

That should be obvious. "I'm rich."

"And sexy." She glared at him. Like he was the one who'd committed a crime. "Bad boy appeal."

Uh, okay.

She pointed at him. "You need to keep your hands off me."

He wanted his hands all over her. "Why is that?"

"Because I don't want to get involved with you. It would be a mistake, for us both."

He took her hand. Yes, he was touching her. He liked doing it, and she didn't pull away. Because she liked his touch?

They didn't speak again until they were near his house. Drake nodded to a guard who was watching them. "Did he even see you slip out?" Drake asked her, curious because the man had his narrowed gaze on Jasmine.

"No, I think he was taking a potty break."

Laughter broke from Drake.

"I had to pick my moment," she confessed.

He tugged her into the house. Shut the door. Instead of heading to the den, he took Jasmine into his study.

Once they were there, Jasmine glanced down at her hand. "You can let go now. You've got me."

Slowly, he dropped his hold on her. "Do you...hurt?"

He should've asked her that before.

Again, surprise flashed across her face. What? Had no one ever asked Jasmine how she felt?

"Just a little ache," Jasmine said as she walked around the study, poking and gazing at different things. "Nothing to worry about. I've had plenty worse."

Drake didn't like hearing that news. "How many times have you been stitched up?" He eased into the chair behind his desk. His hands flattened on the wooden surface.

"Maybe three times. Everyone has accidents."

Bullshit. "That was no accident last night."

She put down the hourglass that she'd been examining "You're right. That was my mistake. I should've moved faster." Her breath expelled on a sigh. "So there are accidents and there are...non-accidents."

Locking his jaw, he motioned to the leather chair in front of his desk.

She didn't sit.

The woman just liked to be difficult.

"Who are you working for?" Drake asked her.

"Myself?" Yes, she made it sound like a question, but then she nodded, as if she'd reached an important decision. "From here on out," Jasmine said softly, "I am."

She was making his head ache. "Who sent you to the Arrow?"

"I came on my own. I figured I had a better shot at getting to you there. Your house here..." She waved her hand. "It was too isolated."

"No, you knew I kept my files there and you wanted access to them."

Her fingers tapped against a bronze statue. Jasmine was touching everything. *But me.*

"If you know all the answers, why ask the questions?"

Because he didn't have the answers for the big questions. "Tell me who sent you."

"So we can both make his hit list? I don't think so."

She looked too confident and in control. Jasmine should have the sense to fear him. She didn't. "Why aren't you afraid of what I'll do to you?"

"Bones can be broken, flesh can be cut. Been there, done that."

He shot to his feet.

"I survived those *non*-accidents," she continued, her voice quiet, calm. "So I figure I'll survive whatever you do to me, too."

His hands had clenched at his sides. "Who hurt you?"

"Lists are long...and boring. The past is over. Let's just stick to the here and now." She turned her back. Gazed up at a painting of wild horses on the wall. "This is hideous, by the way. Why would you ever pick this out to hang it up in your study?"

"I didn't. It came with the house." She was trying to distract him. Nice.

He was ready to distract her, too. So he threw out the question that he *knew* would get a response. "Who interested you the most in that photo?"

He saw her shoulders tighten. "What photo?"

Drake sighed. "Each time you lie to me, I'll expect something from you. An apology, of sorts."

She turned to face him. "I don't understand."

Drake closed in on her. Pinned her between him and that freakishly ugly painting. "You just lied. Make it up to me."

"H-how?"

"Kiss me." He didn't think she would. He just—

She leaned up on her toes and pressed a quick kiss to his lips.

"No, princess, not like that." He tipped up her chin and he took her mouth. Deep, thorough. Rough. "My way."

Her breath rasped out against him.

"Every time you lie to me," Drake told her, aware that his voice had thickened, "you pay for it."

Her gaze searched his. "I probably should confess...I lie a lot."

"Then you'll pay...a lot."

Her hands pressed to his chest. But she didn't push him away. Instead, it was more as if she were trying to get a feel for him. Testing his strength.

"Who sent you to the Arrow? To me?"

"You're a man with enemies. Maybe you can figure that part out yourself."

"What's your role? Seduction?"

She pushed against him. Hard. A shove. But he didn't step back so much as an inch.

Jasmine swallowed. "I told you before, I'm not a whore. Don't *ever* make the mistake of calling me that again."

"There's a difference between seduction and prostitution. From where I'm standing, seduction seems to be one of your key talents." She sure had made him want her easily enough.

Red lit her cheeks again. "*Don't.*"

"You used your body to get to me before." When she'd seemed so eager for him back in his private lounge. "Don't like being called on it now?"

Her lashes lowered, shielding her eyes. "I wasn't going to have sex with you."

"But you knew I wanted you. You used that. And I'm betting you've used men's desires against them plenty of times." The thought had his muscles clenching. He didn't want to think of any others in Jasmine's life.

"Weaknesses can always be exploited."

His hand slid down her neck. Her pulse raced frantically beneath his fingertips. "You're too delicate for the danger you seek."

"Looks can be deceiving."

No, in her case, they weren't. A twist of his hand, and she'd be dead. Maybe he should tell her about his past.

But...

No.

"I don't know why you're wasting time with me. Don't you have a flight today?" Jasmine asked him as her pulse kept racing beneath his fingers. "I remember reading someplace that you were working on some big casino deal in New Orleans."

"The eyes do help you play innocent," he allowed as he studied her. "But that innocent routine doesn't really work for me."

Her gaze held his. She seemed to come to some decision as she told him, "Take some advice from me. You need to pay attention to what's happening down in New Orleans. You've pissed someone off, and that particular person isn't going to stop until he gets his pound of flesh from you."

His fingers lingered around her throat. "A *name,* Jasmine. That's what I want. Neither of us will leave this room until I get it."

"Elvis Presley."

He growled.

"That's a name. My favorite all-time performer."

He didn't move.

"Be careful what you ask for, you just might get it." Her pulse kicked up even more. "Do you know what will happen to me...if I talk?"

"Nothing."

Her lips twisted, but her smile was sad.

"I'll protect you," he added. With his resources, protecting her would be easy.

Her smile slipped. "No, you'll throw me away. Because you'll have what you need from me. I know how it works. I've been a tool before."

"What were you supposed to steal from me?" Drake demanded as his patience fled.

Her breath whispered out. "The plans for the casino expansion in New Orleans. The projections for your future projects in Biloxi. You've got some competition...someone who wants to cut you off at the knees."

And things started to click into place for him. "That's what you do. You don't take jewels. You're an information thief."

"Ah, I prefer the term...information retrieval specialist."

His jaw nearly dropped.

"It sounds better."

He could only shake his head.

"It does. It sounds a lot better than thief."

"The cops *are* after you in Texas." He freed her and stepped back. "Hell, you're wanted and that bounty hunter—"

"I'm not wanted because I haven't been caught before!"

His gaze pinned her. He'd caught her.

"You were the first," she allowed, obviously reading his thoughts. "No one else ever held me."

"Then the others were idiots."

She looked away from him. "Maybe."

He just couldn't figure her out. "You were hired to do a job. You didn't do it...because you saw a wedding photograph."

"I just changed my mind, that's all."

Lie. "You'll pay for that one," he promised her.

She tensed.

He didn't go to her and collect. Not yet. She'd revealed good information to him, and he just had to work this situation out in his mind.

Casinos...it was about the business. His business. Someone wanted him to crash and burn financially.

Hell, there was quite a list out there for that. When it came to the casinos, Drake didn't exactly play nicely. Playing *nicely* wasn't part of his vocabulary.

But Jasmine was afraid of the person targeting him, and Drake didn't think Jasmine scared easily. He *knew* that she didn't.

So it was business, *and* it was personal.

He watched her. Waited. Narrowed down his enemies. Someone tied to the casino industry. Someone who would be willing to destroy a man's life in an instant. Someone he'd recently pissed off...

Luckily, that list was fairly short. At the moment. "Maxwell Case," Drake threw the name out as a test.

Her chin notched into the air. "Is that name supposed to mean something to me?"

He was on her in a flash. "That's lie number three. Collection time." His mouth sank on hers. Damn but he liked her taste. Liked the way she gasped and arched against him. Liked the sting of her nails along his shoulders.

His tongue thrust into her mouth. He savored her. He wanted to taste every single bit of her. He'd gone too long without a woman. Need rode him hard. Only...

It wasn't need for just any soft, feminine body beneath his. It was a dark, aching need for her. *Jasmine.*

His head lifted. "He's the one who sent you after me."

She didn't speak, but she stubbornly shook her head.

"The Arrow used to be another casino." A rundown dump that needed new life. A spot that had been ripe for the picking. "Case wanted the place. I bought the casino before he could. Found out the SOB's bid, and I took it." When Vegas was supposed to be Case's domain. Screw that shit. Drake took what he wanted.

And he'd wanted Vegas.

"I took what was his, and now he's trying to take what's mine."

She gazed up at him with wide eyes.

"*That's* why you told me to head down to New Orleans. He's trying to take my casinos from me. The bastard thinks he can run me out of business."

Her lips pressed together.

"Not happening." He marched for the door. "No one takes what's mine."

"Can I...can I go now?"

"Go?" he repeated as he turned back to her.

Her hands twisted in front of her. "You think you know everything, so you don't need me."

He stilled. "On the contrary, I think I need you very much."

"I don't understand."

The woman's eyes could bring a man to his knees.

But Drake bowed for no one.

"Good thing your bag is packed, princess, because we'll be leaving for New Orleans soon."

Her jaw dropped. "You're taking me with you?"

"I wouldn't dream of leaving you behind."

Fear flashed in her eyes. "You should, though. You need to leave me."

"No." Because he had plans for Jasmine. So many plans. "I'm not letting you go."

***

No one takes what's mine.

Drake's words echoed through Jasmine's head. He'd sounded so fierce and determined.

But Drake was wrong. This wasn't just about his casinos.

It was about his life.

Maybe...maybe if she played things just right, she'd survive what was coming.

Perhaps they both would.

Then Drake would think that she was worthy enough, then he'd help her. He'd—

"Coming?"

She schooled her expression before she glanced up. Drake was back in the doorway. The guy hadn't gone far at all.

"You really should leave me behind." She was trying to be fair. "I told you that before. You don't want the kind of trouble I can bring to your life."

"Ah, Jasmine, you don't know the kind of trouble that *I* am." He flashed her a tiger's grin. "But you'll be finding out. Very, very soon..."

A shiver slid down her spine.

***

He slipped into the Arrow. Headed inside as easily as could be. The security guards at the front of the place didn't notice him—mostly because they thought he *was* one of them. Getting the guard's uniform had been too easy.

He made his rounds, like a good security guard would. Then he went to the area that interested him the most.

"Heard there was some action here last night," he murmured when he saw the two uniformed men near the vault.

One guard grunted. "Damn smoke bomb."

This time, it wouldn't just be about smoke.

But the guard to the right frowned at him. "You aren't supposed to be here. You're not part of the usual rotation."

Ah, so security had been stepped up.

"Let me see your credentials," that guard barked. "Because I don't know *you.*"

Now both guards were eyeing him with suspicion.

He raised his hands. "You don't know me because I'm the new guy on the team." He flashed a friendly smile. "But don't worry, I'm getting out of here. Just wanted to see where all the cash was kept. Curious, you know."

His smile and easy attitude should have reassured them. But one of the guards was pulling out his radio. Dammit.

"I need the chief," the guard snapped. "There's some guy down here who won't—"

"I'm already leaving," he murmured as he edged away. Hell. This wasn't part of his plan.

He turned his back, intent on getting out of there.

But one of the guards grabbed his shoulder.

He stiffened. "Wasn't supposed to go down like this," he murmured, but a smile pulled at his lips.

Sometimes, violence was the best answer.

He turned around and attacked.

CHAPTER FIVE

Jasmine had her nose pressed to the window as the plane landed.

"First time in New Orleans?" Drake asked her, curious. She carried so many secrets.

"First time on a private jet." Her right hand was tight around the armrest. "And this plane is lush." Her tone was admiring.

The plane bounced a bit as it landed.

Jasmine glanced his way. He wondered if she'd be afraid or if—

A wide smile winked her dimples. "And, yes, this is my first time in New Orleans, so I want to see *everything*."

That smile was going to cause serious problems. Carefully, Drake shifted his position. A smile shouldn't make him *that* aroused, that fast.

But hers did.

When they were clear, he unhooked his belt.

Jasmine began, "My bag—"

"It's being taken care of." Everything would be taken care of now.

Jasmine nearly skipped down the runway. An interesting trick, considering that she was wearing stilettos.

"I've heard this city is magic." She was tugging on his arms. "I want to see the Quarter. I want to eat beignets at midnight."

He pulled her to a stop. "It's close to midnight now." But New Orleans wouldn't be sleeping. The jazz music would be drifting in the air, and the place would be alive with people filling the streets.

That smile was still on her face. The one that made him want to think she wasn't a thief. That she was just a woman he desired.

But I know better.

He also knew how to get her to lower her guard.

"Can we get beignets?" Jasmine asked him quickly. "At that place along the riverfront? I've heard people talk about it."

He nodded.

Her smiled beamed even more.

He didn't speak again until they were in his car, and Matthew, his driver/security detail, was leading them through the city.

"You know," Drake finally mused as he carefully watched her, "most women get this excited over diamonds, not beignets."

"I'm not most women." And she was back to having her nose pressed to the nearest window. She stared out at the city as if it were the most amazing sight that she'd ever seen.

He kept his eyes on her.

Matthew dropped them off near the riverfront.

"I hear jazz!" Jasmine exclaimed excitedly.

That was because a man was playing a saxophone less than ten feet away.

Jasmine hurried through the crowd and stopped near the man. Then she just listened, apparently spellbound, as he played.

Drake kept watching her.

She was a puzzle he couldn't quite figure out. What was real with her? The enthusiasm and happiness she was showing now? Or the tricks she'd shown back at the Arrow? The lock picking. The seduction.

He put money down for the musician and led Jasmine toward her beignets. When she bit into one, powdered sugar slid over her upper lip.

His gaze locked on that lip.

Jasmine moaned. "Incredible." She devoured the beignet, licking her lips, savoring the sugar.

"Sweet," Drake muttered.

Her gaze slid to his. "You should...have a taste."

He leaned toward her and licked away the soft powder near her upper lip.

Her breath caught. "Drake..."

He pulled back. Stared at her.

"Thank you."

Drake didn't like it when she thanked him. He didn't want her gratitude, not for buying her a simple beignet. He wanted...*her*.

Thunder rumbled in the distance. Her head turned at the sound, and she stared out at the river.

"We should go," he told her, aware that his voice sounded gruff. "A storm's coming." He could smell it in the air.

"I've never minded a storm."

No, she wouldn't.

They stood there, staring at the water, as the raindrops began to fall.

Then, because he couldn't help himself, because he *wanted* her and he was going to take exactly what he wanted, Drake turned Jasmine in his arms. He kissed her. Tasted the sweetness on her lips. Tasted the rain.

Tasted desire.

Her hands wound around his neck as she leaned into him. She was kissing him eagerly, seeming to hold nothing back.

Good. Because from that moment forward, there would be no stopping or holding back.

Not for either of them.

He had a house in the French Quarter, one away from the wildness of Bourbon Street, and he took her there. His driver was close, and he picked them up quickly. Within minutes, they were heading down the lane that would take Drake to his house.

Then Jasmine is mine.

Jasmine...Now that they were in the car, she was back to staring out the window. And he was watching her. Drake...liked watching her.

Her hair was wet around her shoulders. Her clothes clung tightly to her body.

He wanted her naked.

He'd have her that way.

When they reached his house, he hurried from the car.

"It's incredible," Jasmine whispered as she stared up at the house. Illuminated by faint porch lights, the Victorian stood strong in the surrounding darkness. "Gorgeous."

He caught her fingers with his. The rain was still falling, but Jasmine didn't seem to care. She was laughing as they hurried inside.

For a moment, he almost wanted to laugh, too.

He took her upstairs. Pulled her against him. The wet clothes let him feel every inch of her body. Tight nipples, pebbled hard.

From the cold?

From need?

He stared into her eyes. "I'm going to fuck you."

Her lashes flickered. "You could try making love to me."

His jaw locked. "This isn't about love." Emotions didn't enter into the equation for him.

Sadness swept over her face for an instant. He wondered if she'd pull back. If she'd try to play him.

Instead, her hand slid over the stubble that lined his jaw. "Maybe one day, you'll change your mind. Maybe one day, you'll love someone."

He caught her hand. Held it in a too tight grip. "I want to fuck you. *Now*." He couldn't be more clear.

Her wet hair slid over her shoulders. "Then what are you waiting for?" The sadness was gone, and he wasn't sure if it had ever really been there. He just knew he had the woman he wanted in his arms, and Drake wasn't going to wait any longer.

He stripped her. Peeled those wet clothes from her body even as she kicked away her heels.

Her bra was a lacy temptation. Her breasts full and round, and when he tossed the bra away and her breasts spilled into his hands...*Perfect.*

He threw aside her pants. Nearly shredded her panties. This time wasn't about softness and seduction. This was about need. Want. Desire that was running unchecked through him.

Too long.

He needed to fuck. Hard and fast. More, he needed to fuck *her.*

Her mouth called to him, those plump lips teasing him. He took her lips and thrust his tongue deep even as he backed her up to the bed.

"Your clothes—" Jasmine gasped against his mouth.

Then he lowered her onto the bed. He didn't give a shit about the bed getting wet from his clothing.

He needed to touch her.

His hands learned her first. He started with her breasts. Plucking the nipples. Loving the way they went so tight at his touch. He stroked her, cupped her.

She arched into him. Her breath came in little gasps that made his cock grow even harder.

Want in her.

His hand swept over the curve of her stomach. But when his fingers skimmed along the edge of her bandage, Drake froze.

What the hell am I doing? She's hurt! He tried to pull back.

"Don't even think of stopping," Jasmine said, her voice a sensual demand. "I need you, Drake. I. Need. You."

Every muscle in his body ached for her. "I'm too rough. You're hurt—"

"Pain...is the last thing I feel right now. Don't stop."

And he knew he couldn't. "I'll use care." Somehow, he would. His hands eased down her body. Down...down...right to the heat between her thighs.

"Drake!"

He explored her. Slowly at first, caressing the sensitive flesh, but when her hips arched against him, his touch became more demanding as he thrust two fingers into her.

She was hot and tight and he knew she'd feel fantastic around him.

"I want to touch you!" She was struggling with his wet clothes. "Get these off!"

He pulled away from her, just long enough to toss his clothes across the room and grab for a condom. He rolled it on, hissing out a breath because he wanted to be balls-deep in her *now*.

She was splayed out for him on the bed. Her nipples were pink, tempting. So very temping.

He licked her nipple. She jerked at the contact. He licked her again. Scored her lightly, sensually, with the edge of his teeth.

His hand was between her legs and he felt the rush of arousal as she grew slick for him.

He kissed his way down her stomach. Her legs parted even more for him. He blew lightly over her clit. She tried to reach for him, saying that she wanted to touch him again, but he caught her wrists and held them tightly with one hand.

Then he put his mouth on her.

She came that way, with his mouth against her, his tongue in her, the first time. Crying out, Jasmine arched against him and he loved it.

Her body was shaking, quivering, and it was all for him.

Drake rose quickly and drove deep into her, as deep as he could go—even as the climax still shook her.

Her eyes were wide and dark with pleasure. Her cheeks flushed. She was beautiful and she was—

Begging for more.

"Please," Jasmine gasped, her voice husky and desperate. "Drake, *please!*"

He withdrew. Thrust deeper. He still had her wrists in his grasp and he lifted them up, pinning them above her head. He wanted the control, but he'd sure see to it that she had her share of pleasure.

Enough pleasure to make her scream.

He plunged into her again, his rhythm giving them both just what they needed. Wanted. The wooden posters of his bed thudded into the wall. There was no restraint, no slow build up.

His cock sank into her, again and again.

Her legs lifted and locked around his hips as she tried to meet his thrusts.

It wasn't enough.

He needed *more.*

He withdrew from her.

"Drake?"

In a flash, he'd rolled her over, positioning her on her knees. He wanted in her even deeper.

"Hold the headboard," he ordered.

Her hands curled over the wood.

"Hold tight," he whispered into her ear as his body wrapped around hers. She shivered against him. "Is this...okay...are you hurting?"

He didn't want to hurt those stitches—

"Only pleasure," Jasmine whispered back.

He put his mouth on the curve of her neck. His hand slid under her, fondling her breasts, then moving down, down, and finding the tight center of her need.

He stroked her clit even as he thrust into her.

Jasmine cried out. Her hands flew off the headboard.

"Hold tight!" Drake ordered her.

Her hands slapped back down and he drove into her with a thrust that had them both gasping. He thrust and stroked her, playing with her clit, forcing her closer to another release, one that he knew would be hard and brutal, because the orgasm pounding down on him was going to be that way. It was going to—

Consume.

She screamed his name as he erupted. The spasms of his release had him pounding deep into her. Pleasure made him blind and nearly mad for a moment as he held tightly to her. His whole body ached as the release seemed to go on and on, surging through Drake.

Her breaths were rushed and desperate.

And he was holding her too hard.

Awareness slowly came back to Drake.

Jasmine's knuckles were white as they curled around the headboard. Her body was quivering.

The scent of sex and vanilla and woman hung in the air.

Perfect.

He kissed her shoulder.

Her head turned, just a bit, and her eyes met his. There was pleasure on her face. No denying that, but Jasmine also looked...lost?

Had he hurt her? "Jasmine?" Her stitches—

"I...wasn't prepared for you."

He didn't know what that meant. He'd taken care of the protection. He always did. No way would he go bareback with a woman he'd just picked up.

Jasmine's not just any woman.

She blinked and her expression changed. Now she just looked...happy. Sated.

His.

"That was incredible." Her voice was still soft and husky, and he was already getting hard inside of her. Again.

Round two, coming up.

But first...

He pulled out of her. Settled her down against the covers. Feasted for a moment with his eyes. He'd give her a few minutes to rest, then he'd get more screams from her.

Sex with Jasmine had been fantastic. Far better than—

His phone was ringing. Hell, where was his phone? He'd thrown it aside earlier when he shed his clothes. He'd been so intent on getting *in* Jasmine that he hadn't exactly been paying much attention to the thing.

Ah...there...

He followed the sound and swiped up his phone—it had been under his trousers. "This had better be important," he snapped. *Cause you're taking me away from paradise.*

"Oh, it's important, all right, boss. Some jerkoff just tried to get access to your vault," Chad told him, voice flat and hard. "The guy stole a guard's suit and walked right up here."

His body tensed. "Where is the joker now?" Drake turned his back on Jasmine.

"He knocked out two of the guards."

What?

"And he...hell, it looks like he just left. Must've realized that he wasn't going to be able to break through the vault's security system."

No, that didn't fit. The guy knocked out the guards, then left—with nothing?

"Drake?" Jasmine's voice. Worried.

He glanced over his shoulder. She'd sat up in his bed. Her body was naked. Flushed from the releases he'd given her.

Beautiful, distracting Jasmine.

His jaw clenched as he put puzzle pieces together. "The devices last night were on timers..."

At his words, Jasmine's gaze seemed to double in size. "What's happening?" she demanded as she rose from the bed. Her eyes were wide.

"Those were just smoke bombs..." But now Chad's voice was hard with an edge of worry.

"Tell me what's happening!" Jasmine grabbed for his arm.

He didn't respond to her, but he told his security chief, "Maybe those were just smoke last night, but maybe they aren't tonight."

Her hand tightened on him. "Was someone at the Arrow?"

As if she didn't know.

Such a lying, beautiful face.

"What happened?" Her nails dug into him. "*Tell me.*"

He eased the phone from his mouth. "Someone tried to get to the Arrow's vault. Attacked the men there but left without taking anything—"

"No," the word was a stark whisper from her as horror flashed across her face. "He hasn't taken anything yet. You have to get your men out of there! Close the casino!"

He glared at her. "You know what he's doing." *A set up. She's still playing me.*

"He's pissed. If he went in...or if he sent someone else inside...anyone in that casino could be in danger."

"What will he do, Jasmine?"

She shook her head. "I don't know...I just...I don't want anyone hurt."

Liar. He'd warned her about telling lies.

"*Please,* be safe." She was begging again, but not because of passion. "Get the people out of there!"

He brought the phone back to his lips. "Get a sweep going—now. Close the whole place down." Because even without Jasmine's words, his gut was clenching with an instinct that couldn't be denied.

"Yes, sir," Chad told him instantly.

Jasmine's breath whispered out as Drake ended the call. She backed away from him. Still naked. Still staring up at him with secrets in her eyes.

But he was figuring out those secrets. *And maybe I really did just get fucked.* "You're the distraction."

"Wh-what?"

"You keep me busy, while what...he goes after my money?" She'd been the one to tell him that he had to head down to New Orleans. A ruse, to get him away from the Arrow so her boss could attack.

He'd been lost in her, driven to the edge by his lust, when some of her cronies had been trying to rob him. "What's he got planned?"

"I-I don't—"

"*What?*" Rage erupted inside of him. "Dammit, I have friends in that casino. Innocent people in the club. Don't you try to cover—"

Her chin slipped up a notch. "I don't know anything about another attack on the Arrow! I thought he was trying to come after your property down here, not up there in Vegas."

"You're lying to me." He'd warned her before. There were no more warnings.

"No."

"People could die, Jasmine. Stop screwing around and tell me what you know! You wanted my security guards to do a sweep. You knew that something could be happening."

She was silent.

"Tell me."

Her lashes lowered as she seemed to go limp in his arms. "I'm a dead woman now."

What?

"Like you, Maxwell Case was ex-military."

Maxwell Case. She'd just confirmed the SOB's identity. And she was still talking.

"Demolitions were his specialty," her voice was muted. "He liked to—liked to make things explode. That's what he told me." When her lashes lifted, her eyes shone with tears. "When I was in his office, I...accessed his computer. Found blueprints for the Arrow. Information on the vault. That's how I knew where to put my smoke bombs. I used the plans I found on his computer. The placement was so obvious...I...*it was just smoke for me, but I'm afraid it won't be for him.*"

He pushed her away and called his head of security. "Chad?" The man answered right away. "Get the bomb squad in there."

"Boss?"

"Use your connections. Get them there *now,* and make sure everyone else is *out.*"

Because he would not have anyone dying on his watch.

Maxwell, you bastard...now I'll be coming after you.

"I can tell you where to search," Jasmine whispered. "I can tell you everything I saw on his computer..."

***

The Arrow should've blown. A controlled explosion that would've given him access to all the cash in that casino.

Not that Maxwell Case needed cash.

He wanted to make a fucking point.

But the bomb squad came. The place didn't blow. They found all of his devices. In record time.

As if they knew just where to look...as if they knew exactly what he'd planned.

Jasmine.

That little bitch. She had always seen and understood far more than most people realized. It was that deceptively delicate appearance. When you looked that fragile, people expected you to be weak.

Jasmine was the smartest woman he'd ever met.

She was also a dead woman.

You told him, Jasmine.

She'd figured out his game. Figured out how much Maxwell liked the fire. Ah, now that was a shame. He'd had such grand plans for Jasmine.

But she'd gone and wrecked everything.

He slid into the back of the limo that waited for him. One that had been parked blocks away from the Arrow.

"Home, sir?" his driver asked.

"Yeah." Because there would be no fireworks that night. He pulled out his phone. Pressed the number for the hunter who was proving to be nothing but useless. "Hardin, where the hell is she?"

Silence. Then, voice breaking a bit, the hunter confessed, "She flew away with him...to New Orleans."

Maxwell nearly smashed the phone. Jasmine wasn't supposed to leave town. She should've returned to him.

"I-I'm boarding a flight now," Hardin stammered out. "I'll be right on her tail."

So will I.

Jasmine...beautiful bitch. She'd switched allegiances. Told Archer about the bombs. Even when she shouldn't have *known* about them.

And now...now she'd suffer.

He had a special way of paying back those who betrayed him.

Jasmine, baby, you're going to burn.

CHAPTER SIX

"They found three explosives."

Jasmine's eyes squeezed closed at this news. She was out on Drake's balcony, clad now in jeans and a t-shirt. The rain had stopped, but she knew the storm was far from over.

"They were all right in the exact spots you said." His hand closed around her shoulder as he turned her to face him.

She forced herself to hold his furious stare.

"You knew what he was doing."

The rage on his face terrified her. "I didn't!"

"You knew every spot—"

"N-no one was hurt?"

Grimly, he shook his head and she was finally able to draw in a deep breath. "Thank God." She'd been terrified that someone would get hurt before the bombs could be deactivated.

"You're working for a sadistic asshole who plants *bombs*." His hold was almost painful. "So you've done this before...just stood by while innocent people suffered. While they were hurt, you—"

"*No!*" The scream broke from her because it was too much. "I haven't. I wouldn't." So he really thought that of her, huh? Not surprising. Most people had been sure she was just trash all her life. *Just like dear old mom.* "He gave me the specs to get in to the casino. I told you, he had the blueprints." Blueprints that she'd discovered when she did a bit of snooping on his computer. "I knew about his demolitions past, okay? And I just put two and two together when you told me that someone was back at your casino. I wanted to make sure everyone was *safe*."

He had no clue what she'd just done. Maxwell would discover that his devices had been found. He'd also soon connect the dots and realize that she was the person who'd seen the blueprints. She'd been the one in his office. He would know that. She'd had access to his computer, and getting past his computer's security system had been all too easy for her.

When he realized what she'd done, Maxwell would come after her.

I'm a dead woman. None of her connections would be able to save her this time.

"It's not like he rose to power easily in Vegas." She'd read the newspaper stories. Had done her own research. "He told me once that he had to fight his way to the top of the pack."

"You're working with him."

She shook her head. "I took one job for him. I was supposed to get that business intel on your computer. Nothing more. I swear, I *swear*, I would never do anything to hurt anyone."

"You crawled into bed with the wrong man."

She flinched. The memory of being in Drake's bed was too strong. *I can still feel him on my skin. In me.*

"I'm going to destroy him," Drake told her flatly. "No one comes after me like this. *No one.*"

He pushed her away. As if he didn't want to touch her anymore. Then he turned his back on her. Left her out there on that balcony.

"Drake?" She took a quick step forward.

He didn't turn at her call.

Jasmine hurried after him. "Drake, please, it's not what you think—"

He didn't answer her. Didn't talk to her. Didn't even stop in the den. He left the big, cavernous house. Left her standing there, with her arms wrapped around her stomach.

He said he'd protect me.

But he was leaving her. He'd fucked her, just like he'd said he would.

More like fucked me over.

Jasmine felt as if she were about to shatter into a million pieces.

Maxwell planted bombs in the casino. People could've died. He wouldn't be done, not yet. His attack hadn't worked, so he'd make a new plan. That was how he operated. Why he was so very dangerous.

He didn't stop, not until his enemies were eliminated.

She hurried toward the phone in the den, her whole body shaking. Picking up the phone on the nearby table—Jasmine's phone was some place back in Vegas—she called him blindly.

Maxwell answered on the second ring.

"What have you done?" Jasmine whispered.

"*Jasmine...*"

"Bombs, Max? Dear God, people were in there!"

"You found my plans...naughty girl."

She'd found blueprints. She hadn't realized just how important they were, not until that moment in Drake's bedroom. A robbery was one thing. A bombing was another. "I'm going to the cops." She'd tell them everything she knew about Max.

"The cops won't save you."

Goosebumps rose on her arms.

"You know how I deal with betrayal, Jazz." *Jazz...*a nickname that had followed her for so long that it had become her codename in the business.

You wanted information retrieved from a rival...call Jazz.

You needed a computer hacked...call Jazz.

You need a life destroyed...

A sob rose in her throat. "I'm telling them everything. You're done. You should just...you should get on a plane and get the hell out of the country. Run, while you still can."

His low laughter slipped over the line. "My, but you must be upset...because you didn't even try to block this number when you called me. Such an amateur mistake. But then, I already knew you were with him in New Orleans."

The sob choked her. No, she hadn't tried to block the call. What would have been the point? When she'd been on Maxwell's computer, she'd seen the file he had on Drake...a file that had contained the addresses and telephone numbers for all of Drake's homes. This place in the Quarter, the estate in Vegas, the—

"I know where you are, Jazz, and I'm coming for you."

No. *No!* "Stay away from me. Stay away from Drake!"

"I'll be seeing you in the Big Easy, love. I'll find you, and then I'll finish my business with Drake."

He hated Drake. She didn't even know why. Surely this wasn't just about business?

"I'll show you just how beautiful I can make the flames," Maxwell promised her. "They'll be nearly as beautiful as you."

He's coming to kill me.

"Stay away from Drake," she repeated as she swiped at the stupid tears on her cheeks. "And you need—you need to run. You think he was the only one that I hacked? I was in your office, too, Max. I've got your files. I've got your business. I've got your life."

Silence, then... "You're playing out of your league."

"I didn't want to be in this nightmare at all. You forced my hand." Now...*turnabout, asshole.* "Stay away from him."

He hung up on her.

Her gaze flew around the house.

Then Jasmine did the only thing she could...she ran. It was a good thing that she'd had plenty of practice at running.

I ran away for the first time when I was fifteen. I wasn't going to let her use me...wasn't going to let those men touch me.

I ran then.

And she would keep running, for as long as it took. She'd run until she was safe.

***

Drake stared down at the crowd in his casino, the Masquerade. The New Orleans place was his crown jewel. Right on the riverfront, perfect for the tourists. Perfect for those looking to live on the edge.

The floor was mostly empty below him. Dawn had come, and in a few hours, the place would begin to fill.

Coins would fall into the slot machines. The tables would be surrounded. Roulette, Black Jack, Craps...

They'd come for the thrill. The thrill drew them back again and again.

Like moths to the flame...they'd all get burned sooner or later.

"We all do," he muttered as he turned away from the scene below.

He'd been burned. *Jasmine.* She was so tangled up with Maxwell. A lying, deceiving, murderous—

"Mr. Archer? There's a...a federal agent here to see you."

He turned at his assistant's hesitant voice. Janet stood in the doorway, her hair pulled back in its usual elegant twist. Her hands hovered nervously in the air. "He said it was urgent."

Great. Just what he didn't need then. Trouble with some government jerk. "Tell him I'm not available—"

"Like I'd buy that BS," a male replied as he shouldered in after Janet. The man's sharp gaze flickered assessing over Drake. "Especially since I saw you saunter up here five minutes ago."

Janet had actually *brought* the guy to his office?

"It's the badge," the fellow said with a hard grin. "And the gun...they tend to get action."

"I'm sorry," Janet whispered.

"Forget it." Drake rolled back his shoulders. "Just shut the door on your way out." He'd have this guy hitting the street in moments. Not like it was the first time an agent had paid him a visit. Sometimes, the visits were about his past. About the missions he'd done. And sometimes, they were even about Uncle Sam needing him to help again.

You couldn't really leave the business. Not for good. Some ties were never broken.

The door softly closed behind Janet.

Drake took his seat and motioned for the agent. "Didn't catch your name—"

The guy flashed his ID. "Special Agent Victor Monroe."

The name meant nothing. "And what can I do for you this incredibly early morning, agent?" Drake didn't bother keeping the impatience from his voice.

The agent eased into the chair across from him.

"I was informed of the scare you had at your Vegas casino recently."

Drake let his brows climb. That had been *very* recently. "Your intel is fast."

"Three bombs," the guy reminded him. "That's the kind of news that has to pass quickly."

Drake waited for the agent to continue.

Victor cleared his throat. "I couldn't help but notice those bombs were found rather easily, as if you had a map leading straight to them..."

Drake kept staring.

Victor leaned forward. "Tell me where she is."

The hell, *no.* "Who?"

"We're alone in here, so cut the bull. I need to find Jazz."

Jazz? The agent's tone had far too much familiarity for Drake. "I don't know who you're talking about."

"Cut the crap. She left Vegas with you. My intel put her on your plane, and the way you found those bombs, so damn fast, I *know* she told you about them."

"This little visit is over." Drake rose and glared at the guy. *Get the hell out of here.*

"I'm taking her in," Victor said as he stood. The agent was almost as tall as Drake. Victor's hair was a dark brown, and his eyes, a light blue, were hard with intensity. "So save me some time and tell me where she is. If she's here at the casino—"

"Find criminals on your own time. Not mine."

Victor's jaw hardened. "Ah, so you know what she is?"

"Find her on your own," he gritted out again. He'd walked away from her. There was no way she was still at his house.

Hell, he hadn't even locked the door on his way out. Hadn't even put a guard on her.

Because I don't want her anymore. Because I won't let another beautiful, lying woman try to destroy me and the people close to me.

I. Don't. Want. Her.

And there was no one there to call him a liar.

"I don't think you actually grasp the urgency of the situation." Victor leaned over Drake's desk, resting his hands on the old wood. "I need Jazz, and I need her now. She's to be placed in federal custody immediately."

"And she said that she wasn't running from the law," Drake muttered. "Another lie." How unsurprising.

Victor's eyelashes flickered. "I don't think you understand—"

"Yeah, I understand just fine. Jasmine is a liar and a thief, and she's not my problem anymore." The words were hard. They had to be.

He would *not* think of the way Jasmine had looked when he'd last seen her on that balcony. The pain that he'd heard in her voice as she called out after him.

She was playing him.

Just like—

No. He slammed the door on that memory.

The FBI agent pulled out a card. Tossed it on his desk. "If you should see the liar and thief, call me. I'll take her off your hands." But Victor's whole manner had changed. He seemed pissed.

Join the club, buddy.

Victor gave him a little salute then he strode from the office. Did he mutter "Dick" on his way out? Drake's eyes narrowed. The door closed with a near slam.

Drake waited about twenty seconds, then he grabbed his phone. The text he shot to Trace was blunt.

What the fuck did you find?

His fingers drummed on his desk. He waited for a text back, but instead, his phone vibrated. He answered immediately. "You called back, so I know the shit is bad."

"I'm still working on the details, okay? Your girl's past is tangled and twisted."

"She's not," Drake managed to push out, "*my* girl."

Silence. "Well, that plays, since I'm getting rumors she's been claimed by Maxwell Case."

His blood burned, then turned straight to ice in Drake's veins. "She's his lover?"

"That's what I'm picking up, and, man, that guy is trouble."

"Tell me something I don't know." Jasmine and Maxwell. Jasmine *fucking* Maxwell. His hand was a fist on the desk. His temples felt as if they were about to explode.

"I don't have proof on that relationship, just rumors. But it's looking like—"

"He sent her to me."

I'm not a whore. Grim pride had cloaked around her as Jasmine spoke those words to him.

He pushed back his shoulders as he tried to shove her image away.

"She was born in Kendall, Texas. Her mother was Shirley Bennett, and no father was listed on her birth certificate. Shirley had over a dozen arrests for prostitution so—"

I'm not a whore.

His fist slammed into the desk. That pain in her voice had been real.

"So maybe Shirley didn't even know who Jasmine's father was. Seems your gir—uh, Jasmine ran away when she was fifteen, and that's when things get harder to track."

Fifteen? He straightened. "What about before then?"

"Uh, before? She was just a kid—"

"What was she like?" Why had he just asked that shit?

"Straight A's, actually. I got access to her grades. Schools are always the easiest to hack. She was one of those never-in-trouble types."

His thief had been a good girl?

"She was taking AP classes in math and science and her teachers had been hoping she'd be able to get a scholarship, but then she...left."

Ran away. To something?

Or ran *from* something?

"I'll keep digging but the woman's life after fifteen—"

"She's good with computers." He rubbed his hand against his throbbing temples. "Very good. So good I think she—"

"Might be able to cover her own trail." Now Trace was annoyed. "You should have mentioned that point before." He rallied quickly. "Don't worry. I've got my own team of hackers. It'll take us some time, but we'll discover her secrets."

Drake headed out onto the balcony that overlooked Canal Street. Glancing down below, he saw Victor storming from the casino. "An FBI agent named Victor Monroe just left my office. He was looking for her."

"And did you give her up?"

"She's not mine to give. I don't know where she is." Her image flashed before him once more. On that balcony, her face had been so pale. She'd almost looked broken. *Appearances can be deceiving.* "She's definitely working with Maxwell. I won't let another woman set me up for death."

"Well, if she's working for him, then how come she told you all about the bombs?"

Of course, Trace would already know about them. After the visit from the FBI guy, Drake was wondering who *didn't* know. "She told me about them because Jasmine didn't want anyone at the casino to get hurt."

"Wow, quite the cold-blooded bitch, isn't she?" Now Trace's voice was mocking. "Just like Anna Jean."

"*Don't,*" Drake bit out. "Don't say her name to me." Because he was so sick of remembering. Anna Jean's lies. Anna Jean's life.

Her death.

At his hands.

"Not every woman is like her," Trace's voice was soft.

"You mean your woman isn't like her." Skye. Trace had been obsessed with Skye for years. But the bastard was lucky—Skye loved him, too. Enough to risk her life for him.

Silence hummed on the line, then Trace said, "It wasn't your fault."

Drake had to laugh at that even as he kept staring at the street below. "Really? You mean someone else drove the knife into her? Because I sure as hell remember her blood being on my hands." The agent had disappeared. "Call me when you learn more."

"Wait man, look, don't do anything stupid, okay?"

What?

"You take too many risks. You've been walking on the edge for a while, and I don't want you falling over."

Too late. He'd gone over the edge long ago.

"Maybe Jasmine can help you," Trace added. "If she's valuable to Maxwell and the guy is gunning for you, then maybe you should team up with her and—"

Valuable. The wheels began to spin in his head. "Maybe I can use her." The idea had whispered through his mind once before.

"No!" Trace's voice was a bark. "That's not what I meant. I said work *with* her. But wait until I can find out more, okay? Leave this to me and you—"

"I'll be waiting on the edge." Drake ended the call. Maybe he had been too hasty when he walked away from her. If Maxwell was screwing Jasmine, wouldn't the guy plan to come after her? And to think, Jasmine had tried to act afraid of the fellow.

I'm dead...

The fear had sounded so real to him. She was one fine actress. Maybe even better than Anna Jean had been.

She'd asked Drake to protect her from Maxwell. She'd given him her body. Told him enough to keep his casino safe. Yes, he could use her. He could learn more.

And he would make absolutely sure that he never gave the woman the chance to betray him again.

***

Jasmine hadn't expected the sheer number of people who packed Bourbon Street at nightfall. They drifted in and out of the bars, some hung over the edge of the balconies, and some made out in doorways. Drinks were flowing heavily. Laughter filled the air, and everywhere Jasmine turned, bodies seemed to brush against her.

Getting lost in the crowd here would be easy. It would be—

Her gaze fell on a brightly lit doorway. A woman stood there, barely dressed. Only the woman looked young. So very young. She was motioning toward some frat boys, inviting them in for a dance.

A private dance.

Jasmine's gaze slid to the left. Another brightly lit doorway. Another woman beckoning for a dance.

It wasn't just the drinks that were flowing on Bourbon Street.

Jasmine stared at those women, and her own past stared back at her.

Mama's tired tonight, and he...he likes you, baby. Why don't you help me out? Just do a little dance for him. Come on...he'll pay you.

Jasmine turned away from those women and she began to shove her way through the crowd. It had been the perfect place to hide earlier, but now, now this place was suffocating her. Too many bodies. Too many hands brushing against her.

Too many memories that she could never forget.

"Hey, where's the rush?" A man was in front of her. Blond hair, just like Drake's, big with stretching shoulders. Only...he wasn't Drake.

Drake was gone. No protection. No hope.

"I've got a date," she muttered as she tried to step around him.

But he stepped with her. "I can be your date." He had an overflowing drink in his hand, and under the streetlights, his eyes gleamed. "I can be anything you want me to be."

I want you to be out of my way. She bit those words back and gave him a weak smile. "Not gonna happen tonight, handsome. I'm taken."

He shrugged and eased aside, moving off in search of new prey.

Jasmine exhaled heavily and took a step forward.

"Taken?"

She stilled. That voice was low and deep, and she knew it could only belong to one man. Because that voice—that man—had been the one to break through the careful wall that she'd put around herself.

He'd hurt her. When no one else had, not in so very long.

The crowd seemed to part around him. Drake wasn't wearing his expensive suit and coat. He wore jeans. A battered jacket. He looked big and tough and dangerous. Sexy, damn it.

"Didn't realize you were taken. Didn't realize you belonged to someone."

That seemed to be anger hardening his voice and eyes.

Good. She had plenty of her own anger.

You made me feel like a whore. No, she would *not* say those words to him. But when he'd left her there at that house, her body still humming with pleasure even as fear swamped her, and he hadn't looked back...Drake had changed everything for her.

"You don't know me, Drake. And you never will." This time, she was the one who turned on her heel and walked away. *See how it feels, jerk.*

"Jasmine."

He said her name like it was a demand. No, a command. Like she was just supposed to stop because he was there and actually speaking to her again.

Screw. You. Jasmine lifted her hand, waving one fun finger back at him, then she picked up her pace. So what if she'd just left this particular corner not two minutes ago? She could retreat this way if she wanted.

Her gaze slid over, and she noticed that the women weren't in those doorways anymore. Wait, *new* women were there.

She swallowed.

Drake didn't call her name again. She didn't look back to see if he was still standing there, a big, unbreakable statue, or if he was following her.

When she hit the next intersection, Jasmine turned and snaked down the other street. A much quieter street. Then she ducked into an alley. Sure, she was almost running now, but she'd left the bustle of Bourbon behind her. Actually, by just heading over a few blocks, she'd seemed to leave everything behind.

Silence surrounded her.

Shadows loomed.

And...

"Jasmine."

That voice hadn't come from behind her. A man stepped from the shadows. "We always seem to meet in alleys," he said.

It was just not her night.

That voice didn't belong to Drake. It belonged to another man who she'd hoped to never see again.

Wayne Hardin. So-called bounty hunter.

Hired thug.

"You followed me? All the way to New Orleans?" Jasmine had thought that she had a little more time on her own. She slanted a quick glance around the area. She didn't see anyone else. Thankfully, there was no sign of Maxwell.

There was also no sign of Drake. She figured he was still back on Bourbon Street. Maybe he hadn't even been looking for her out there. Maybe he'd been looking to party. He'd been dressed casually, and he hadn't exactly fallen at her feet and begged for forgiveness...

"I don't stop until I bring in my bounty."

Her breath felt cold in her lungs. "I'm not in the mood for another knife wound."

He lifted his hands toward her. "Got my orders. You're to be brought in, with not so much as a scratch on you."

Now that was just a mistake. He shouldn't have told her that. Because she planned to do more than just scratch him.

"The boss wants you," Wayne added.

"We can't always have what we want." She reached into her bag. A cute little bag that she'd picked up in town at a boutique next to a Voodoo shop.

She'd also picked up something else. Not at the Voodoo shop, but from a very helpful man she'd met.

Jasmine drew out her gun. "Here's how this will play out. You're going to turn around and walk away. You're going to tell Maxwell that you never saw me. And, in return, I won't shoot you. I'll be super generous and call us even."

He laughed at her. "You're not gonna shoot me. You don't have the guts."

Idiot. This wasn't the time to insult her. "Of course, I do."

"You hack computers. Snoop in files..." He was closing in on her. "You don't get blood on your hands."

She kept a tight grip on the weapon. "Turn around and walk away." He couldn't scratch her. She could shoot him. The wound in her side seemed to throb. It would be both payback and self-defense.

"What's he gonna do, when Maxwell gets you back?" Wayne asked her as he kept closing in. "I don't get to hurt you, but I'm betting he does."

She wasn't planning to find out. "I'm going to count to five, and if you aren't out of here by the time I get to five...I will shoot you."

It was too dark for her to see his face.

"One."

He was still coming toward her.

"Two."

Jasmine heard a faint rustle of sound. Close by. But she wasn't about to look away from the threat before her.

"Three," she snapped. Did he think she was bluffing? Jasmine aimed for his shoulder. *Come on, man. Back off.*

"Four." Her hands were sweating. Her heart racing. He wasn't going to stop. She'd have to shoot.

Jasmine squeezed her eyes shut. "Fi—"

A thud had her eyes flying right back open. She saw that Wayne was on the ground and another shadow loomed over him. Wayne surged upright and attacked that shadow.

Great. Fabulous. Those two could just fight it out. She didn't know if that was a mugger or another one of Maxwell's henchmen, and she wasn't sticking around to find out.

Jasmine sprinted on down that alley.

"*Jasmine!*" The roar of her name came from the mystery shadow. That roar belonged to Drake.

She spun around. He was already running toward her and he—

Snatched the gun from her hand. "A gun? Are you serious?"

She had been. Only... "It wasn't loaded," she whispered.

"*Fuck me.*" He grabbed her arm and started hauling her to who the heck knew where.

Frantic, Jasmine glanced over her shoulder. "What about Wayne? Is he—"

"Alive and running away."

She heard the thud of footsteps then. Well, she thought that she heard them. It was hard to tell because of her frantically beating heart and her own rushed footsteps. "Guess after last time, he didn't want to mess with you again."

He shoved the gun into the waistband of his jeans. "What the hell were you thinking?"

"I was mostly thinking about survival." She struggled to keep up with his fast pace.

"A gun? No bullets?"

"I've never used a gun before." Wayne had been so right on that one. "I didn't want to accidentally shoot myself." She also hadn't been prepared to shoot anyone else. Score another point for the bounty hunter. He seemed to know his prey pretty well.

"I don't believe this." Drake finally stopped the dragging and stalking routine. His hand dropped away from her.

They were in the darkness, no street lights around, so she couldn't see his face, but Jasmine was sure she didn't want to read his expression anyway. "I didn't ask you to follow me. Why don't you just wander right back over to Bourbon Street and forget all about me, okay? I can handle myself."

"Doubtful."

Jerk. "I've been doing it just fine for twenty-eight years," she bit out.

"And you've got a bounty hunter on your tail! Him and an FBI agent!"

Her breath huffed out in surprise. Was he talking about Victor Monroe? "Wh-what FBI agent?"

"The one who is chomping at the bit to get you into custody. The way I see it, I'm the only thing standing between you and two very bad spots."

Wayne.

The FBI.

"You don't know what's happening." She inched away from him.

"Then why don't you explain things to me."

"You *left* me." Wow, okay, that was a lot of rage cracking there. She hadn't meant to say— "You said you'd keep me safe, and at the first opportunity, you walked away without a backwards glance. I trusted you!"

She had *not* meant to say any of that. Not a word. How had all of that just erupted out of her mouth?

Jasmine snapped her lips closed.

Drake just stared down at her.

"Leave me alone," Jasmine ordered as she started to brush by him.

His fingers caught her wrist. "Or what? You'll count to five and pretend to shoot me?"

So he'd heard all that? He'd been in the shadows, silent and watchful, while she'd been terrified? Jasmine tried to yank her wrist from him. "This isn't funny! It's not a game. It's my life—"

He pulled her flush against him. "I know it's no game. The people in that casino that your lover tried to bomb—they matter to me."

Her lover? "He's not."

"What?"

"He's not my lover, okay? I don't know what you *think* you know or what you've heard, but he isn't."

"Right. Like I'm supposed to believe your lies. You screwed me. You screwed him—"

"Stop it." Her voice was flat and cold.

And...Drake stepped away.

"Don't you stand there and judge me. Don't *ever* say things like that to me again, do you understand?" That rage was back, and she didn't care that she was on a street corner in the Big Easy. She didn't care that a bounty hunter and an FBI agent could both be hunting her.

Her pride was too brittle. Her pain too strong.

"I wanted to be with you. You gave me pleasure, and I-I thought I gave you the same thing." His hands lifted as if he'd touch her again. She couldn't let him do that. Jasmine jumped away from Drake. "Then you turned your back on me as if I were nothing. You wouldn't even talk to me."

"Jasmine..."

"My sex life is my own. I don't judge you. Don't question you. And you have *no* right to throw accusations at me." She turned away from him, her shoulders hunching. "And you have no right," now her voice was hoarse, "to make me feel like I'm a whore—"

"*No!*"

She tried to draw in a shuddering breath but she couldn't because he had his hands on her. He'd spun her around to face him. "You're not a whore, and I'm sorry..." His words roughened. "I'm so sorry I made you feel that way. You touched me, got to me too deep, and I struck out at you." He wrapped his arms around her and pulled Jasmine against his chest. She could feel the frantic rhythm of his heartbeat beneath her ear. "You were too close, and I was an idiot for trying to push you away."

Stupid hope started to grow in her chest. No one...no one had ever said anything like that to her before. *You were too close.* He spoke as if she mattered to him, and he sounded so sincere.

Believe him. That was the voice of the desperate girl she'd been, so long ago. The one who'd imagined that people could be good. That life wasn't always about the darkness she saw all around her every single day.

She'd imagined that men could love. It wasn't always just about buying pleasure for a night.

"I want you to come back with me."

Such beautiful, tempting words. But... "I can't..."

"Jasmine, come back with me. *Please.*" Ah, that strangled word was lovely, but he didn't understand.

"I made a mistake. I-I called Maxwell from your house. He would've had your address already," she said, rushing out those words but they didn't exactly alleviate her guilt. "But already he knew that I was there, with you." He would've already known the exact location of that house. "He said he was coming after me."

"Let him come. I want to face the bastard."

"No, you don't." Drake was tough, sure, and he'd done his time in the military, but he wasn't on Maxwell's twisted level—Maxwell had no conscience. He would hurt anyone who got in his way. "He sent Wayne after me, and Maxwell won't be far behind." She should pull out of his arms. She didn't. "I have to go so that Maxwell will follow me."

He eased away. Just enough to stare down at her in the darkness. "You think that if you leave, he won't come after me? That he'll focus just on you?"

No, she thought he'd still go after Drake, but she had a plan.

"I should've kept that bounty hunter," Drake said, the words low and hard. "Made him talk."

She shivered.

Drake shook his head. "Wait. What the hell am I doing? I know better. We can't just stay out here." And he was back to pulling her down the street. Or rather, he pulled her back to Canal

Street and she was sure grateful to see the bright lights and cars again. Drake opened the door of a Porsche for her, one that had been parked near the edge of the street.

Another Porsche?

Before she could question the man's choice of cars, he was driving away with her.

And she just let him do it.

The city passed in a blur and she pounded her head against the seat rest.

She felt his eyes sweep over her. "Want to tell me what that's about?"

That? Her head-pounding routine? "I shouldn't be trusting you."

"Why?"

That point should be obvious. "Because you'll hurt me again."

They stopped at a red light. Jasmine looked toward Drake, and she saw his fingers tighten around the steering wheel.

"You get to me," she confessed. That was the whole reason she was in the car with him right then and not running like mad down the streets of New Orleans. "You make me feel...feel in ways I haven't before."

His head turned. He held her gaze.

"You were looking for me." It hadn't just been a walk on the wild side of Bourbon Street.

Drake nodded.

"Why?" So much depended on what he had to say. Her fingers curved around the handle of the door. She could jump out. Flee fast right then and get on the trolley.

"Because I need you."

Jasmine's breath left her in a rush.

A car horn sounded behind them.

"Don't take me back to your house in the Quarter. He'll just have eyes there." Maxwell would have eyes everywhere.

"Don't worry, princess," Drake said as he drove them forward. "From here on out, I've got you."

***

"She's here," Wayne said into his phone as he hurried down the New Orleans street. "But Archer is still sticking to her like glue—"

"And you didn't think to pull her away from him?"

Wayne glanced to the left. To the right. The street looked deserted. "The bastard is tough. I'm just biding my time until I can attack."

"No, you're being a coward. And your services—they're rather disappointing."

Lights flashed on then. Bright and blinding. Lights from a car that shouldn't have been so close.

If I'm watching Jasmine...who does he have on me? That thought rushed through his mind once more. Too late, this time.

"No..." Wayne whispered.

"Disappointing and no longer needed. And...by the way..."

The car was accelerating toward him. Wayne tried to run.

He had to make it across the street. Maybe he could break down the door of that old voodoo shop and—

The car didn't hit him.

Bullets did.

And then Wayne hit the pavement.

CHAPTER SEVEN

When she walked through the casino, she could hear the slot machines, playing like music. No, playing over the music that filled the Masquerade. She spun around, her gaze caught by the glitter and glamour all around her. The casino was decorated in a Mardi Gras style, with purple, gold, and green colors featured prominently. Large masks hung on the walls, masks that seemed to watch the casino-goers with glee.

The place was gorgeous. Phenomenal.

Then Jasmine looked up—up at the chandeliers that shone like diamonds above her. *Amazing.*

Drake's arm wrapped around her waist. "Do you like it?"

She thought about the home she'd had as a kid. The old trailer on the rough patch of land that no one else wanted. "It's...a little excessive."

He laughed lightly. "It was the trees in the lobby, right?"

She didn't even know how those trees—real trees—were alive out in the lobby.

"When you come from nothing," Drake said as he guided her toward a private elevator.

"Sometimes you want everything." He swiped a keycard over the security control panel, and the elevator's doors slid open.

The mirrored walls of the elevator tossed Jasmine's reflection right back at her.

"What do *you* want?" Drake asked her.

The elevator was rising. He was close to her. So very close. Drake seemed to fill that small space.

She had decided to be as honest with him as she could be. Because Drake mattered and, most shocking of all, he seemed to be saying that she mattered to him, too.

I need you.

"I want to belong." To some place. To somebody. She wanted a home. A real one. When the holidays came around, she wanted to bake cookies and stare up at a Christmas tree and be held in the arms of a man who loved her.

She didn't want to be alone forever.

"You can belong to me."

Her knees did a little jiggle. Had the elevator stopped rising? The doors hadn't opened but it felt as if they weren't moving any longer.

He came toward her and put his hands on either side of her, pressing his palms flat against the mirror behind her and caging Jasmine against his body. "Do you want to belong to me?"

Her head was spinning. She'd thought that he'd just walked away from her. But he'd searched for her. Protected her, *again,* and now he was offering her...

Hope.

"I want to be with you." The attraction she felt for him was unlike anything she'd experienced before. When he touched her, Jasmine's heart raced. When he kissed her, she went molten. And when he was in her, she exploded.

"Then be with me." His head lowered. His lips brushed against hers.

The kiss was tender. Open-mouthed. Hot. And she was molten—again. Jasmine knew her panties were getting wet. She wanted to shove off his clothes. To have sex with him right there. Then.

No restrictions. No fears. She wanted the pleasure he could give here once more.

Without the shame.

Her hand pushed against his chest.

Drake's head lifted.

"Don't walk away again." She couldn't handle that. Not from him.

Drake nodded. His gaze held hers. "And don't run from me."

Her eyes searched his. There was something there, in his stare. An emotion that she couldn't quite define.

"Because if you ran, then I'd be like Maxwell. Chasing you through the streets." His laugh held a rough edge. "Or I guess I already am like him."

"No." Her denial was swift. "You could never be like him."

A muscle flexed near his jaw.

"You're safe here," Drake told her. "Security has been doubled. Maxwell and his men won't get to you." He backed away. Used that keycard again and the doors opened. "I have an apartment here that we can use for the night. Private quarters that I keep."

Sleeping wasn't exactly high on her priority list.

She followed him from the elevator.

But he stilled in that small hallway. "I'm going to destroy him."

"Drake—"

"You won't like what I do. But it's going to happen. Then you'll never have to worry about running from anyone again."

His words caused fear to rush through her, but in the next moment, he had her in his arms. He was carrying her—*carrying her!*—into his private quarters. Into the bedroom attached there. He stripped her slowly. Using so much care, when, before, he'd been frantic in his need.

His hands slid over her body. His caresses seemed to cherish her. She had to blink away tears because she *knew* what he was doing.

I felt like a whore.

"I want to see your pleasure, princess."

And now he was treating her like someone precious.

He stroked her and caressed her until Jasmine was about to go out of her head. He'd been demanding before, and he still was—but only demanding her pleasure.

He caught her nipples in his hands. Thumbed the peaks, had her gasping. Fire rushed to her sex as he kissed and stroked his way down her body. He seemed to be even more careful around her bandage, but Jasmine didn't even feel an ache from her wound. She was too focused on him.

His mouth pushed over her core. His tongue licked her clit, and when she arched off the bed, he locked his hands around her hips and took even more of her.

She climaxed with a fury so hard that the room went dark. Her heart was a drumbeat in her ears. Her breaths panted out. The pleasure twisted her up, shook her. It was amazing. *He* was amazing.

Then he...he pulled away.

"Drake?" He left her there on the bed, still shuddering and quaking. His hand smoothed over her, once, so carefully, then he retreated.

She watched, heartbeat still not back to its normal rhythm, as he stopped near the window.

Drake gazed out at the city below. She could practically feel the intensity of his desire filling that room. *But he'd walked away.* "Drake, you—"

"I want the pleasure to just be yours."

"That's not what I want." She rose from the bed. Naked.

He turned toward her. "You don't have to give me anything," he seemed to push out the words. "This time was just for you. I can be more than a selfish bastard."

She lowered onto her knees before him. Did he know that she'd never done this for another man? No, he couldn't know. But she'd never really wanted to, until now.

"And this is just for you." Her hands fumbled a bit as she reached for the snap of his jeans, then she pulled down the zipper with a hiss of sound that was far too loud in that quiet room.

His cock sprang toward her. No underwear for her tough guy. Just a full, long cock. One that she had to stroke as she explored with her hands.

Her knees pressed into the lush carpet as she leaned toward him. Her breath blew lightly over that heavy length and his cock swelled even more.

"Jasmine...be careful..."

Oh, crap, maybe it was obvious this was her first time. "I'm new at this," she confessed as she glanced up at him, "so tell me when I do something wrong."

The darkness of his pupils swallowed the green of his eyes. "New?"

"You're my first." She felt like she could tell him anything in that moment. "So if I do it wrong—"

"You can't. No damn way."

His hands bit into her shoulders.

She pressed a kiss to the head of his shaft. Then she opened her mouth and took him inside.

"Wanted you to...be careful..." His words were so low and rough. "Because you're making me want you...too much..."

She liked his taste. Wanted more. So she tried to take more of him as she licked and sucked.

His hand moved to curve around her nape. He tilted her head and she took more of him.

He was—

"*Jasmine!*"

He had her on her feet. Two steps and he had her on the bed. Her legs fell apart as she hit the mattress, and he was right there. He'd put on a condom in an instant and now he had her in his sights. Still standing, at the side of the bed. He pulled her toward him. Her hips were at the edge of the mattress and he thrust into her, deep and hard, filling every inch of her.

"Warned you," Drake bit out. "Want you...too much."

And there it was. The wild, frantic mating that she'd secretly craved. The rush that wasn't controlled. The need that wasn't safe.

In and out. He drove into her again and again, and Jasmine loved it. Her nails scraped over his shoulders as she fought to get closer to him. To hold him as tightly as she could and take everything that he had to give.

She arched against him, her head tipping back against the bed. His mouth pressed to her throat. The sting of his teeth electrified her.

When she came, Jasmine felt Drake erupt inside of her. Biting her lip, Jasmine tried to hold back a scream. She didn't want—

"Give it to me," Drake demanded. "Give me everything."

So she cried out her pleasure.

And he growled her name.

***

He was watching her sleep.

Drake stared down at Jasmine as she lay curled in his bed. His arm was under her head. Hell, he was her pillow. And he...didn't mind.

She looked innocent. Sexy.

Right.

And that was wrong.

No woman was supposed to look right in his bed. He had a rule—his lovers didn't stay the night.

So why was he pulling her closer and inhaling the vanilla scent that clung to her?

She'd been so hesitant when she knelt before him and told him that it had been her first time. He hadn't wondered if the words were a lie. Her eyes had flickered with nervousness and desire, and she'd touched him almost reverently.

She'd also nearly made him fall to *his* knees when that sexy mouth had closed around his aroused cock.

But the desire was sated. The passion had cooled.

Or, at least, that was what Drake was trying to tell himself. The twisted truth was that he'd fuck her again. And again. He wanted to take her endlessly. Sex with her had been even better the second time.

He loved to see her eyes go blind with pleasure. Loved her taste.

She snuggled closer to him.

His hand smoothed over her shoulder.

His phone vibrated. He'd moved it to the small nightstand, and he reached out, being careful not to disturb her as he read the text.

Got info you need.

The text was from Trace.

Drake glanced at Jasmine's sleeping face.

The phone vibrated again. His gaze slid over the screen.

Be careful. There's more going on than you know.

Right. Because, of course, Trace would've found out that Jasmine was trying to screw him over.

He almost texted back...*I don't want to know*. Because he just wanted to stay in that bed with her, and act as if the rest of the world didn't matter. He wanted Jasmine to simply be the woman that she appeared to be in his arms.

No secrets. No lies.

That wasn't the way his reality worked.

Carefully, he rose from the bed. Jasmine had said that she'd called Maxwell from the phone at his home in the Quarter, so getting that number hadn't exactly been hard.

Instead of responding to Trace's text, Drake called Maxwell Case. The call was already overdue.

The phone rang once. Twice. Then...

"Who the hell is this?"

Drake smiled. "I'm the man planning to destroy you."

Jasmine stirred a bit on the bed, moving restlessly.

"*Archer.*"

"You shouldn't have started a war with me." Because if there was one thing that Drake knew how to do, it was fight a war.

"You're the one who started this. You think I don't know what you did? To *her?*"

Drake's gaze narrowed on Jasmine. She was still sleeping.

"If she didn't come back, she told me to look for you. She thought she could count on *you*."

A cold fist squeezed his guts. "This is personal," he said. Not about business. Not about casinos.

"She trusted you, and you killed her."

A chill encased Drake's body as those words sank in. Drake realized that his past was coming back to bite him in the ass.

And Drake couldn't take his eyes off Jasmine. *Did she know?* Did she realize what this nightmare was truly all about?

"What did she matter to you?" Drake asked. He didn't make any confession.

"She was mine, far longer than she was yours. My Anna Jean..."

Dammit. The man had just confirmed Drake's suspicion.

You killed her...Anna Jean...

This wasn't about casinos. Money. Power.

It was about a woman. Betrayal. Vengeance.

His past—and a reckoning.

Jasmine had mentioned that Maxwell had been in the military. Drake should have paid more attention to those words.

Maxwell had been enlisted and so had Anna Jean. Beautiful, lying Anna Jean.

Beautiful, *dead* Anna Jean.

"We were going to take down your friends," Maxwell said. "Anna Jean and I had a plan, but then you *killed her.*"

Jasmine's hand fluttered against the covers, as if she were seeking him in her sleep.

"Now I will take everything away from you," Maxwell promised him. "And in the end, you'll beg to die."

"I don't beg for anything." Never had. Never would. "And you've made a mistake. The same mistake she made. I won't be played. And anyone who comes after me...well, you're going to be finding a swift trip to hell waiting on you."

Laughter was Maxwell's answer.

But then the laughter stilled. "What will you do..." Maxwell asked him. "When another woman dies in your arms?"

That cold fist squeezed him tighter.

"Jasmine shouldn't have turned to you—"

She didn't just turn to me. She gave herself to me. Came in my arms. Screamed for me.

"I'll punish her, but, don't worry, you'll be there. You'll watch it all."

Jasmine's lashes fluttered open.

"You're a dead man," Drake said flatly.

Jasmine gasped as she heard his words. She shot upright in bed, clutching the covers to her.

That mocking laughter came again.

The call ended with a fast click.

With wide, unreadable eyes, Jasmine stared up at him. "M-Maxwell? That was him on the line, wasn't it?"

He nodded.

"He's on his way to New Orleans. He may already be here." She scrambled from the bed. Dragged the covers with her. "What are you planning?"

"To kill him."

Jasmine flinched. "No, go to the cops. Talk to them."

What? That was the *last* thing he'd expected her to say. "That's not an option." Not with Anna Jean's death being tangled in this mess.

"You don't know what he's capable of doing—"

His hand sank into her hair and he tipped her head back. "But you do, and you're going to tell me everything you know about him."

"Drake..."

"You want to be free of him, don't you? I'll make sure you're free."

But Jasmine's body trembled. "I don't want you to kill him! That isn't who you are! That isn't—"

Now it was his turn to laugh. "Ah, princess, and here I thought you'd done your 'research' on me." With a mocking smile on his lips, he said, "I'm very good at killing. You should have discovered that by now."

She pulled away from him.

"Maxwell won't hurt you again because we are going to take him down. You're going to tell me his weaknesses. Every single thing that you know about him. And I will use that information to break him."

"He hates you," Jasmine whispered. "So much...*why?* I could never figure out *why*."

Why not tell her? Drake shrugged. The move was careless, his past wasn't. "Because it seems we were both dumb enough to fall for the same woman."

Her eyes doubled in size. "What?"

"We fell for her, and then I killed her."

***

"Has the situation with the bounty hunter been handled as I asked?"

Maxwell Case stared out at the glittering New Orleans skyline.

"Yeah, boss, he's been left just as you ordered."

He'd been enraged when he found out just what Wayne had done to Jasmine. Good thing that doctor in Vegas had been so chatty...

With the right leverage, anyone would talk.

Anyone would break.

"Pressure has to be applied," Maxwell said. "Archer has such a perfect cover now. The legitimate businessman. We're blowing that cover to hell. The world will see him for who he is, and he'll pay for his crimes."

"What about...what about Jasmine?"

He turned at the question. His guard, Saxon, had been with him for a while. Saxon could always be counted on to get the job done—no matter what that job might be. The man was a loyal employee.

And he had wonderful, deadly skills that Maxwell so enjoyed using on his enemies.

"You're not...you're not really going to kill Jazz are you?" Hesitation slowed Saxon's words. It was the only time Maxwell had ever heard hesitation in the man's voice.

Saxon had been the one to first bring the lovely Jasmine to Maxwell's attention. Saxon and Jasmine had worked together before. Smaller jobs. Little heists.

They were friends, of a sort.

"If it weren't for *Jazz,* the Arrow would be nothing more than a pile of rubble in Vegas." Anna Jean would've liked that. She would've laughed as the flames hit the sky. "She turned on me. She must have hacked *my* computer, and she told Archer everything she knew."

Saxon was sweating. "But..."

Maxwell waved his hand in the air. "Don't worry, I'll handle Jazz."

"She's going to suffer?"

It was such a shame. Saxon seemed almost concerned for Jazz. But then, Jasmine had a talent for getting to people. For slipping right past their guards before they even realized it.

Maybe it was those eyes of hers. So deep and dark. Or it could've been her dimples. The woman had a beautiful smile.

He'd caught himself watching her smile once or twice. Waiting for those dimples to flash. Perhaps in another time...another place...

He shook his head. He only had this time. "Jasmine isn't who you think she is."

He'd recently uncovered more intel on her.

Saxon backed up a step.

"So the hell, yes," Maxwell narrowed his eyes on the guard, "I will make her suffer." He would make her beg, bleed, and *burn.* "And if you have a problem with that, then—"

"N-no problem," Saxon managed.

Good. Because if it *had* been a problem, then Saxon would've been dead.

In his organization, people either followed Maxwell's orders completely—or those people were eliminated.

***

She watched the sun rise over the city. Sleep hadn't exactly been an option for Jasmine, not after Drake's big reveal during the hours of darkness.

And not with his endless questions.

Where is his money—all of it, Jasmine. Off-shore accounts, properties...

I want his business associates. Every name that you know.

Why did he pick you? Why you?

He'd seemed enraged when he asked that question.

Her answer hadn't exactly thrilled him. *Because I was convenient.*

She'd worked with one of Maxwell's bodyguards before. Saxon had been the one to tell Maxwell about her particular skill set.

"He's out there." Drake's arm brushed against hers as he came to stand with her on the balcony.

A dull headache pounded behind her eyes. "Yes, he is." Waiting. Planning to strike. How would he attack first?

He'll come after me.

Jasmine figured that Maxwell would save his big game for last.

"I answered all of your questions." She'd given Drake as much information as she—safely—could. "Now, I need you to answer mine." Squaring her shoulders, she turned to face him. "Who was the woman?"

He was staring at the rising sun. She knew just how that sunrise looked—like blood flashing across the sky. "Anna Jean. Beautiful Anna Jean."

The name meant nothing to her. That would be changing as soon as she got near a computer. "Did the beautiful Anna Jean have a last name?"

His gaze slanted toward her. "That doesn't matter."

It did. Everything in this vendetta mattered.

"How did you meet her?" Jasmine pressed.

"We worked covert operations together. After I got out of the military." His lips twisted. "She was my friend's girl."

Hold up, wait, that didn't make—

"But I had sex with her. One drunken night." He ran a hand over his face. "Because that's what a *good* friend I was to Tucker."

She backed up a step. Her hips hit the balcony's railing. "Did you...did you love her?" Jasmine held her breath as she waited for his answer.

He kept staring at the sun. "Maybe."

That wasn't really an answer.

His head turned. "But that didn't stop me from killing her."

Those words were supposed to terrify her. Okay, they *did* terrify her. And after dropping that big bombshell, Drake just turned around and started to head toward the bathroom.

"No!" So she'd yelled. That yell had stopped him in his tracks.

She ran around and faced him. Jasmine jabbed her index finger into his chest. "I deserve more than that. I talked until I was hoarse for you." That would be why her voice sounded so husky. *Not* because she was scared and sad and close to breaking on the inside. "So don't just spout a line about killing her. Tell me what happened. Everything that happened."

"Why?"

Seriously? He made her want to yell, again. "Because I want to know! I want to see past this cold mask you're giving me! You didn't kill her in cold blood. You couldn't have."

"How would you know?"

"I think you're more than that."

"You want me to be more." His lips twisted. "You need to accept that I'm not."

Her heart shook her chest. "What happened?"

"She betrayed me. I killed her."

She grabbed him and she shook him. Okay, she tried to shake him, but Drake was an unmovable object of stone. "Stop it!"

He blinked at her. Then his gaze lowered to her clutching hands. A furrow appeared between his eyes. "Why are you drawn to the danger?"

She didn't let him go.

"I tell you that I killed the last woman who told me that she loved me, and you...you hold on to me as tightly as you can." He looked back up at her. "Something is wrong there, princess."

Something has been wrong with me for a long time. "There's more to the story," she said stubbornly even though his words had hurt. "You're trying to scare me, but you don't have to do that. Don't you get it? I was scared of you before we even met."

His head cocked to the right as he seemed to study her. "Yet you came to my bed."

"I'm scared every single day of my life." If he lived her life, he would be, too. "Fear can't stop me." If it could, she'd be hiding in a closet some place, with her eyes squeezed tightly shut against the darkness. "Now drop the bullshit, and tell me what really happened."

"You're so sure I'm not a monster?"

"Yes."

"You're wrong."

She wanted to slug him. "*Tell me.*"

At first, she didn't think he would. That glittering gaze of his seemed to weigh her and judge her. How many times had she been judged before and found lacking? Too many. She tried to stiffen her shoulders and straighten her spine. If he closed her out, then fine, she'd walk away. She wasn't going to just hang around for *nothing.*

"The first time she died, we were in a wasteland of snow and ice. On a mission gone bad, bad because she'd betrayed my team. She'd set us all up to die so that she could make away with a fortune."

"The...first time?" Just how many times could one person die?

His gaze stared into the past, and, judging by his expression, she knew it wasn't a pretty sight. "I was taken on that mission. Held. Tortured because they wanted more intel on my team."

"Your team?"

"My buddies and I formed our own covert reconnaissance group after our tours were over."

His buddies...Trace Weston and Noah York.

"Trace and Noah came for me. They got me out—them and Tucker." His voice roughened on the last name. "Anna Jean was supposed to be Tucker's girl. Of course, he didn't know that I'd taken her behind his back. One time." A muscle flexed in his jaw. "I was drunk and I woke up afterwards, *hating* what I'd done. But Anna Jean...she was the kind of woman who could get beneath your skin."

She pulled her hands away from him.

"She wanted me to be with her. Only I wasn't going to betray Tucker like that again...hell, maybe that was why she was so eager to sell us all out. I pissed her off, and she got her payback."

"The scars on your back..." The scars that she'd felt in the darkness. Felt but hadn't seen. Her hands had stroked more scars, too. On his stomach. His chest. So much pain. So much hell.

"Those scars are mementos from my captivity. They remind me of the price for betrayal." He exhaled on a rough sigh. "Noah and Trace got me out of there, but before we could make it to safety, we came under enemy fire. Enemies were all around and Anna Jean...she used that moment to come at me. I turned and saw her gun, and I did the only thing I could..."

She couldn't breathe.

"I stabbed her. She fell back into the snow, and Tucker—he went crazy. He shot me. Cause I deserved it." He raked a hand over his face. "I don't remember much after that. Noah and Trace got me out, but...they had to put Tucker down because he wouldn't stop. He was too crazed over Anna Jean. Even knowing that she'd sent us all to die, he still loved her—and he...he died with her that day."

Goosebumps rose onto her arms. "So you stabbed Anna Jean. It...it was self-defense—"

"Anna Jean was an unusual woman."

Did he even realize how he sounded when he spoke of her?

"Beautiful, deadly. She could fly any plane or chopper, and she could bat her eyes and make men fall at her feet."

Men like you?

"Somehow, she even managed to make it out of that pile of snow and death in Russia."

What?

"She survived and came looking for her vengeance. Only she didn't realize that I'd been the man who put that knife in her chest." His lips curled in a humorless smile. "Funny thing about those life or death moments...when you're bleeding out in the snow, your mind will play tricks on you. She blamed Trace for what happened. She thought he'd attacked her and killed Tucker."

Jasmine's muscles were aching because she held herself so still.

That mocking smile slipped away. "She went after Trace's fiancée, Skye. Anna Jean was going to kill her. His whole life, Trace has only loved one person on this earth, and no matter what I had to do, I wasn't going to let Anna Jean take Skye away from him."

Her lips were bone dry. She licked them and managed, "You talk about him...as if he's a brother to you." The emotion in his voice revealed so much about his relationship with Trace and Noah.

"Brothers in battle," he muttered. His shoulders rolled back. "Anna Jean wanted some payback. She nearly gutted me with a knife, then she went after Skye. I was Skye's protection, and I'd promised Trace I would keep her safe. That I would do *anything necessary* to protect Skye."

She nearly gutted me.

"I could barely move, and she was attacking Skye right in front of me. There were only seconds left. Seconds. And I had to make a choice..."

"Drake..."

"When I stabbed Anna Jean that time, I didn't miss her heart."

Jasmine's body swayed a bit.

"I killed her, and I didn't hesitate."

She blinked away the moisture that wanted to fill her eyes.

He turned away from her, giving her the broad expanse of his back. "Still think I'm some kind of hero? Because I'm betting heroes don't go around killing women like that. Heroes don't do half the shit I've done."

In that instant, she could only stare speechlessly at him. Jasmine just didn't know what to say. Because he was right. Heroes wouldn't do half the shit he'd done.

"That's what I thought," Drake murmured.

A loud peal—a doorbell?—reached her ears and Jasmine jumped at the sound. Drake just slowly sauntered off the balcony as he headed back inside. He walked toward the apartment's front door. Jasmine ran to keep up with him, hurrying through his quarters.

The pealing cry was soon followed by a fierce pounding on the door. Drake glanced through the peephole at the entrance, then swung the door open.

Swung it open...

As if he didn't have a care in the world.

As if he hadn't just confessed the darkest secret of his past to her.

Maybe that's not his darkest secret. Maybe there are more secrets.

Jasmine wasn't sure she could handle more right then.

"Janet," Drake said softly to the woman in the well-cut suit who stood there, wringing her hands and looking terrified, "why are there cops behind you?"

Jasmine backed up a step.

"Because a body was found on your property this morning," another woman said as she pushed into the apartment. A woman with light blonde hair and a cold, gray gaze. "I'm Detective Nancy Taggert, and I've got a few questions for you, Mr. Archer."

Not so much as a ripple of surprise crossed his face as he looked from Nancy Taggert to the two uniformed officers who still shadowed the woman he'd called Janet.

"A body?" Drake repeated. "At my home?"

Jasmine was pretty sure her blood had turned to ice.

"Um...yes." Detective Taggert was watching him like a hawk. "Seems a bounty hunter named

Wayne Hardin was shot on your property. A neighbor called to report hearing shots fired, and then we found Hardin spread-eagle on your sidewalk."

No, no.

"Were you acquainted with Mr. Hardin?"

"Our paths may have crossed." Wow. Talk about having no emotion in his voice.

"It appeared as if Mr. Hardin had been the victim of a recent...physical altercation. His nose was broken. Bruising clear on his face, and well, I can't help but notice...you've got some bruising, too."

This couldn't be happening.

"That bruising is right along your knuckles," the detective murmured. "As if...as if you'd recently given someone a beating."

"I box," Drake said flatly. "Sometimes I go bare-knuckled. So, yeah, I bruise, and I don't even notice it."

This wasn't going to end well, and Jasmine couldn't let Drake be pulled into Hardin's murder investigation. "Drake didn't shoot Hardin." Jasmine stopped backing away and forced herself to approach the cops. There was no way she was going to let him get railroaded for this.

"It's all right, Jasmine," Drake said, and there was a bite in his words.

"No, it isn't." Did he think she was just going to stand there and let him get interrogated? Or worse—hauled away to jail?

Detective Taggert's gray gaze focused on Jasmine. "And you are...?"

"I'm the woman that Hardin was after. It's me that you should be questioning, not Drake."

"*Jasmine.*" Drake's voice was downright lethal.

"He didn't have anything to do with Hardin's death. Drake was with me all night long. I swear that he was."

Taggert's eyes were cold and flat. "Why was Hardin after you?"

"I..."

Drake stepped in front of her. "Don't say another word."

Detective Taggert marched to Jasmine's side. "You just confessed to having a bounty hunter on your trail. That's making me think you might be a wanted fugitive, ma'am."

"I'm not. Not wanted at all." She glanced at the detective. "But I'm afraid I can't tell you more here."

Taggert's face hardened. "I think we need to take a little trip down to the station."

"Probably," Jasmine agreed. "We do, but Drake doesn't. He wasn't involved at all in what happened."

There was enough fire in Drake's eyes to singe Jasmine.

"I think we should *all* go downtown," Taggert said.

"No." Drake caught Jasmine's wrist and pulled her away from the detective. "You want us downtown, you get an arrest warrant. But that won't be happening and we both know it." He flashed the cop the tiger's grin that always made Jasmine feel nervous. "So you need to leave now, and any further communication can be conducted through my attorney."

Taggert's own gaze flashed. "You listen to me. You can't just—"

"I'm coming with you," Jasmine said, cutting through the cop's words. Because she knew her time had run out. If Hardin was dead, then she'd be next on Maxwell's hit list.

Surprise rippled over Drake's face. "The hell you are." His hand tightened around her wrist as he leaned in close to her. "Do you know what she'll do to you down there?"

"Question me? Toss me in a cell?" Jasmine shrugged. "A girl can't run forever."

He shook his head. "What are you doing?"

Ah, this was the crazy part. "Believe it or not, I'm trying to keep you safe."

Judging by the floored expression on his face, that possibility had obviously not occurred to him. Jasmine leaned up on her toes and pressed a quick kiss to his lips. "It's my turn to protect you," she whispered. "Consider it payback."

Then she stepped away from him. She'd known that she was living on borrowed time, but that time was gone now. *Hardin is dead.* A cold chill had wrapped around her spine. She didn't want to wind up like him.

Her gaze connected with the detective's. "You'll be needing to put a call in to the FBI. Ask for Agent Victor Monroe."

"The FBI?"

Jasmine nodded. "And I won't be answering any more questions. Not until Victor arrives."

She sent Drake one last smile. *Thank you.* For a little while, she'd felt so good with him. Safe.

But safety was a lie.

And her death...it had been a certainty from the very beginning.

"I'll miss you," she told Drake.

She meant the words. She wouldn't miss much about the con that was her current life but...she would never forget him.

He didn't say anything back to her. Not surprising, really. No lover had ever really missed her when she left.

Story of my life.

She turned and walked away.

***

What. The. Hell?

Drake stood rooted to the spot, unable to believe what had just happened. Jasmine had given herself up, sacrificed herself for—him?

"I'll be back," Detective Taggert promised as she pointed at him. "And maybe even with that warrant."

He growled out some kind of response as the cops left. Like the threat of a warrant scared him.

Janet hovered nearby. When the coast was clear, she whispered, "What do you want me to do?"

Get Jasmine back.

But Jasmine was gone. Heading off with the cops.

He rushed out onto the balcony. He stood there, waiting, furious, and in a few moments,

Jasmine was led out of the Masquerade. The cops loaded her into the back of a squad car. The wind caught her hair, tossing it lightly around her face.

She'd wanted to see the city. Now she was going where—jail?

"Drake?" Janet queried.

"You don't have to do anything," Drake said as he watched the door slam and seal Jasmine in the car. "I've got this."

Like he was really just going to sit back while Jasmine vanished from his life.

Hell, *no*. He'd get her back, and he knew just who he'd use to help him. He spun away from the balcony and pulled out his wallet. The card he needed was inside.

Federal custody, my ass.

He'd be the one watching over Jasmine.

***

They hadn't handcuffed her. Hadn't barraged her with questions. They'd just locked her in an interrogation room. Then the cops had appeared to forget about her.

Her chair was hard and cold and after about two hours, Jasmine's ass was definitely aching, so she marched around the tiny room. She tried to peer into what she was sure was a one-way mirror. She leaned in nice and close, cupping her hands around her eyes—

The door to the interrogation room opened with a click behind her.

"Well, well...aren't you a hard woman to find."

She whirled around.

FBI Special Agent Victor Monroe stared back at her. Tall, handsome, all law-abiding and solid-looking.

That was Victor.

His square jaw locked as he crossed the room to her side. His dark brown hair was swept away from his high forehead. "I hear you've been causing trouble."

"I'm rather good at that." Her best talent.

He leaned in toward her. His blue eyes swept over her face.

"How the hell am I supposed to get you out of here?" he whispered.

Ah, but it was good to have some friends in the right places.

"You're the special agent," she murmured back, keeping her voice low. "I'm sure you'll figure something out." Then she smiled because it was nice to finally be with someone who trusted her.

Even if he shouldn't.

Too bad Victor had never seemed to learn that lesson.

CHAPTER EIGHT

Jasmine was being led out of the police station in handcuffs. Drake staggered to a stop at the sight of her. He'd been trying to call the FBI agent all morning, but that jerk Victor hadn't answered, and now Drake saw exactly why the agent had been dodging him.

Victor was the one pulling Jasmine toward a dark SUV. Victor had one hand securely on Jasmine's shoulder. As he walked, Victor's jacket parted, and Drake glimpsed the gun holster beneath the man's arm.

Detective Taggert stood a few feet back, up at the top of the steps, and she was frowning as she watched Victor and Jasmine.

She was just letting the guy take Jasmine away?

"Stop!" Drake called out.

"Uh, I don't think we should interfere here..." His lawyer muttered nervously from his position beside Drake.

"Screw what you think right now." Drake rushed toward Jasmine. Her head had lifted at his call. Why did she look so shocked to see him? Had she really thought that he'd just let her walk away?

Before he could reach out to her, Victor stepped in his path, totally blocking Jasmine's body. "You need to back away, Archer," Victor told him curtly. "You don't want to get involved in federal business."

Didn't he? "Why are you taking her?" Drake demanded.

"Because she's involved in some active investigations that we're working," Victor responded smoothly. "Now, get out of our way."

Drake put himself in their path even more. "I need to talk with Jasmine."

"The liar and the thief?" Victor tossed back. "I don't know why you'd want to waste your time with her." He eased to the side a bit, glancing back at Jasmine. "I mean, that is what you said, right? That she was 'a liar and a thief,' and she wasn't your problem any longer."

Pain flashed on Jasmine's face.

"That's not what I meant," Drake snapped.

"Sure about that? Because I think those words were exactly what you meant."

Jasmine's gaze jerked away from Drake. As if she couldn't stand to look at him in that moment.

What the hell? Why do I feel like shit right now?

Because Jasmine turned herself in to the cops...because she was trying to protect me.

She could've stayed silent at the Masquerade. Could've let him be dragged off. Then Jasmine would've had her opportunity to run.

She hadn't.

Jasmine had sacrificed herself for him, even after he'd told her about his past. He didn't understand *why* she'd done it, and not understanding was driving him crazy.

"You were right," Victor told him as he put one hand on Drake's chest and pushed. "She's not your problem anymore. She's mine from here on out."

There was something in the guy's voice. A deeper note that set off alarms in Drake's mind.

Possessiveness.

Drake glared down at the hand pressed to his shirt-front. "Move it."

"Or what?" Victor wanted to know. "You'll assault a federal officer?"

"Uh..." Footsteps rushed toward them. Drake's lawyer huffed closer. "Sir, sir, I'd really advise against that!"

Screw Thomas Morley's advice. Drake had pulled the guy down there to help Jasmine, not so the man could get in his way.

"I have to go, Drake," Jasmine said, her voice soft. "It's time."

No, no, it wasn't.

He needed to know more about what was happening. He needed...her.

"What are you going to do?" Drake asked Victor. No, the question should have been..."What has she done?"

He'd told Jasmine his crimes. Didn't that mean he deserved to know hers?

"You're better off not knowing," Victor replied. "Ignorance is damn bliss, right?" Then he leaned in close to Drake. "Just pretend you screwed an angel and not a devil in disguise."

Fury erupted in Drake. He pulled back his fist and drove it right at the agent's smug face.

"No, no, no!" The frantic voice of Thomas Morley shouted.

Victor didn't even take a swing back at Drake. "Poor impulse control." He motioned to Detective Taggert. She was already running down the stairs. "You and your men should take him inside. Get him to calm down."

Drake lunged for the agent again.

But Jasmine was there. She stepped in front of Victor.

Drake froze.

"I'm a liar and a thief," she admitted and her eyes had never seemed so dark. "And I'm not worth what you're about to bring down on yourself."

His jaw hardened even more. "I think you are worth it." That was the problem. She'd inched beneath his skin. Gotten to him when she shouldn't have ever been able to pierce his armor.

Her dark eyes widened. "Drake?"

"I'm not pressing charges," Victor said.

"Thank God," Morley muttered.

He seriously needed a new lawyer. One with some balls.

"But I want this man held until he cools off..." Victor pulled Jasmine away when uniforms surrounded Drake.

"This isn't over!" Drake called out to her.

She shook her head.

"It isn't!"

Victor opened the passenger side of the SUV. Jasmine slipped inside, still wearing the cuffs. When the door shut, she glanced back at Drake through the window.

Her hand lifted and touched the glass. Then Victor drove her away.

"Why don't we go work on that calming down..." Detective Taggert suggested.

Screw calming down.

Drake didn't take his eyes off that SUV.

***

When his phone rang, Maxwell knew it was the call he'd been expecting. The cops had been tipped off, the stage had been set...and Drake Archer should be getting a little taste of hell.

"Were the reporters there when Archer was hauled to jail?" he asked as he put the phone to his ear.

"No reporters," Saxon told him flatly. "And he wasn't the one the cops brought in. They pulled in Jazz."

Maxwell shot up. He'd been lounging in bed with a slumberous blonde. Sex always took the edge off for him. The blonde mumbled something and tried to reach for him, so he kicked her ass right out of bed. "*Jazz?*"

"Only she's not with the cops now. She just left with an asshole I think you know...*Special Agent* Victor Monroe."

His temples were about to burst. "Monroe has been trying to nail me for years."

"Yeah, well, he's got Jazz. And now I'm wondering...is he going to get her to turn on you?"

"She won't have the chance," Maxwell vowed. And it was also time that he eliminated Monroe. That bastard had been a thorn in his side for far too long. "Follow them, and wait for orders."

"Yes, sir."

Saxon had been friends with Jazz, but there was no hesitation in his voice now. Maxwell knew the man realized that Jazz couldn't be given the chance to turn on them.

Death was her only option.

***

"So how much longer do I have to wear the cuffs?" Jasmine asked Victor as they rolled through the city. The traffic seemed to pass her in a blur. "I mean, don't get me wrong. Being led out in handcuffs was a nice touch."

"I thought so," Victor said, voice a bit amused as he kept his eyes on the road. He was taking them away from the busier streets. The traffic around them began to thin. "Made us look all official."

She looked down at the handcuffs around her wrists. "They're a little tight."

"Well, they aren't supposed to be fashion bracelets." He braked at a red light and reached for her wrist. A quick turn of his key, and the handcuffs popped off. His fingers slid over her wrists, massaging quickly right before the light changed to green.

The SUV shot forward. This time, they were the only car on the road. Victor knew how to find all the forgotten streets in a city—that was his talent.

We have to vanish, and he's making that happen.

"How's your jaw?" she asked him quietly.

"Throbbing like a bitch," was his immediate reply. "Archer has a killer punch."

"He boxes," she heard herself say. Her lips quirked. "Or at least, he said he did." Would Drake be surprised to know just how much she knew about boxing? Maybe she'd tell him. Maybe—

He'll never know. Jasmine swallowed and tried to push the lump in her throat far, far down.

"Jasmine?"

She straightened in her seat. "Th-thanks for not having him arrested."

"I might be able to use him later. Figured it was to my advantage to have the guy owing me."

Yes, Victor did like to use people. Use or be used...that was his motto. Always had been. "I'd...prefer that you didn't."

His gaze slid to her when he braked at another deserted light. The buildings around them were all old, boarded up. A street that had been forgotten after the hurricane.

"Let him have his life," Jasmine said. "Just leave him alone."

Victor laughed. "Ah, Jazz, don't go soft for him. He told me you were little better than trash and that he wanted you out of his life." He accelerated once more.

Her chest burned. "It doesn't matter what he said about me. I want you to leave him alone."

"A little late for you to be making demands, isn't it?"

"No, it's not because I'm the one here with all of the—"

Gunfire erupted.

The SUV's front windshield shattered. Jasmine screamed. Victor swore and jerked the wheel to the left, and as the vehicle lurched, a hail of gunfire slammed into Jasmine's side of the SUV.

"Get down!" Victor yelled.

She was already in the floorboard. "Get us out of here!" Jasmine yelled right back at him.

The SUV's engine revved and—

Then the vehicle lurched once more. Harder this time.

"Tires," he snarled. "They shot at—"

The SUV twisted, turned, and Jasmine clamped her lips shut to hold back her screams as they flew toward a tall, metal lamp post.

Then more gunfire erupted...

***

Drake's foot shoved down the gas pedal as he raced through the back streets of New Orleans. Jasmine and that FBI agent didn't have much of a lead time on him. He sure as hell hadn't planned to stay at the station with Taggert and calm down.

Jasmine had looked so hurt. Victor was a prick, and Drake wanted to do more than just drive his fist into the guy's face.

Jasmine had been cuffed. Helpless. He'd just wanted to take her away. To protect her.

He turned another corner, his gaze scanning the empty streets. They were gone. Dammit. Finding them now was going to be nearly impossible.

Rat-a-tat.

When he heard the sound of gunfire, Drake didn't slow down. He sped up even more as his heart thundered in his chest. He cleared the next set of red lights, and then his heart nearly stopped.

The FBI agent's SUV was on its side. Glass littered the narrow street, and two armed men—wearing black ski masks—were pulling someone from the wreckage.

Jasmine.

She was fighting them. Kicking, twisting her body, but they were dragging her toward a gray van that waited just a few feet away.

He slammed on his brakes. Grabbed for his own weapon—good thing he'd brought it from the Masquerade—and rushed out of his car. *"Let her go!"*

One of the men turned at his shout. The guy lifted his weapon and took aim at Drake.

The other masked asshole heaved Jasmine back against him and nearly succeeded in tossing her into the van.

"Drake!" Her scream chilled him.

Drake dove to the ground, and the bullet missed him. But in the next instant he was firing, and Drake found his target. The jerk who'd shot at him grunted and staggered back.

Then Drake was moving again. Staying low and going in fast, he raced right toward Jasmine. Her hands had locked around the side of the van and she was kicking out at her captor.

The guy was so busy keeping her in check that he didn't turn to face Drake, not until it was too late. Then Drake hit him hard and fast, and the guy's head slammed into the side of the van.

"Drake," now her voice was a stunned whisper.

He grabbed her and pulled her into his arms. She was shaking and there were scratches on her hands, but she seemed okay.

He locked his hand with hers and rushed back to his car. He pushed her into the passenger seat.

"Victor!" She grabbed for Drake, holding on tightly. "You have to make sure he's okay. He-he wasn't moving when they took me."

She was worried about the FBI agent?

Giving a grim nod, he spun back around. The two jerks who'd tried to take Jasmine were retreating into their van. They thought they'd just get away? Oh, the hell, *no.*

He took a lunging step toward them, his weapon up.

"Help!"

That cry was coming from the wreckage. The agent?

"I'm stuck, and I smell gasoline—*help me!*" Yeah, that was definitely the agent.

And he was right. Drake could smell the acrid odor filling the air. Shit, *shit.*

He took aim at that van. Fired. Once, twice. The van careened when the bullets crashed into the back, but it kept going.

Drake rushed to the wrecked SUV. He heard the clatter of footsteps behind him. He spun— "I put you in the car!" So she'd be safe.

"And I got myself right out!" Jasmine tossed at him. She tried to shove by him.

He pushed her right back. "There's gasoline leaking out. You need to stay back." He quickly shoved his weapon in to the back waistband of his jeans.

Fear flashed across her face. "We have to get Victor out of there!"

In the distance, he heard the wail of a siren.

This street was deserted, but someone must have heard the shots and called the cops. The question was...would the cops get there in time?

Jasmine broke free of his hand and ran right to the driver's side. "I'm here, Victor!"

Part of the driver's side window had shattered. Victor pushed his hand through the hole there and his fingers curled around Jasmine's. "Dammit, baby, I was afraid they were going to take you, and there wasn't anything I could do."

Drake stiffened. That didn't sound like an FBI agent talking to his charge.

Jasmine isn't wearing handcuffs.

"But it's too dangerous," Victor snarled. "There's gasoline pouring on the ground, and I can...I can smell smoke..."

Drake's gaze shot to the rear of the SUV. The rear...and the front. Tendrils of smoke were escaping from both areas. The SUV had been littered by bullets and some of those bullets had hit with a very, very dangerous impact.

The driver's side door had slammed into a lamp post, and it was a dented heap.

"My left leg is pinned," Victor said, voice gruff. "Archer, I need you to break out the rest of the driver's side windshield and see if you can help me get free."

"Victor..." Jasmine's voice was low. And scared.

Drake grabbed a chunk of metal that had fallen down—part of the SUV's front bumper?—and headed toward the driver's side. Jasmine stepped back when Drake slammed the metal into the glass. The rest of the windshield shattered easily as it rained down on Victor.

The smoke grew thicker. The wail of the siren seemed to be coming closer. But it wasn't close enough.

From the corner of his eye, Drake thought he saw the flicker of flames. He ignored that flicker and crawled half-way into the vehicle. The air bag was in his way, so Drake used the knife he normally kept in a sheath at his ankle, and he cut right through it.

"Hold on, Victor," Jasmine whispered.

The agent's leg was caught all right, the dash had thrust in around him, and the steering wheel sagged, keeping the guy trapped.

"Jasmine." Victor's voice was low and calm. He had blood dripping down his face, and Drake was pretty sure the man's leg was broken, but the agent didn't sound as if he were in any pain. "I want you to wait for me in Archer's car, okay?"

"I'm not leaving you," she said right back. "*I'm not.*"

Drake's gut clenched. "Hold still," he ordered Victor. "Don't make me cut you more than I have to—"

"What?" Victor barked. "Wait, hold the hell up—"

"The vehicle is about to blow, and we both know it." Drake was half-in, half-out of the car. He drove his fist into the remnants of the dash, determined to push it back, then he sliced out with his knife, trying to make the material weaker. "Hold. The fuck. Still."

"Get her out of here!" Victor yelled. "I can see the flames!"

Jasmine's hands had locked around Drake's hips. She was helping to hold him while he fought to free Victor.

"It's too late," Victor snapped at him. "Leave me. *Get her out* or we'll all burn!"

Jasmine was yanking on him. "Drake, Drake, you need to run! I'll get him! You have to go—I don't want you hurt. *Go!*"

She thought he'd just leave them both there?

He dropped the knife onto the floorboard—well, what was left of it, then he drove his fist into that dash again and again and again—

"*Drake!*" Jasmine yanked him back with a surprising force, and they tumbled onto the sidewalk.

Flames were racing over the front of the SUV. When they merged with that gasoline...

"I'm free," Victor gasped out.

Jasmine let go of Drake. He reached for the other man and hauled the guy through the driver's side window. But when Victor's feet touched the cement, his right leg crumbled. *Definitely broken.*

So Drake put the jerk in a fireman's carry even as he locked one hand around Jasmine's wrist. They ran forward, as fast as they could as the flames grew behind them.

As he looked ahead, Drake saw the flashing lights of police cars rushing down the street.

The cops would be there in moments.

A boom sounded behind him. The blast knocked Drake off his feet, and he hit the ground.

"Get...her...out...Get Jazz..." Victor had crashed right along with him. Jasmine was on her knees beside Drake. "Before the cops...come...get her..."

The SUV was blazing behind them. The men who'd attacked Jasmine and Victor were long gone, and now the FBI agent wanted him to help a supposedly wanted woman escape?

Since that had been his plan all along, Drake rose and pulled Jasmine with him.

"But you need help," Jasmine cried out as she stared down at the injured man. "Victor, your leg—"

"I'll come to you, Jazz. Just...*go!*"

She turned with Drake and they ran for his car. In seconds, they were inside the vehicle and racing away from the blaze. The heaving sound of their breaths filled the car. When Drake glanced in his rear-view mirror, he saw smoke and flames and the blue lights of patrol cars.

He sped up and turned hard to the right. He knew these roads—streets usually not traveled by many because this was the side of town that the tourists avoided.

Drake didn't know if the cops were following him or not, but, either way, he wasn't going to leave a trail for them.

Jasmine's hands were clenched in her lap. She didn't speak, and small shivers shook her body every few moments.

"You should...you should probably drop me off somewhere," she finally said, her words hushed.

What?

"That corner looks good." She pointed.

"I'm not," Drake snarled out, "dropping you off any place."

He was taking her back to his casino. Since he had extra security there, he figured it was the safest place in the city.

"I'm just...I'm trouble you don't want."

"If I didn't want you, do you really think I would've followed you from the police station? Do you think I would've shot a man for a woman I didn't want?"

They were hitting the busier streets now. A few more turns, and he was sliding into his private entrance at the Masquerade. He stopped long enough to bark orders to the guards. Then they were inside the parking garage. He couldn't get her out of the car and into his private elevator fast enough. When the elevator doors closed behind them and they shot up, heading toward his quarters, he pulled her into his arms.

"Drake, look, I—"

He kissed her. Deep and long and desperately. If those SOBs in the van had taken her, he never would have seen her again. He knew that fact with utter certainty.

His hands sank into her hair as he tilted her head back. Drake felt as if he were starving, as if he'd spent his whole life on the edge of hunger—and she was everything that he needed.

I'm as bad as Trace and Noah.

No, he was worse. Because he knew that Jasmine was no angel. And he didn't care.

He turned their bodies, pushing her back against the mirrored wall of the elevator. His aroused cock thrust against her. He was rock hard for her, and he needed to be *in* her.

He tore his mouth from hers. Pressed hot kisses to her neck.

Adrenaline heated his blood. Fear. Fury. A deadly combination.

Won't let her go. No one will take her from me.

Jasmine wasn't standing docilely in his arms. She arched against him, and her moans and gasps just drove him on.

His hands slid down her body. He caught the snap of her jeans. Yanked those jeans open. Shoved them down her legs. The material got tangled in her shoes, but Jasmine kicked herself free.

"Drake..."

He kissed her again. Kissed her, even as he grabbed the lace of her panties and tore them away.

There was no finesse this time. No seduction. He needed in her.

He needed the certainty of knowing that she was his. She was safe.

He lifted her up against the mirror. "Wrap your legs around me."

She did. Drake thrust into her. Deep and long, and the desperate fear finally eased.

But the arousal didn't. The consuming lust just grew as he withdrew and plunged into her. Again and again. He held her hips tightly, moving her to match his rhythm, forcing her to take all that he had.

She cried out his name, and he felt the clench of her delicate inner muscles around him as she climaxed.

His thrusts grew faster. He wanted to take and take from her. Take until she realized that he was the one she needed.

The only one.

Her lips pressed lightly to his throat. She kissed him. A delicate, tender caress in the maelstrom of passion that surrounded him.

He came with a release so strong that his heart seemed to stop for a moment as the pleasure pulsed through every vein in his body. It swept over him, through him, and it was so good. So incredibly good. He never wanted it to end.

It was as close to paradise as Drake knew he'd ever get.

And she was climaxing again. He heard the quick catch of Jasmine's breath and felt her stiffen against him. He kept thrusting, drawing out his own pleasure and forcing more pleasure on her.

He always wanted to give Jasmine pleasure.

He wanted to spoil her for any other lovers.

Just me, princess. Always...me.

And that last thought scared the hell out of him because he wasn't supposed to want any woman that way. Wasn't supposed to care about her other lovers. Wasn't supposed to care at all.

But for her...with her...he did.

Jasmine would have no idea just how dangerous that was.

***

Saxon marched into the office that Maxwell had claimed. Maxwell noticed that the guy was moving a bit slower than normal, and...

"You're missing someone," Maxwell pointed out.

Saxon's chin jerked up into the air. "We encountered a problem."

Maxwell rose and circled around the desk. The scent of the river drifted through the window. "I don't care about problems. I care about Jasmine."

Or rather, he cared about silencing the bitch.

His eyes narrowed. "Is that blood on your shirt?" Because it sure as shit looked like blood soaking the shirt near the guy's shoulder.

"I took a hit," Saxon muttered. "Archer was there. He shot me, and he got Jazz."

Maxwell grabbed the man, and he made sure that he dug his fingers into Saxon's injured shoulder. "Jasmine was with the FBI agent. You were supposed to take them both out. A simple enough order. It wasn't time for Archer. Not. Yet."

"He followed them!" The lines near Saxon's mouth tightened as pain rippled across his face.

Maxwell dug his hand in a bit deeper.

"W-we had the agent controlled. Jazz was almost in the van, then Archer flew up and started shooting. We didn't have any choice—we had to get the hell out of there."

"One man, and you ran from him? I'm very, very disappointed in you." When he got disappointed, people died.

"Avery was already back in the van. He was going to leave me," Saxon snarled at him. "I was bleeding all over the street. I didn't have a choice."

Avery. Ah, yes, he was still a fairly new employee, and the man didn't understand just how much Maxwell hated disappointments. He would. "Send Avery in to me." He released Saxon. "Get your shoulder stitched up."

Saxon backed away, but he didn't leave. "Drake isn't about to give that woman up again. You should've seen the way he fought to get her."

Interesting. So Archer wouldn't be surrendering Jasmine to the cops again. And if he had a twenty-four seven watch on her, well, that would make things a bit more complicated.

Not impossible, of course, just complicated.

"You both wore ski masks?" His order, but he wanted to make sure it had been followed.

"Yes." Blood dripped from Saxon's soaked shirt and splattered onto the floor.

"Then Jasmine has no idea you were the one who went after her."

A quick, negative shake of Saxon's dark head was his reply.

"Excellent." Because if force hadn't worked, then they'd try another method for getting to Jasmine. They wouldn't worry about going through Archer's guards—and the man had certainly upped his security force at his New Orleans casino—they'd just get Jasmine to come right to them.

A lamb, to the slaughter.

CHAPTER NINE

She'd just had sex in an elevator.

Jasmine lifted her head from Drake's chest. He was slowly pulling out of her body, and that glide sent off little aftershocks in her core. Helplessly, she felt herself squeeze him tight, one more time.

Her breath sighed out at the rush of pleasure. "I...didn't mean what I said."

Her lashes lifted. He was straightening his clothes. She should probably do the same. Especially since her half-naked image was being tossed back to her courtesy of those mirrored walls.

But Drake beat her to the punch. He bent and eased her jeans back on her. Carefully. Slowly. He even paused to check her bandage. Like those stitches would have slowed her down.

Then he tucked her torn panties into his pocket.

"Ah...what you said?" She had to clear her throat because her voice came out way too husky. Jasmine had no idea what he'd said before. She was pretty lost.

Still kneeling before her, Drake glanced up. His eyes seemed to blaze at her. "I'm not done with you."

He should be. "Drake..."

In one quick, fluid motion, he rose before her.

She put her hand on his chest. "I am a liar. And I'm a thief." The words had hurt, but the truth often did.

His gaze narrowed. That green stare seemed to measure her as it moved slowly over her face, then down to the hand that pressed not just over his chest, but right over his heart. She could feel the strong, steady beat beneath her fingertips.

"Maybe," he allowed.

There was no maybe.

"But you're *my* thief," and his voice had hardened. He kissed her. That mind-numbing kiss of his and she pretty much sank into him. "Don't forget it," he muttered against her lips.

As if she could.

Then he pulled away. Put in his security code and had the elevator doors opening. He exited the elevator and offered her his hand. Taking it, Jasmine hesitated. "This is the first place the cops will look for me. You know that, right?" They might as well flash a neon sign.

He didn't appear concerned. Not even a little. "Then we'll just have to make certain they don't find you here." He sounded so confident. "It's not like you'll be staying long."

Uh, she wouldn't be?

"Give me a bit to make arrangements. I can have you out of town in an hour. I'll get us on a private flight and I can make you vanish."

So tempting. But... "I can't leave Victor." As it was, she'd have to find out which hospital he was in. As soon as it was safe, she'd contact him again and find out what needed to happen next.

Drake's jaw locked as they entered his home— that was what she thought of that place as, anyway. It sure had all the comforts of home. And had she really just left from that exact spot hours ago? So strange. It had seemed like much more time passed. "I didn't think I'd be coming back here."

"You sacrificed yourself for me."

She glanced back at him. His shoulders were propped against the door, and his arms were crossed over his chest. Jasmine couldn't read the expression on his face, no matter how hard she tried.

And to think, she was usually pretty good at reading people. She pressed her lips together a moment, then said, "Maxwell killed the bounty hunter, we both know that. I was just trying to...to make less trouble for you."

"Maybe I want trouble."

Her eyes widened.

"No more lies, Jasmine."

Ah...

"I've been playing nice with you."

He had? Wow. What was he like when he played rough?

"I warned you about lying, and you are already due some punishments."

Kissing hardly counted as punishments.

"But I've got questions for you, and I want the honest truth." He advanced toward her, a lion stalking his prey. "Do you understand?"

Jasmine shook her head. "I'm sorry, but there are some things I just can't tell you." More than her life was at stake.

Her answer didn't even slow him down. "Why weren't you in cuffs?"

"Um, what?"

"At the crash site, you weren't in handcuffs, but when Victor loaded you into the SUV, he had both of your hands cuffed."

She glanced down at her wrists. "He took them off."

Drake reached for her hands. That was when she realized that she had scratches and cuts on her palms.

Drake must've noticed the damage, too, because he swore and pulled her toward the bathroom.

"It's all right," Jasmine tried to tell him when he began to wash the wounds. "I just...some of the bullets hit the windshield, and I put up my hands so that my face wouldn't get cut by the glass."

He stilled and the air in the bathroom seemed to grow very, very tense. Drake's head turned, and his eyes met hers. "The bullets could have torn right through you."

"They didn't," she whispered back. "I'm all right. I'm here, with you."

"What if I hadn't appeared on that street?" The words were hard, but the fingers moving against her skin—cleaning her so carefully and bandaging her wounds—they were gentle.

"I'd be dead."

"*No.*"

Drake was incredibly powerful, but even he couldn't stop death.

"I think my hands are okay. The scratches were light." She'd had so much worse. Good thing she had such a high pain tolerance.

He eased away from her. His broad shoulders seemed to fill the doorway. "I keep forgetting how fragile you are."

Jasmine laughed. "Actually, no, you don't."

His brows shot up.

"Even when we were in the elevator, and I was so wild I wanted to scratch my way down your back, you held me still...you moved me, made sure that I didn't pull any stitches." His hands had been so secure on her. Controlling her movements. Giving her so much pleasure. "You don't forget anything." She was certain of that.

His lips twisted in a humorless smile. "Princess, that wasn't about your stitches. I'm a selfish bastard, and I just wanted to screw you deep and hard."

"Liar," she barely breathed the charge but Jasmine knew it was the truth.

For a moment, he looked lost, then he blinked, and that image was gone.

"You play so tough, but I can see through you. You didn't hurt me in the elevator. You didn't hurt me *any* time that we've been together. Because at heart, you aren't a killer. You aren't the bad guy." That was what made him different from Maxwell.

"What am I?"

"A protector." That was why he'd fought so hard for her on the street. Why, when the SUV exploded behind them, he'd tried to shield both her and Victor.

Drake wasn't a deadly threat. He was a hero, the man just didn't realize it.

She did.

Drake's expression tightened. "Tell that to the dead I've left in my wake."

Her gaze didn't drop. "You won't scare me. No matter what you say or what you do, because I know the real you."

He laughed. "You've been with me for a few days. How can you possibly know anything but what's on the surface?"

Jasmine swallowed. "You've known me for less than forty-eight hours, and you shot a man for me today."

They stared at each other. "What would you say," Drake asked her, softly, "if I told you that I would have killed for you? If I hadn't been able to get that jerk to free you...if he'd tossed you in that van..."

She gave a sharp, negative shake of her head. "I don't want you to kill for me. I don't want anyone to do that." She edged closer to him. "I want to get the hell I've brought *out* of your life, and I just want you—I want you to be happy."

He gazed down at her. "This war isn't on you. Maxwell and I were set to battle long before you came into the Arrow."

Because of Anna Jean. The mysterious Anna Jean. A lover Drake had confessed to killing.

Goosebumps rose onto her arms.

She knew how Maxwell thought. He was old school, an eye-for-an-eye type.

There is no escape.

A low, pealing ring filled the air. The same peal that had sounded right before the cops arrived on their last terrible visit. Drake turned at the sound, heading back into the main living area. Jasmine followed, grabbing for his arm. "Drake, no, it's probably the cops!" And without Victor close by, she did not want to deal with them again.

"Cops wouldn't have gotten past my security—only a very select few could get to me now."

Great. Wonderful. *Not.* He was almost at the door. Jasmine jumped in front of him. "Drake, I get that you seem confident about whoever might be on the other side—"

"I am confident, because I told them to get their asses down here."

Wait, what?

He slipped around her. Took an instant to glance through the peephole—*at least he checked that much*—then Drake was opening the door.

"You made better time than I thought," he said as he offered his hand to the first man in the doorway.

Jasmine inched back. Her guts were twisting into knots and she was so hoping that she was wrong about the identity of the men in Drake's doorway.

She took another step back and realized she didn't have on her shoes. They were still in Drake's private elevator. She lifted a hand to her lips. They felt swollen—from Drake's mouth. She touched her hair—oh, hell, yes, it no doubt looked as wild as it felt to her touch.

"Well, well..." A deep voice said, and Jasmine dropped her hand as she realized that the three men were now inside the apartment—and all gazing at her. "You must be Jasmine Bennett." The man speaking was tall, with midnight black hair and startlingly bright blue eyes. He wore a suit cut perfectly to his broad shoulders, and he seemed to ooze both money and danger.

Trace Weston. She recognized him instantly.

And if Trace was there...

Her gaze slid past Trace and Drake, and her stare locked on the third man. A man who wore jeans and a jacket, but still came off with a heavy air of power and affluence. His eyes were green, a shade that seemed less...cold...than Drake's. His face was magazine perfect, his cheeks high, his nose slanting. He was about an inch shorter than Drake, but he was built along powerful, deadly lines.

She stared into his eyes and realized she'd seen those eyes before.

"Jasmine?" Drake stepped forward, cutting off her direct line of sight with the man she knew to be Noah York.

This can't be happening. This can't be happening.

"Are you okay?" Drake reached for her hands. "You're shaking."

Noah shouldn't be standing there. Not Noah.

"What happened to her hands?" Noah asked as he inched closer. His voice flowed over her. No accent. No hint of Texas.

Because he hadn't been to Texas. Not in so very long.

"Some assholes shot at her SUV, and the windshield shattered around her," Drake said this so matter-of-factly. "Jasmine, shit, I knew I should've used more care—"

"Uh, used care *when*, exactly?" Trace asked, his eyes gleaming as his stare raked from Jasmine's mouth to her hair, then back down to Drake—and Drake's gentle hold on Jasmine's hands.

"I think I should sit down," Jasmine managed. She had to figure something out, fast.

Drake pulled out a chair and got her settled. Then he stayed there, right beside her, frowning worriedly down at her.

He was worried? This was bad.

Because now all three of the men were crowding around her. Her gaze kept wanting to slide to Noah. He looked different in person. More approachable. Not that she would've ever approached him.

This wasn't supposed to happen.

She yanked her gaze off Noah, only to find herself caught by Drake's hard stare. He'd realized that she was staring at Noah. Staring too long at him.

"It happens," Trace suddenly said. "Women look at him and get a little crazy. I knew we should've broken his nose a few more times, Drake."

Drake grunted. "Yeah, seems like a good idea right now."

She felt heat race to her cheeks. "Wh-why are you here?" Jasmine turned her focus to Trace when she asked that question. Because of all the three men, he would be the one most likely to wreck her plans.

Trace *was* Weston Securities, and if he wanted to uncover secrets about her past...

Understanding hit and her focus shifted to Drake. "You had him investigate me." She said it like the accusation it was.

Trace coughed into his hand. "You did try to rob him, correct?"

Her flush was just getting worse. So Trace *and* Noah thought that she was a thief—*I am*—and they also knew she'd just had sex with Drake. The floor could just open up and swallow her at any time—that would be awesome.

"There's a lot going on that you two don't know about," Drake said to his buddies. "The past still isn't dead."

Jasmine focused on breathing, nice and easily. Unfortunately, her breaths came out sounding all ragged and desperate.

"Anna Jean's lover is trying to destroy me," Drake said. "Seeing as how you were both involved in what when down a few months ago, I figured you deserved to know what was happening."

"Her lover?" Noah's brows climbed. "I thought that was you."

"Not this time." Drake was still staring at Jasmine. "I think you might know him. It's a jackass named Maxwell Case."

Noah whistled.

"He wants Jasmine," Drake revealed. "And I need you both to make sure that doesn't happen."

"I'm guessing his men were the ones shooting up her SUV?" Trace threw out.

Drake nodded.

Jasmine straightened in her chair.

"You guys can't go after Maxwell." That comment had all their eyes turning back to her. "You can't," she repeated, wondering if perhaps the men were a bit crazy. Or a lot crazy. "You all need to get out of town and let the FBI handle things."

"You mean your buddy Victor Monroe?" Drake's voice was flat. "Because you told him what was happening, didn't you?"

Victor knew plenty. "He's with the FBI. I figured he was my safest bet."

"Didn't look safe to me," Drake said, hands tight at his sides. "When he was trapped in that SUV and you were being hauled into that van."

She shot up from the chair. "We were ambushed!" That hadn't been Victor's fault.

"And he should have done a better job of keeping you safe, ambush or no ambush!"

"Uh, excuse me..." Noah murmured.

"Victor is a great FBI agent," Jasmine defended fiercely. "He's one of the most decent men I know and he's—"

"Another lover?"

She had *not* seen that one coming. Jasmine's jaw dropped.

"No handcuffs," Drake pointed out. "And I don't think he calls most of his suspects 'baby' but I could be wrong."

This wasn't a conversation that she wanted to have in front of Trace and Noah, and those two were avidly watching.

Why am I trying to pretend? She was sure that Trace had already briefed Noah on all the information he'd discovered about her.

Daughter of a prostitute.

Did Trace know that? Yes, yes, of course he does...

Teenage runaway.

Hacker.

She drew herself up to her full height. But her toes curled in the carpet. "Just to be clear, I haven't slept with Victor or with Maxwell." She pointed at Trace. "And I don't care what your intel says. Intel can be wrong. It's wrong this time." Her glare swept back to Drake. "You're my lover. The only one I've had in a very long time, and you know what? That shit should be private! I shouldn't be having to explain and justify myself to you and your buddies!" Chest heaving, she turned on her heel. "Now I'm tired. I was shot at, nearly abducted, and then, well, you *know* what went down in that elevator. I'm going to bed, and I don't want anyone so much as knocking on that door for the next two hours." Jasmine didn't glance back over her shoulder as she gave that order.

Her knees didn't knock as she made her way to the bedroom. She slammed the door behind her. A nice touch, at least, Jasmine thought so.

When the door closed, yes, her knees definitely trembled. And her gaze flew around the room.

I have to get out of here.

Because she had to stop Drake and his buddies before they all wound up dead.

Jasmine inched toward the air vent in the corner. No way could she fit in there. That just left the doors that lead out onto the balcony...

The balcony. Being as quiet as possible, Jasmine opened the French doors that led outside. She tiptoed onto the balcony. They were about ten stories up. She could see the flash of cars below her. So very far below her.

Not like she had a choice, though. Jasmine squared her shoulders and inched closer to the edge of that balcony.

***

"So...out of curiosity...what did go down in the elevator?" Trace asked, him voice mild.

"Shut the hell up," Drake fired at him. His gaze was on the closed bedroom door. There had been something about Jasmine's expression when she stormed away...

Noah strode closer to him. "Give the woman a few minutes to rest. She looked exhausted." He cocked a brow. "And since when are you the kind of guy who wants to keep twenty-four seven tabs on a woman, anyway?"

"Since he met a woman who tried to rob him blind." Trace dropped onto Drake's couch. "And trust me, with a woman like her, you're gonna need to keep watching, carefully."

Drake narrowed his eyes on his friend. "A woman like her?"

"Sexy, smart, and dangerous."

Noah's hand slapped down on Drake's shoulder. "Ah, that makes her just your type, am I right? Women with an edge are always more interesting."

Drake growled at him.

Noah sobered. "Though I am a bit confused. If some jerks were hauling her into a van, how'd you get her away from them—"

"I shot one of them."

Noah and Trace exchanged a long look.

What? "I wasn't going to let them *kill* her."

"But obviously they wanted her alive," Trace pointed out, "or else they would've killed her on sight."

For an instant, Drake saw red. The red of Jasmine's blood. "He wanted to take her away so he could torture her. So he could hurt her because she was helping me. Everything that he wants to do to Jasmine, every pain, is because of me." Then, softer, "And Anna Jean. He wants to pay me back, and he's going to use Jasmine to do it."

Trace's fingers drummed on the couch as Drake paced the room. "She's no innocent. Her file—"

"Screw the file! She took nothing. She helped me." His gaze swung back to the closed bedroom door. "And I will help her. I'm not going to let Maxwell get anywhere near her."

"That would be where I come in," Noah said with a slight nod. "Am I still supposed to be the woman's ride out of town?"

Drake knew the cops would be monitoring his movements, so he'd decided that it would be best for Jasmine to slip away with Noah. "Yes. You fly her to New York. I'll be there as soon as things are cleared up down here."

Noah tilted his head toward Drake. "You mean as soon as you eliminate the threat posed by Maxwell Case."

Drake stared back at him. He thought that was obvious.

"You can't kill a man in cold blood," Trace warned.

"Don't give me that bullshit." Drake stopped pacing. "For your precious Skye, just what would you do, Trace? What *have* you done?"

Trace's mouth tightened.

"Trace loves Skye," Noah said, voice soft, thoughtful. "Are you saying that you have...feelings for this woman? Do you love her?"

Drake's eyes narrowed. "Love has nothing to do with this."

***

Wind whipped against Jasmine's body as she stood on the balcony. Her hands gripped the edges of the railing. It was high. It was terrifyingly high.

But you're not going down. You just have to go across.

She'd found her escape path.

A thin ledge connected two balconies. The balcony in Drake's apartment, and a balcony that waited about ten feet away. If she got to that other balcony, she could slip away and vanish into the casino.

If she got to that other balcony.

Lightning crackled across the sky, illuminating her deadly walk. Thunder rumbled.

And raindrops hit her.

She really had shit for luck.

***

"Oh, I forgot," Noah declared as he flashed Drake a hard smile. "You don't love. Love is for fools like—"

"You." Because he'd seen exactly how crazy Noah had become when he fell for Claire. Crazy and desperate. Obsessed.

Drake had no intention of becoming obsessed with anyone. "Just take Jasmine back to New York with you, okay? When Trace and I are done eliminating Case's threat, you can stop playing guard."

From outside, Drake heard the hard rumble of thunder.

"You guarded Claire for me..." Noah sighed. "So I guess I can return the favor."

"Be warned, Jasmine is *nothing* like your Claire." Noah's wife Claire was sweet and charming, and when Drake had looked into her eyes once, he'd seen all the pain of her past. Claire had nearly been broken by the nightmare that had been her life.

Jasmine—Jasmine wasn't broken in any way. She was wild, a firestorm, strong and ready to meet any challenge head on.

"Hell." He rushed for his closed bedroom door as realization dawned. "That woman isn't tired at all."

He threw open the bedroom door. The room was empty.

That wasn't even possible.

"Jasmine!"

"The doors to the balcony are open," Trace noted as he ran in behind Drake.

The doors were open—and rain poured in from those open doors.

"It's storming," Noah said, sounding lost. "Why would she go out in a storm?"

Drake leapt out onto the balcony. Lightning flashed overhead. He looked down—*no Jasmine*. She wasn't sprawled, body twisted, on the pavement below.

Thank Christ.

He heard a faint gasp then, and his gaze shot up and to the left. Jasmine was there, about ten feet away from him, reaching out for the railing on the other side of an incredibly small ledge.

Drake stopped breathing as he stared at her.

"Oh, shit," Noah whispered from behind him.

Her hand closed around the railing. Drake knew he should be rushing back through his apartment and around to that other balcony, but he couldn't move, not until he was sure that she was safe.

Every muscle in his body had turned to stone.

Slowly, inch by inch, she climbed over the railing and onto that balcony. Her feet were bare, and when her toes touched down, he finally took a breath.

"Jasmine." Her name was on that breath.

And even though his voice had been low, her head whipped up. Her gaze met his.

Then she turned and ran.

CHAPTER TEN

Adrenaline had her whole body quaking. Adrenaline and fear and oh, God, but she *never* wanted to do anything like that again.

Desperate times make for desperate women.

She had to get out of Drake's sight. Get to Victor. End this nightmare before anyone else was hurt.

She yanked open the balcony door and found herself inside an office. A long conference table waited to the right. She ran past it and toward what she hoped would be an exit door. She had to find the stairs or an elevator and get—

"Going somewhere?"

Trace Weston lunged out of the darkness of that room. He stood between Jasmine and her precious exit door. And he was a definite immovable object. His head was cocked as he studied her.

She staggered to a stop.

"Unlike Drake, I didn't stay around to see if you'd make it to the other side of that little ledge." He took a step toward her. "I'm the one who's been investigating you for the last few days, so I know just what you're capable of doing. What you *have* done. I knew you'd dance right across that ledge."

"Y-your wife is the dancer, not me." Trace was married to an ex-prima ballerina, so that taunt just rolled right out of her mouth. This big, tough, *scary* guy had hooked up with a woman as delicate as fine china.

Maybe opposites really did attract.

She choked back her fear and said, "You have to get out of my way."

Her lead time was dwindling fast. Drake would be running in there soon.

Trace looked genuinely confused. "Why would I want to do that? I don't think Drake planned for you to disappear from his life."

Her gaze flew to the door behind him. She only had *seconds*. "I'm going to hurt him."

"*How?*"

"I'm not a woman to be trusted, but I think you already discovered that." She inched toward him. "Please, I need to get out of the Masquerade. I have to go see Victor—"

"The FBI agent?"

She nodded quickly "He's the only one who can stop this."

His arms crossed over his chest. "You should have more faith in Drake."

It wasn't about faith. It was about what *would* happen. "I don't want to hurt him," she confessed. "So you have to get out of my way."

He shook his head.

Her back teeth locked. She hadn't made it across that scary-as-sin ledge to be blocked by this guy. Footsteps were pounding outside of the door. Drake—rushing after her.

"Why did you try to run?" Trace asked her. "We were making plans to fly you up to New York."

"Oh, how wonderful," she muttered. "Plans for *my* life. Thanks, but I've already got plans of my own."

And since he wasn't getting out of her way, Jasmine did the only thing that she could—she made a break for it. A fast, desperate run.

But Trace caught her before she'd taken more than three steps. His arms locked tightly around her, and he yanked her up against his chest.

"I don't trust you, and, unlike Drake, I wasn't taken in by your innocent eyes."

Her eyes were innocent? Since when?

"You aren't getting away," he promised.

The door burst open. Drake stood there, chest heaving, eyes blazing.

"Not from any of us." Trace's whisper slid into her ear.

She heaved in his hold. Trace just tightened his grip, so she slammed down her heel. She hit his foot, then his shin, then anything she could find.

"*Stop it!*" Drake yanked her out of Trace's arms. "What the hell were you thinking? You could have *died* out there."

He didn't get it. "If I stay with you, I am dead. We both are. I'm a target, big and red, and Maxwell is coming for me fast and hard. Or did you miss that *shoot out* on the street? He wants me, and he'll take out anyone who gets in his way." Her gaze darted from Trace to Noah. Lingered on Noah. "I can't have collateral damage. I won't." Just looking at Noah *hurt*.

He had no clue who she was to him. And, seeing as how Trace had no doubt given the guy an earful about her many sins, it was better that way.

"I'm leaving," she told them. "Even if I have to climb over a dozen balconies, I'll do it."

Noah stalked closer to her. "Balcony climbing isn't necessary. You *are* leaving. With me. Our plane will take off within the hour."

Jasmine shook her head and flinched away from him. "I'm not going anywhere with you." No way could that be an option. Not ever. Noah had to be safe. He had a life. A wife. A family.

I wanted a family. For so long.

And she was staring right at the family that was hers.

Noah frowned at her. "Are you...okay?"

Dammit, she was almost crying in front of him! Jasmine blinked away the water that filled her eyes.

"Jasmine..." Now Drake was sounding all worried and his hand was slowly stroking her arm. "You don't have to be afraid. I won't let Maxwell hurt you."

Seriously? It wasn't about her. It was about them! Him. Noah. Even asshole Trace. She straightened her spine. "Tell them," she demanded with a fast glare at Trace. "Tell them that they're wasting their time. That I'm not worth any help they want to give."

Trace's eyes narrowed to near slits as he studied her.

"Tell them!" Jasmine yelled. Her heart was breaking. She couldn't be this close to Drake...and to Noah.

Noah doesn't know me. I'm a stranger to him. A stranger who could rip his life apart.

She'd never wanted to rip apart Noah's life. She'd wanted to meet him. Just see him.

When she'd been a kid, she used to dream about Noah...she'd known he existed, of course. Her mother had told her all about the baby boy she'd given up for adoption.

She gave him away...but she kept me.

Jasmine knew Noah was the lucky one.

Her brother. Standing right there. Staring at her.

"I'm not worth it," Jasmine repeated again. "I'm a criminal, a thief." Her lips twisted into a humorless smile. "A liar. If I had the chance, I'd betray every single one of you." Her gaze came back to Drake. She made herself say, "Every. Single. One."

A muscle flexed in Drake's jaw.

Jasmine laughed, and the sound was bitter to her own ears. "Didn't you learn anything from Anna Jean? You don't want to trust me. You can't. So get the hell out of my way before I destroy you all." Such tough words. Such hard words to say.

Because she didn't want to run from Drake and Noah.

Those two men—they were all she'd ever wanted.

A lover who made her forget the hell of her life.

And a brother...*family*. Real family. Not the kind that was always drunk or high or...willing to sell you.

Her lips clamped together and she stormed around Drake. He wasn't stopping her. Good. He'd gotten the message. She was trouble. She was also going.

"You'll be dead before the sun sets." That was Trace making that grim prediction. "Do you *want* to die?"

She couldn't have what she wanted. That was why Jasmine planned to leave Drake behind.

Her hand touched the doorknob.

"I don't trust you." Drake's voice stopped her cold.

But that was what she wanted, wasn't it? No trust. No attachment.

"Maxwell wants you. He wants you very badly."

She opened the door.

Saw the guards in the hallway. Four of them. Hell.

Drake's hand closed over her shoulder. "And I'm not going to let that bastard have *anything* that he wants." He turned her to face him. "I don't trust you," he said once more, like he was driving a nail into her coffin.

Her chin lifted.

"But I am going to use you, princess. You're going to be the bait that brings down that bastard. Then we'll both be free. You can vanish from my life, and I'll stay the hell out of yours."

***

He didn't like the way Jasmine stared at Noah.

Drake frowned as he watched Jasmine send yet another furtive glance toward his friend. Why did she keep gazing at Noah with that lost expression in her eyes?

Yeah, okay, fine, Noah was a ladies' man. Or he had been, until he had settled down with his Claire. Now Noah was full-on obsessed with his lovely new wife, and the guy *wasn't* playing the field.

Jasmine needed to stop watching Noah.

Fucking now.

"That's jealousy."

He turned at Trace's voice. They were in a small, private airport outside of the city. Noah's plane was supposed to be taking off soon.

Taking off *with* Jasmine.

She's bait, all right. But she doesn't have to actually be here when the trap is sprung. He wanted her safely away because he...well, he just wanted her safe.

"The way you're glaring at Noah, it's a dead giveaway." Trace sighed softly. "You really sure you want your woman flying off with him?"

"I trust Noah." He did.

"Ah, right. But not *her*? What if she tries her hand at seducing him? I mean, she can't seem to keep her eyes off the guy."

He was growling. Drake tried to stop. He wasn't an animal, no matter what he might be feeling at that moment. "Noah doesn't see any woman but Claire."

"Huh. Is that how it works?"

Drake shifted a bit because he'd just noticed that Noah was staring at Jasmine with a guarded, assessing gaze.

As soon as Jasmine caught the other man's stare, she immediately stiffened and glanced away.

"Maybe he was another target for her," Trace mused. "I mean, the way she's acting, the woman *knows* him. Or she knows something about him."

Fuck. "The photograph."

"The what?"

He marched away from Trace and headed for Jasmine. Noah stood near her, and his friend nodded as he approached. "About fifteen minutes until take-off," Noah said. "Once we're safe in New York, I'll call you."

Drake didn't glance his way. "You never told me why the photograph mattered."

"What photograph?" Jasmine immediately asked as her chin notched up.

Back to that old game, were they?

He caught her sexy little chin between his thumb and forefinger. "It's a dead giveaway," he told her.

Her eyes widened. So dark and deep. A man could get lost in those eyes.

Noah would *not* get lost there.

"When you lie...your chin rises up a bit."

"No it doesn't," she whispered back. "It does that when I get scared."

He blinked.

"Uh, we should get on the plane," Noah announced. "The pilot told me that we'll be—"

"Why do you watch Noah so much?" Drake demanded, and he heard the bite of jealousy in his own voice. He'd never been jealous over a woman. Not like this.

Noah coughed a bit. "Okay, I think I'll wait on the plane..." He started to back away.

"Don't go anywhere," Drake ordered because he was trying to figure this thing out.

Jasmine had paled. The sun was up, and he could easily see the sudden pallor of her skin and the flash of fear in her eyes. "That was Noah's wedding picture," Drake added.

Now Noah was crowding in closer. "What are you talking about?"

The pilot advanced toward them. "We should board the plane now." He shifted a bit nervously, from one foot to the other. "The pre-flight checks are all clear. We've got the okay to take off."

Two mechanics were over in the corner, packing up gear.

Jasmine tried to head toward the plane. Drake moved with her, blocking her path.

"What is with you?" Jasmine exploded. "You want me to go, you want me to stay. Make up your mind!"

"I want to know why you took one look at Noah's wedding picture, and you decided not to hack my computer. I want to know why one look at that picture changed everything for you." And it had. She'd betrayed Maxwell and set this deadly chain of events into motion.

But she didn't betray him for me.

Jasmine's gaze slanted toward Noah.

She did it for him.

"I saw you on the security footage." There had been such longing on her face. Longing for Noah? Rage pumped through his blood.

Jasmine wet her lips with a quick, nervous swipe of her tongue. "I don't know what you *think* you saw—"

Drake's stare lasered onto Noah. "Have you met Jasmine before?"

Surprise flashed on Noah's face. "No."

Trace had closed in next to Noah.

"Are you sure?" Drake pressed. "*Think* about it."

Noah's stare swept over Jasmine. A very tense Jasmine. "I don't think I'd forget a woman like her," Noah said.

Drake unclenched his back teeth.

"But...but I swear," Noah continued, voice roughening, "there's something familiar about you, Jasmine. I look at you, and I..."

Jasmine pushed through the men and headed for the plane. "We need to get this show on the road."

"How do you know him?" Drake pressed.

She kept marching toward the plane.

Drake shot a glare at Trace. "Are they connected? Did you see anything in her past that is tied to Noah?" Why had she changed everything for him? Yeah, that jealousy was back and twisting hard in Drake's gut.

Trace shook his head. "I didn't see a connection, but so much of her life is shrouded. The woman is *good* at covering her tracks. Hell, if

I didn't know better, I'd think..." But then Trace broke off. "I've seen government agents who have less security in their lives than she does. She wanted years of her life hidden, and she made them vanish."

"What can I say..." Jasmine's words drifted back to them. "I'm amazing." But her voice was flat. "Now, the plane's ready. The plane that you *insisted* I board."

The pilot hurried by her and rushed up the steps that led to the plane.

The mechanics were still lingering in the corner. Watching.

Waiting?

Jasmine climbed two of the steps.

Drake turned away from her and focused on those mechanics. One had a faint smile on his face as he watched Jasmine board the plane. He was still smiling as he turned away...and started heading for the door.

"Stop!" Drake shouted at him.

The mechanic jerked and glanced back.

"I want to talk with you," Drake barked as he hurried toward the man, his instincts on high alert. "To *both* of you."

"Uh, Drake..." Noah began.

The mechanics were grabbing their gear and they weren't slowing down for a little chat. They were trying to haul ass out of there.

"Stop!" Drake yelled again. His phone started ringing, vibrating like mad in his coat pocket. He ignored the phone and focused on the men. The two guys were full out running now and the plane's engine was growling behind him. That didn't make any sense. Mechanics wouldn't run—

They're not mechanics.

He spun back around. "Jasmine, get away from the plane!"

She was on the stairs. Her eyes widened.

"Get away from it!"

Trace was now running after the fleeing mechanics but Drake ran right toward the plane. Toward Jasmine.

He saw understanding on her face. But she didn't leave the plane. That insane woman turned toward the plane's entrance and began yelling for the pilot. She disappeared inside.

No! "Jasmine! Get the hell out!" His legs burned as he raced toward her.

All he could think was...a bomb. *They planted a bomb, and I'm about to lose her. Maxwell likes his bombs...I'm going to lose her.* "Jasmine!"

His phone was ringing again. Drake ignored the thing because he was rushing to her.

She was back on the steps now—and hauling the pilot with her.

Drake rushed up the stairs toward her. He grabbed her hand and pulled her against him. Then they ran down the last few steps as fast as they could.

They'd just cleared the tiny airstrip when the plane exploded.

***

"Boom," Maxwell whispered when he saw the smoke fill the sky. Ah, but it paid to have eyes and ears everywhere.

Noah York and Trace Weston were on Maxwell's hit list. He'd planned to take them all out...because they'd all played a part in Anna Jean's death.

But they'd been targets for later. Less important. Drake had been his main goal.

Then Drake had made the mistake of calling in his friends.

"It was time for them to die." Maxwell rolled his shoulders. He'd made the little bomb. All his men had needed to do was plant it.

"So beautiful," he murmured. Saxon stood a few feet away. "Head toward the scene for me," Maxwell ordered. "See who survived...and who didn't."

Face expressionless, Saxon nodded. The guard turned and climbed onto his motorcycle.

Maxwell admired the blaze for a moment longer, then he headed toward his car and driver.

It sure was a beautiful morning.

A plane, my love...ah, Anna Jean, isn't that fitting? She'd been such a wonderful pilot. He definitely thought she would have appreciated the send-off he'd just given to Noah York and Trace Weston. After all, two passengers had been scheduled to depart. A little cash to the right hand had given him that information.

And a little more cash had been paid to end those two lives...

***

His phone was ringing again.

Drake stared at the blaze, aware of Jasmine's hand clutching his arm.

She'd nearly died.

Jasmine blinked. "I, um—"

His arms wrapped around her and he hauled her as close as he could get her. She was warm and soft against him. Alive.

"Sending you away isn't an option," he snapped. The smoke had turned the sky black.

His phone stopped ringing.

Jasmine looked up at him. "Noah was going to be on that plane." Her words trembled.

He couldn't look away from her.

"He's at risk now, too, because of me." A tear slid down her cheek. "I never wanted him in danger."

Him? Still on Noah? "What the hell is the connection?" he demanded.

His phone rang once more.

Swearing, he pulled away from her—just a few inches—and yanked out that phone. He didn't recognize the number on the screen.

Sirens were screaming once more. Story of his life these days. Where he went, police cars followed. "We need to get out of here," Drake said.

"We'll handle things," Trace told him, giving a hard nod. He stood just a few feet away. "You get her out of here." He motioned toward the two men who were slumped at Noah's feet. Trace and Noah had made sure those men didn't flee the scene. The "mechanics" hadn't gotten away. "We've got this," Trace promised simply.

Drake didn't want to leave. He wanted to interrogate those SOBs and force them to lead him back to Maxwell.

But Jasmine had to be protected. He'd nearly messed things up royally just then. *He'd* been the one to demand that she get on that plane. If he hadn't gotten suspicious in those last moments, the plane would have exploded with her inside.

Then what would I have done?

Jasmine was staring at Noah. A-fucking-gain. He wanted to slug his friend and drag Jasmine away.

So he *did* drag Jasmine away.

But she called out, "I'm so sorry!"

She was apologizing to Noah?

"I never wanted this to happen. It wasn't supposed to touch you."

He pushed her into his car. Had that Porsche purring and bursting out of the lot in seconds.

"What is the deal?" Drake demanded between gritted teeth. "Why him?"

His phone rang. He yanked it out as a motorcycle passed them. "*What?*"

"Don't let her on the plane!"

His hold tightened on the phone.

"Do you hear me? This is Agent Victor Monroe. I've got intel that York's private plane is going to be targeted. Do *not* let Jasmine get on that flight—"

Drake's gaze slanted to his rear-view mirror. "Too late," he muttered as he stared at that smoke-filled sky. "The plane's burning."

There was a swift inhalation of air. "But you have Jasmine. You *have* Jasmine!"

His stare drifted to her. She sat stiffly next to him. "I've got her."

"Good...good...if you want her to stay alive, you'll listen very, very carefully because I am the only one who can help her."

"Cause you did such a stellar job last time," Drake snapped at him. "The way you had her safe in the city—oh, wait, she was being *taken* by those jerks in the van—"

"St. Laurence Street. Five-oh-eight. Get her there, understand? I'll meet you, and this will end."

The line went dead. Asshole agent. He shoved his phone aside. Jasmine didn't ask any questions, she just sat there in silence, and that silence was driving him crazy.

Why Noah? "He's got a wife." Yeah, so Noah was the one who laughed easily. Who didn't scare small children. Who—

"I'm not interested in him that way."

"You *cried* for him."

From the corner of his eye, he saw Jasmine's fingers twist in her lap.

"Tell me why he matters. Why he changed everything for you." And maybe he'd stop wanting to punch his best friend.

"You won't believe me." Her words were so soft that he had to strain to hear them. "I keep seeing the plane...if he'd been on it..."

"Screw Noah! *You* were the one nearly blown to hell!" And he couldn't get that image out of his mind. Jasmine should have been safe. This wasn't the way the plan was supposed to work. Not at all.

Drake had underestimated his enemy. Maxwell's reach was greater than he'd realized. *Were you watching Noah and Trace?* Hell, if Maxwell was looking for payback because of Anna Jean, then, dammit, yes, Maxwell *would* be keeping eyes on them, too. There was no telling how long the bastard had been putting them all in his crosshairs.

Rage churned within Drake. Rage and fear. *I almost lost Jasmine.*

"The pilot nearly died, too." Her voice was even softer than before.

"No, he didn't," Drake snarled back. "Because you risked your life to go back in after him! You should've gotten out, you should've—"

"That's not who I am."

He spun the car off the main road. They hit dirt and gravel and flew forward toward the swamp. It was a path most wouldn't have known. It was a path he took every time he needed to escape.

He kept driving, kept going until he was sure they were out of sight and that all the fire trucks and cops wouldn't see him.

Good thing he knew the area so well. Once upon a time, he'd spent summers on all these back roads when he stayed with his grandfather. They'd hunted. Fished. Stared at sunsets and snakes.

"I couldn't leave him to die. I-I couldn't let anyone just...die."

He braked the car. Dust shot into the air around them.

"Um, I'm not so sure this is the best place for your Porsche..."

He jumped out of the car.

She followed him, much, much more slowly. "Is that a cabin?" She was staring at the dense vegetation around them. The swamp had nearly swallowed the cabin. "We should get out of here. This is someone's property—"

"Mine."

She glanced at him in surprise. "What?"

"The cabin is mine."

Her eyes squinted as she looked at the cabin once more. "You drive a Porsche, you have luxury homes in Vegas and New Orleans and you—"

"I grew up dirt poor in Mississippi until I was ten. Then my dad cut out on me, and my mother and I moved in with my grandfather." He pointed to the cabin behind him. "I spent the best years of my life in this place."

Her expression softened.

"Other than Noah and Trace, no one else knows about this cabin. We'll be safe here until I can make contact with Trace again." He knew that Noah and Trace would be able to handle the cops. Trace had connections all over the place. "Let's get inside."

She glanced toward his now dirt-covered Porsche. "You surprise me."

He paused on the first wooden step. Sure, the cabin might not be much to look at, but he felt at home there. Always had. He came out there at least four or five times a year, when the city was about to choke the life out of him, and he remembered who he'd been a lifetime ago.

A boy who fished on the dock. A boy who jumped into the water and laughed at the freedom. A boy who looked up at stars and dreamed.

Not just a man with too many nightmares.

"I didn't see this for you," Jasmine added as her hand waved toward the cabin. "It doesn't seem to fit."

"Then maybe you should've checked more into my past, and not just my present."

She gave a jerky little nod as she came closer to him. "My past is so screwed up. I have a rule that I try not to poke too far into anyone else's—"

He caught her hand in his. "Because you don't want them knowing about yours?"

"Yes." So soft.

"I want to know everything."

She smiled, but her dimples didn't flash. "Isn't that what Trace is for? So he can give you a file on me?"

"I want you to tell me."

He waited a beat.

"You *will* tell me."

One way...or another.

***

Saxon braked his motorcycle a good distance from the old cabin. The Porsche waited, covered in dirt and dust, about fifteen feet from the place. Drake's car. He'd recognized it on sight.

So he'd followed them. Carefully.

His eyes slid over the cabin. *Drake and Jazz were in there.*

This was the perfect opportunity. Just what his boss had been waiting for.

Now, if he could just get the go-ahead to act.

Saxon pulled out his phone. "Guess who I've got in my sights…"

CHAPTER ELEVEN

"So I'm supposed to reveal all my secrets to you?" Jasmine asked as she rubbed her arms. There was no reason for the sudden chill, but she still felt it. "Is that the way this works?"

He was seated at a small, wooden table. His legs were stretched in front of him.

"I tell you mine," she heard herself say, "and I'll want to know yours." She thought those words might scare him. She should have known better.

His head inclined and her heartbeat raced.

"You first," Jasmine blurted because she was a coward at heart. Had he realized it? Sure, maybe she could walk on a three inch ledge to a balcony ten feet away, but sharing anything personal?

Terrifying.

"What do you want to know?"

She sucked in a deep breath. "The woman...Anna Jean...did you love her?"

"No."

Such a flat response.

"I wanted her, I cared for her, but...I never loved her. I don't think I've loved any woman."

Jasmine cleared her throat.

"Have you slept with them?" Drake demanded.

"Them?"

"Victor Monroe. The too familiar agent."

Jasmine shook her head.

"And Maxwell?"

"No. He was an assignment, nothing more."

His eyes narrowed and she realized that she'd slipped up. Jasmine hurried toward him. "Why casinos? You were in the military, and going into the casino business seems like a serious one-eighty to me."

"Life's a gamble." He shrugged. "You realize that when you spend your days and nights dodging bullets. When you cheat death over and over again, you realize you've hit a lucky streak."

Hell, his whole life was a gamble. Now it made sense to her.

"Then your luck runs out."

She stopped near his side and stared down at him. "Is that what happened to you?"

A faint smile tilted the corners of his mouth. "My turn now."

Oh, right.

"Why did you run away at fifteen?"

Talk about getting right to her darkest, most carefully guarded secret. "I don't like this game anymore."

He caught her hand. Held it in his. "It was never a game."

His touch scorched her.

"Tell me."

She stared at their entwined hands. She didn't want to look in his eyes when she revealed her shame. "My mother...I realized what she was when I was nine years old. Before that, I just...I thought she had a lot of boyfriends. That was what she called them, you see. Her boyfriends."

Mommy's going out with her boyfriend tonight. You just stay inside and keep the lights turned off. I'll be back soon.

"She liked drugs and she liked to drink and she needed money...so she got it the only way she could." Had her mother been different once? Maybe before Jasmine had been born? Long ago, she *must* have been different.

Drake's hold tightened on her.

"When I was fifteen, she tried to give me to one of her boyfriends."

His hold became painful.

"She said she was tired and that he liked me, and it would just make things easier if I...if I..." No, Jasmine would *not* say it. "I left, and I never looked back." Her breath whispered out. "Maybe ease that grip a bit?"

"Sorry." He immediately lightened his hold. Then he brought her hand up to his lips. Kissed her wrist. Her palm.

Jasmine could only stare at him. "That wasn't how you were supposed to react."

He looked up at her.

"I'm the daughter of a drugged out prostitute. She overdosed a week after I left her. She died and they found her naked and alone in that trailer park." She shoved back the pain. "You're not supposed to react this way. You're not supposed to just sit there and stare up at me and—"

He kissed her hand again. "The first time we talked, I realized how strong you were. I thought you might just be the strongest woman I'd ever met."

She shook her head. She wasn't strong. She was weak. A—

"You should see what I see," he told her, tilting back his head. "When I look at you."

"A liar and a thief." She already knew what he saw.

"No." He pulled her down, and Jasmine sprawled over his lap. "I see a beautiful, smart, *strong* woman who needs to believe in herself. Life's been hard, damn brutal to you, but you've survived."

He was making her heart hurt. "Like life hasn't been brutal to you?"

"We all have our scars." His thumb moved lightly along the inner column of her wrist. Jasmine knew he had to feel her racing pulse.

Yes, they did have their scars. "When I was a little girl, I wanted another life. Any other life but the one I had. I would dream of starting some place new. A new name. A new past." She swallowed. "A new future."

"Is that why you're still running? Because you want that new life?"

Her lashes lowered. "Sometimes it doesn't matter how long or hard you run, there's no escaping the past."

"Don't I know it. You can't even bury that shit sometimes."

Her gaze jerked back up to his. "Is that what you want to do? Bury your past? Forget about Anna Jean?"

"Her blood will always be on my hands." His voice roughened. "I hate what I did. I hate that I got drunk and screwed my friend's girl. Tucker and I...we were close and that destroyed him. Tucker mattered to me. Tucker, Noah, and Trace—they were my family after my mother and grandfather died. And I wound up hurting them all because I couldn't keep my pants zipped."

"Drake..."

"She was the only woman who ever got close to me. She looked at me and lied, and I didn't even realize it." He paused. Studied her with a hard gaze. "I know when you lie, but the problem is...I don't seem to care."

She needed to pull away. Instead, she leaned in closer.

Their lips were almost touching.

"Why do you stare at Noah York and look as if you're losing your whole world?"

His question sank into her, nearly piercing her heart. Too late, she did try to pull away, but there was no place to go.

"I won't betray my friends. Not ever again," he vowed. "There's something between you and Noah. He doesn't remember you—"

"Why should he? We never met." *He was the lucky one.*

"What is he to you?"

She didn't want to answer him.

"Jasmine..."

"Promise not to tell." Her whisper. Like a child's voice.

Surprise rippled across his face.

"He doesn't need to know, so promise me. Promise that you won't tell. When all of this is over…" And it would be, one day. One day soon. "Don't tell him."

He gave a curt nod.

"I think he's my brother." Such a quiet confession. One that made Drake's muscles tense beneath her. "Actually, I *know* he is."

"What?"

"My mother…she had a little boy before me. She gave him up at birth. She was just sixteen then." The words tumbled out in a rush. "She gave him up, gave him to a family who couldn't have kids of their own."

"You don't—"

"She regretted giving him away. She told me that, she'd scream that at me when she drank. So when she got pregnant again, she…she kept me." *And I'd wished, so many times, that she hadn't.*

Just as Jasmine had wished, so many times, that her brother would come back for her.

A girl, dreaming of a rescue that never came.

"Why do you think Noah is your brother?" No emotion was in his voice.

"Because she had one photo of the family who took him. I found it when I was six and…when I was fifteen, it was the only thing I took with me when I left her." Because she'd thought—stupidly then—that she'd find her brother. That he'd take her in.

And she had found him. But Noah York had been fighting in battles overseas, and she...she'd found her own wars.

"You're certain?"

She stared into the warmth of his eyes. "Tracking him wasn't hard. I had a photograph of his parents. Of him. And when I got access to the right computer equipment...photo imaging software, hospital databases...it all fell into place for me." Her lips tightened. "He even has her eyes."

"Shit."

Just like that, Jasmine found herself *off* his lap and back on her feet. And Drake had paced across the room, putting a good ten feet between them.

"Drake?"

He glanced at her. Jasmine's hands were curled around her stomach and his—his were fisted at his sides. "His sister?"

She nodded.

"Noah's fucking sister?" Then he squeezed his eyes shut. "What have I done?" Then softer, "*Again.*"

"You haven't done anything." Nervously, she edged toward him. The floor creaked beneath her feet.

He threw up a hand, halting her. "Do *not* touch me right now."

She was so lost.

"When you touch me, I want to strip you. I want to take you. I want to make you scream my name."

Oh, well, in that case...Jasmine took another step.

"*You're his sister!*" He backed away from her. "All Noah has ever wanted was to find out about his real family. He used to talk about them for hours out in the field..."

"He was better off not knowing." No... "He *is* better off not knowing." Noah had a wife, a home. He didn't need the mess of the past.

He stared at her with both rage and pain in his eyes. "You're what he's wanted. You were right in front of him, and he didn't even know it."

This wasn't good. "You can't tell him."

"Bullshit. I *have* to tell him."

"No!" Then she leapt across the room and grabbed tightly to his arms. "You really want to tell him that his mom was a drugged out prostitute? That she couldn't remember his father's name? That his sister..." The breath she expelled burned her lungs. "Trace will tell you that I have a criminal history. I've been hacking for years. I've got enemies...so many. You *don't* want to put this at his doorstep. You don't want to put me there."

"Noah can handle enemies."

"I don't want him to know. Please, Drake. There's no point in it."

"He'll want you in his life."

"But I can't be a part of his life." That ripped her up. She'd realized that truth, though, long ago. "So let it go." Her hands slid up his chest. Curled around his shoulders.

He was so stiff in her embrace. "I fucked you."

Did Drake have some moral opposition to "making love"? Because she didn't.

"Noah's sister." His eyes closed. "Knew you were trouble. From the first glance."

"I knew you were, too." And she hadn't cared. She rose onto her toes. Pressed her lips to his.

He immediately jerked away.

"Drake?"

His eyes were open. Blazing. "I won't betray a friend again."

"You aren't betraying anyone." But he was hurting her when he pulled away.

He yanked out his phone. Turned his back on her.

"Drake?"

He took a few more steps away. That phone was to his ear and he said, "Trace, what's the status? Do you have things contained?"

A faint growling sound reached Jasmine's ears. She crept toward the window on the right.

Still talking into his phone, Drake snapped, "Yeah, well, we have another problem."

Her shoulders tightened as she peered out the window. She couldn't see anyone outside, and that growling had stopped.

"How fast do you think we could get a DNA test?"

No. Jasmine whirled around.

"Right. A DNA test. Comparing Jasmine and—"

She flew across the room and yanked the phone out of his hand. She hung up on Trace. "What are you doing? You can't tell them!"

"If you're really his sister, then Noah deserves to know."

He couldn't do this. "No, Drake. *No.*"

His phone was ringing again. He tried to reach for it. She put it behind her back.

One blond brow rose. "Seriously, Jasmine?"

"Yeah, seriously, Drake." She hurried away from him. "This is *my* life we're talking about."

"Noah is filthy rich." Drake spoke those words bluntly. "If you're his sister, he's going to want to take care of you."

"And when I was fifteen and stealing food to survive—"

He flinched.

She didn't. "I would have appreciated his money. I don't now. I *don't* want him knowing." Jasmine wanted to toss that phone. To shatter it. "Trace isn't going to forget this." Now he'd start probing. "Dammit, *why* did you have to say anything? Why—"

That growling was back. Only this time, she wasn't the only one who heard the sound. Drake's head jerked toward the window. In two fast steps, he was there, peering outside, then swearing when he saw the lights that hit the cabin.

"Motorcycles," Jasmine whispered. She counted at least three. And was that an SUV rushing in behind them?

It was.

She answered the ringing phone. "Trace, I think you need to get your ass over to Drake's old cabin...cause we've got company."

Drake had already whirled away from the window. He marched to a closet and started pulling out—weapons?

A gun. A knife.

"What kind of company?" Trace barked in her ear.

"The kind that isn't friendly." She was backing away from the window. How had they been found?

Drake was back. He grabbed the phone from her. "My grandfather's place. Get here as fast as you can...because this party isn't going to wait." He shoved the phone into his pocket as his eyes glittered down at Jasmine. "Do you know how to shoot a gun?"

She did. That didn't mean she'd want to. Or had he missed that whole no-bullets-in-the-gun scene before with her?

He put the gun in her hands. She realized he had a second handgun tucked in the waistband of his jeans. "Aim and fire, princess."

She gulped. "How did they find us?"

The growls died away.

Drake put a finger to his lips, then he killed all the lights in the cabin.

Then...

"There's nowhere to run, Archer! This is the end for you."

That voice...she knew it. *Saxon.* Her heartbeat quickened. Jasmine opened her mouth to call out a fierce reply, but Drake's hand clamped over her lips.

"We know Jazz is in there," Saxon shouted. "So you both need to come out, now."

Drake's hand fell away. He took up a position near the window. Drew his weapon.

Jasmine didn't want him to get caught in the middle of a firefight. And if Saxon was out there...

I can't let this happen.

"It wasn't just fucking," she heard herself say because she knew the end was near for her.

Drake fired. The bullet blasted into the night. "Stay the hell back!" he roared.

"It wasn't just fucking," she said again, her voice louder even as her body trembled.

Drake's head whipped toward her. "This isn't the time—"

"It might have just been for you, but it was more for me." *Tell him.* "I thought I was making love with you."

Gunfire hit the side of the cabin.

"I've never been in love, Drake, but I think...I really think I came close with you."

"*Jasmine...*" Her name was a growl. "We're gonna talk about this later. When bastards aren't *shooting* at us."

But she knew there wasn't going to be a later. "I recognize that guy's voice. It's Saxon—he's...he's good at his job."

"And I'm good at mine." He fired again, and she heard a man cry out.

The gun was heavy in her grasp.

"Burn them out!" That bellow reached her ears and sent ice through her veins.

"Oh, the hell, no, they aren't," Drake snarled right back. Then he was firing, again and again.

Jasmine peeked through the window. Saw the men getting hit by Drake's bullets—saw the guns being aimed back at her and Drake.

And she saw the flash of flame. What in the hell were they doing?

Then some of those flames started flying toward the cabin. Something crashed through the window. Exploded.

Molotov cocktail. Flames licked against the floor. Talk about coming dangerously prepared!

"No!" Jasmine ran toward the flames and tried to stomp them out.

Drake tackled her and sent her flying away from the fire. "Are you crazy?" he demanded. "Dammit, princess, you have to be careful—"

"It's your cabin," she whispered. "Your grandfather's cabin..."

And another Molotov cocktail splintered inside.

"And you're worth more to me," Drake said, voice fierce, as he rose with her. His gaze locked on a door to the right. "Come on. We're getting out of here."

But Saxon and his men would just be waiting outside.

"Stay close," Drake told her. "I won't let anyone hurt you."

And she didn't plan to let anyone hurt him.

Drake rushed toward that door. She followed as closely as she could, still holding tightly to that gun he'd given her. A few more feet, then they were bursting through the cabin's rear door. The light was bright and hard and men were waiting for them. Drake shoved her to the side just as a bullet blasted right where her head had had been five seconds before.

Then Drake was firing. Firing and hauling her toward the swamp. Drake hit with deadly accuracy. She'd never seen anything like him. Men cried out and fell in his wake, and Drake was easily getting them toward the thick safety of the swamp that waited.

Then he ran out of bullets. She saw a man rising, smiling, as he aimed at Drake.

She fired.

She also screamed.

And she hit her target. As the man fell back, Jasmine and Drake rushed into the swamp. She didn't know where they were going. Didn't care if they were headed straight into snake central. They were getting away from Maxwell's goons when she'd been so sure that it was over for her and—

"Hello, Jazz."

A hand grabbed her. A strong, callused hand. Saxon yanked her against his body and took her gun in an instant.

At the man's voice, Drake spun back around. His eyes locked on Jasmine.

"Run," she told him, desperate. "*Go!*"

But he didn't. He smiled, a smile that chilled, and took a step toward her.

Jasmine felt a gun press against her temple. "I don't have orders to kill Jazz here," Saxon said. "But if you take another step, I will."

Drake stopped advancing.

"Go," Jasmine shouted at Drake. "Get out of here!" Why wasn't he hauling ass?

"Kill her, and you'll be dead five seconds later," Drake promised Saxon.

She could hear the thunder of footsteps. The men who could still move were giving chase—hunting them in the swamp.

Saxon has just been one step ahead of the others. He usually was. He'd known they would flee out of the back door. He'd been ready.

She knew exactly how deadly Saxon could be. Once upon a time, he'd been her only friend. She knew him so well...

Well enough to know how this would end.

The sunlight flickered through the top of the trees and fell on Drake, turning his hair a shade brighter.

"Another time," Jasmine whispered as she stared into Drake's eyes, "another place, and things could have been so different." She wished they had been different.

"Move the gun away from her head," Drake snarled. His body was so tight with fury. She knew he was about to advance and attack Saxon.

And Saxon's team wasn't far behind.

"Put your hands up, hero," Saxon ordered right back. "And get on your knees."

"Let him go, Saxon," she cried. "Just take me, and let Drake go."

Saxon laughed.

"Not happening." Drake's voice was lethal.

"Maxwell can't get him," she told Saxon. "He *can't.*"

Then she spun in his hold. The gun was still at her head. She stared into her friend's eyes. *He won't pull the trigger.* "I want Drake safe. Please, I'm begging you..."

But the others were there then. Surrounding them. And Jasmine found herself being forced to walk back toward the SUV. *Two* SUVs were there. A few scattered motorcycles.

Maxwell had sent a full force after them. And now...

Drake was pushed toward the second SUV.

Saxon hauled Jasmine toward the first one.

"You so much as bruise her," Drake shouted, "and I'll make you pay."

Saxon tilted his head as he studied Drake. "Am I supposed to be scared?"

A gun was at Drake's back. Another pointed at his head. He smiled. *Smiled.* "No, you're supposed to know that I'm stating a fact."

Saxon lifted Jasmine up and tossed her into the SUV. When another guy tried to climb inside, Saxon snapped, "Watch the jerk. I've got her."

The door slammed. She was in the passenger seat of that SUV. Saxon was in the driver's seat. He had his gun on her.

"What in the fiery hell am I supposed to do now?" he whispered to her.

"Saxon..."

"There was a plan, Jazz. A *plan*. Now it's all screwed."

Because of her.

"There's no way out. Not for you. Not for me." His gaze slid toward the second SUV and Drake. "And not for him."

"*Please.*"

Would begging even work?

Saxon cranked the vehicle. "Maxwell's waiting on you, and, sweetheart, what he's got planned won't be pretty."

***

They were idiots. Fucking idiots. They didn't cuff Drake's hands. Didn't tie him. Didn't restrain him at all.

They loaded him into the backseat of that SUV. Idiot Number One sat beside him, with a gun shoved into Drake's side. Idiot Number Two climbed into the front seat and cranked the engine.

"You got him?" Number Two called back.

The gun dug deeper into his side. "Hell, yeah."

The SUV shot forward, sending mud flying in its wake.

The others were behind them. Still at the scene. Collecting the wounded. Watching the cabin burn.

Assholes. You'll pay for that fire.

Jasmine was in the SUV in front of him. He didn't want to be away from her. Drake needed to make sure she was safe.

"Hope that piece of ass was worth all the trouble..." Idiot Number One muttered. "Cause you're gonna be in a world of hurt soon..."

Drake waited until they'd put some distance between the SUVs and the cabin. Was Trace on his way? Had to be. And since there was only one old dirt road that led to his cabin, his buddy might even be waiting for them up ahead.

"Always thought Jazz would make for a good screw," Idiot Number One told him.

Slowly, very slowly, Drake turned his head to stare at the man. "She was more than good."

The guy's mouth dropped open, then he gave a surprised laugh. "Hell, yeah!" The gun slipped away from Drake's side, just a few inches. "With that red hair, I knew—"

Drake slammed his head into the man's face. Then he rammed his elbow into the jerk's throat. The gun discharged, but Drake had already heaved up, and the bullet blazed past him, shattering the window. The man in the front seat was yelling, trying to turn and grab his own weapon.

Not going to happen. Drake surged toward the front seat even as the SUV started to careen toward the trees.

***

"What in the hell...?"

The sound of a crash had Jasmine jerking around in her seat. The second SUV had just plowed into a tree. "Drake!"

Saxon slammed on the brakes. His head snapped back as he glanced at the wreckage behind them.

And as they watched, Drake emerged from the vehicle. Only Drake.

He was armed.

"Interesting new boyfriend you have," Saxon murmured. He started to lift his own weapon.

Jasmine's fingers clamped around his wrist. "No, not him."

Saxon's gaze held hers.

"Let's go," she urged. "It ends now."

"Jazz..."

"Not him." She was pleading again.

"*Give me Jasmine!*" Drake yelled.

Saxon's foot slammed down onto the gas pedal and they lurched forward.

She glanced back once more at Drake. He was running after them. Bleeding from a cut high on his cheek. This would be her last sight of him.

"Thank you," she told Saxon.

"Don't thank me." His voice was hard. "Because you're going to die."

***

Drake ran after the SUV. "*Give her back to me!*"

The SUV was flying fast, and Jasmine was vanishing. "No!" Drake roared.

The SUV didn't stop.

Neither did he. He ran back to the wrecked SUV. Shoved the two limp bastards out of the vehicle, got that piece of shit working, then gave chase.

There was no way that he'd just let Jasmine go back to Maxwell. He knew what the man would do to her. Jasmine would suffer. She'd hurt. Jasmine should never hurt.

He drove as fast as the beat-up SUV could travel, but it just wasn't fast enough. When he hit the main road, there was no sign of Jasmine.

Drake glanced to the left. To the right.

He turned right. Tried to floor the SUV, but that was then the thing died on him. "*Sonofabitch!*" Smoke billowed from under the hood. Drake got out. Started running.

He was still running when Trace and Noah found him. Only they weren't alone. Detective Taggert was with them.

Their vehicle pulled to a stop right in front of Drake. He stood there, chest heaving, the gun still in his hands.

Trace was the one who approached him first. "Drake...want to tell us what the hell is happening?"

Drake's gaze slid to Noah. *Her brother.* "They took her." The words were like knives in his own chest. "I'm sorry...so sorry...*they took her.*"

Slowly, Taggert advanced. "I need you to lower that gun."

And he needed Jasmine. "I'll get her back," he promised Noah, frantic. "I swear, I'll get her back." His gaze shifted to the long, twisting expanse of road. *I'll get her back.*

He'd destroy anyone who tried to stop him.

CHAPTER TWELVE

Her arms were tied to the chair behind her. The rope was rough and thick, and it had made her wrists bleed. Jasmine could smell the river, and when she strained really hard, she could even hear the faintest sound of music. Jazz music.

"I expected more from you," Maxwell said as he walked around her, moving in a slow circle. He reminded her of a tiger, closing in on his prey.

"Sorry to disappoint," Jasmine managed. But she wasn't sorry. Not at all.

"It was a simple job. Get close to Archer. Use him. Help me to *wreck* him."

She hadn't looked Maxwell in the eyes. "You—you shouldn't have set those bombs at the Arrow. Innocent people could've died—"

He lunged toward her. Maxwell grabbed the arms of the chair and put his face right in front of hers. "Do you think I give a shit about those people?"

She had to meet his white-hot gaze then. Jasmine shook her head. "I don't think you care about anyone."

"You screwed that up for me. The Arrow should've burned—the place was meant to blow—"

"Because of you." Jasmine wouldn't let him see her fear.

He smirked at her. "Because of me."

"How many others have you attacked?" Jasmine wanted to know, even though she feared the answer. "With your bombs...with fire?"

Laughter was his answer. "Oh, Jazz, I don't always need those tactics. Destroying a man's life is easy these days. A matter of business." His right hand lifted and picked up a lock of her hair. "I use tools. Tools like you. I hack into accounts. I learn secrets. I use them."

She hated his touch. Her gaze slid away from him. Saxon was in the room with them, and he watched impassively from his position near the door. There was no expression on his face. Not even pity.

And pity had been there before, when he'd tied her up.

"Why did you betray me?" Maxwell asked her. "I was paying you well."

"There's more to life than money," she murmured.

He stopped stroking her hair. Instead, he yanked it, twisting it in his hold as he jerked her head back. "*Why?*"

Tears stung her eyes. "Why did you want to go after Drake? Because of some dead ex-lover—"

The blow took her by surprise. The pain was fast and hot, just as fast as his punch had been.

Not a slap. *A punch.*

Fury bubbled inside of her because she could taste blood in her mouth. Jasmine lifted her head up. She saw that Saxon had lunged away from the wall.

She shook her head.

"He told you about Anna Jean," Maxwell said, his voice as sharp as a knife. "Did Drake confess to you? Did he tell you how he killed her?"

She had to be so careful what she revealed. "He told me that she'd betrayed his unit and that she came after Trace Weston's wife—that Anna Jean was crazy and had to be stopped—"

His fist came at her again and Jasmine tensed.

But the blow didn't land. Saxon had caught Maxwell's fist before it could make contact with her again.

***

"We need to be out there!" Drake snarled as he paced the small confines of the interrogation room at the NOPD. "This is bullshit." He stopped to glare at Trace and Noah. "If it were Claire or Skye, you two bastards would be ripping apart the town." Instead, they were standing in his way.

And they were in the *police* station of all places.

"You shouldn't have told Taggert anything." Drake wanted to punch and destroy. Maxwell could be hurting Jasmine right then. "You shouldn't—"

"She already knew everything." Noah's voice was quiet. His expression appeared worried as he stared at Drake. "Man, you have to get your control back—"

"The way you had yours when Claire was in danger?" He couldn't look at Noah, not too long, because guilt knifed through him every time he peered into Noah's eyes. *His sister.* "You don't know how important Jasmine is!"

"Easy," Trace told him as he put a hand on Drake's shoulder. He almost lost that hand, friend or no. "We get that she matters to you."

"She—" *She does.* And when had that happened? When had she gotten beneath his skin?

"Taggert had intel she *shouldn't* have possessed," Trace continued in his annoyingly calm voice. "The detective contained the scene at the airport."

He wasn't about to jump on the Taggert bandwagon. "She's a cop. She's just going to slow me down—"

The door opened. Taggert stood there. Only Taggert wasn't alone. FBI agent Victor Monroe was right behind her. Taggert advanced into the room. Using crutches, Victor followed her. The door shut behind them, sealing their group inside.

"I briefed Detective Taggert on the Maxwell Case situation," Victor said. The agent looked like shit. His face was bruised and scratched and a cast covered most of his right leg. "She's working under my authority now."

"Who the hell are you?" Noah wanted to know.

"FBI Special Agent Victor Monroe."

Noah didn't look impressed. He never did.

"Noah York." Victor nodded toward him. "Trace Weston...Weston, I've certainly admired your work."

Trace lifted his brows.

"Fantastic." Drake's fury erupted. "How about you all just stand here and shoot the breeze all day while *Jasmine dies.*" Drake stormed toward Victor. "Maxwell has her. She betrayed him. Just how long do you think he'll let her keep living now?"

"Hopefully, long enough..."

When Drake lunged for the FBI Agent, Trace leapt forward. Trace's arms locked around Drake before he could do more damage to that FBI prick.

Amusement flashed over Victor's battered face. "Relax, Archer."

Screw that. "Cops should be out searching for her!" He fired a glare at Taggert. "*I* should be searching for her!" Instead, he'd been dragged in for questioning. "Make those bozos you took into custody talk." Back at the cabin, a few had been left—conscious enough—to talk. The police had swarmed on them before they'd all had a chance to clear the scene.

Victor shook his head. "Those men won't turn on Maxwell Case. They're too afraid of him and of what he'll do."

Drake could make them talk.

"But we don't need them," Victor revealed as he leaned forward on his crutches. "I already know exactly where Jasmine is."

"And we're just standing here?" Drake gritted through clenched teeth. "What. The. Hell? Do you want her to die?"

Victor's face hardened. "I have a man on the inside. He'll make certain that Jasmine survives."

As surprise hit him, Drake's jaw dropped. "An inside man?"

"Um...the FBI has been working to take down Maxwell Case for a very long time." He glared at Drake. "And you almost screwed up that takedown."

***

Jasmine's breath came out in hard, heaving gulps as she stared up at Saxon and Maxwell.

"What are you doing, Saxon?" Maxwell demanded, voice silky with menace.

"You keep hitting her, boss, and you'll just get your DNA all over Jasmine. If the cops find it, they'll tie her death to you."

Maxwell's eyes narrowed. "There's not going to be a body to find, so DNA evidence doesn't matter to me."

Saxon dropped his hold. "My mistake."

Maxwell crossed his hands over his chest. "Was it?"

Saxon stared back at him.

"You never like it when the women get hurt, do you, Saxon?" Maxwell pushed. "Noticed that about you. A weakness, for a man who should have none."

Maxwell's attention was shifting too much to Saxon. In another moment or two, Jasmine knew that Maxwell would be totally turning on the guard. And if he turned on Saxon...*Saxon would die.*

"I don't think she loved you," Jasmine blurted.

There. Those words had Maxwell's furious stare swinging back to her.

"Your Anna Jean. The woman who caused this whole hell." She licked her lips and tasted blood once more. "I don't think she loved you or Drake...or anyone."

"You don't know a *thing* about her—"

Jasmine laughed and proceeded to BS her way straight ahead. "I'm a hacker, remember? As soon as I found out about Anna Jean, I dug up every piece of intel on her that I could." If she'd actually had access to a computer, Jasmine would have done exactly that job. Since she hadn't... "You two were working together for years, weren't you? Drake and the others—they thought she was on their side, but she was always betraying them."

He gave a sly nod. "I met Anna Jean right after my enlistment. She was the most beautiful woman I'd ever seen."

Wonderful. Fantastic. "Was her psychotic nature part of the appeal?"

He leaned toward her. "She had an edge."

Right. An edge of insanity. "Like to like," Jasmine mumbled.

Maxwell frowned at her. Well, at least he wasn't punching her. For the moment. So she continued, "When she started turning on Drake and his team, you were the one helping her, right?"

"It paid to play both sides," he said, shrugging. "I didn't join the military for the glory."

No, she suspected he'd done it because he wanted power. Violence.

"The paydays were big, and it should have lasted forever." His jaw hardened. "Then they ruined everything."

"You mean Anna Jean did, when she tried to kill Drake—"

"He left her for dead! He and York and Weston—they left her bleeding out in the snow. Hell, even I thought she *was* dead. All that time. Until she walked into my place in Vegas." His eyes flickered as he seemed to remember. "She looked different, but when I touched her, I saw right beneath the mask."

"Did you?" She wasn't so sure.

"She told me what they'd done to her, and I gave her everything she needed. I knew she wanted to go after Trace and—"

He stopped, but she wasn't about to let that go. "You were all for taking him down, weren't you? Bet you thought a slice of that Weston fortune would be coming your way."

"I was backing the right player in that game." *Anna Jean.*

He shrugged. "And more than just a *slice* should have been coming to me. I should have gotten it all."

Her hands twisted against the ropes. Saxon could've given her a little wiggle room. "Instead, Anna Jean died."

"*And I got nothing.*"

"Maybe you should've cut your losses."

"No." He caught her chin between his fingers as he glared into her eyes. "Anna Jean made me the man I am."

Um, that was a good thing?

"She gave me the money I needed. She set up the contacts. I owed her." He gave a grim nod. "And I pay my debts."

"Even to the dead? Because I don't think they're so concerned with collecting."

"I loved her," he said flatly and she believed him. Anna Jean might have been jerking this guy around just like she did all the others in her life, but Maxwell had cared for her—in his twisted, warped way. "And those who took her...they will *suffer*."

Right. "Is that why you bombed Noah York's plane?"

His lips curled. "Seemed an easy enough way to get rid of him and Weston."

He was confessing all to her. *Because he planned to kill me.* She tried to clear her throat. "S-sorry I got in the middle of your war. I didn't realize what was at stake."

"Now you do."

Love for a woman long dead.

***

When Drake grabbed Victor, the crutches hit the floor with a hard clatter. "You *know* where she is? And we're just standing here with our thumbs up our asses?"

Trace didn't try to pull him away this time. Taggert did. She put her hand on Drake's arm, sighed, and said, "Do you think we don't have a rescue plan?"

Victor's eyelids flickered slightly.

"If you do, then we need to get moving." Drake's hands had fisted in the Victor's shirt. *"Now."* Or did the jerk like knowing that Jasmine was in pain?

I don't. It's tearing me apart.

"My team will handle her rescue," Victor assured him. "I've got agents in position now."

Taggert tapped Drake's arm. He still didn't release the FBI agent.

"Tell those agents to act!" Drake nearly roared.

"I will," the agent snapped back. "As soon as we have Maxwell Case's confession on record. My man has a wire on in there—*this is the chance we've been waiting for. We can nail him for so many crimes—"*

Drake slammed Victor into the nearest wall. "He's kidnapped Jasmine! Nail him on that shit! And stop playing with her life!"

Victor's breath heaved out. "You're not the only one who cares about Jazz." His voice was low, pitched to only reach Drake's ears.

"Jasmine," Drake forced out. "Her name is Jasmine, and you're going to tell me where she is. Right now. I'm not waiting on your team. I'm not waiting on a confession. I'm going to get her out of there."

A knock sounded at the door. Seconds later, a woman poked her head inside. Her blonde hair was pulled away from her face, and her eyes glinted behind the frames of her glasses. "We got him, sir. The confession was recorded."

Victor's body sagged. "Warehouse district," Victor murmured to Drake. "Building thirteen-oh-four. Niles Street."

Drake lunged for the door.

"By the time you get there," Victor called after him. "It will all be over! My team has this!"

***

She should have kept her mouth shut, but Jasmine pushed, "Are you sure Anna Jean wasn't going to betray you, too? What if she was just going to use your resources, then vanish with Weston's money? I bet she even had a back-up lover around. Some fall guy waiting in the wings...seems like her style—"

He didn't punch her then. His hands just dropped to her throat and he squeezed, cutting off the words and her airway. "I don't want you speaking of her again. Compared to Anna Jean, you're nothing."

Story of my life.

"Boss...are you going to use Jazz against Archer?" Saxon's voice came quietly from behind Maxwell. "Because he sure went crazy when I got away with her."

His hold tightened even more. Red spots began to dance before Jasmine's eyes. Her temples were throbbing, the blood surging as he squeezed and squeezed.

Drake, I'm sorry.

He eased his hold. She gulped in air, but those red spots didn't vanish.

"Does Archer care about you?" Maxwell asked her.

"No." The one word sounded like a frog's croak, but she wasn't about to let this man use her against Drake.

"Will he come for you, try to save you?"

Her chin lifted. "No."

He swore. "Then what good are you to me?"

She stared into his eyes. "I'm not."

***

The cars were going too fucking slowly. "Faster, Noah! Dammit, I should've driven!"

The police were behind them. Rushing with their lights blazing. They were driving desperately to the warehouse district.

To Jasmine.

Victor had told them that his team on site would be moving in, but Drake intended to be there, too. He had to see Jasmine with his own eyes. Had to hold her and make sure she was safe.

If Maxwell had hurt her...

"Go faster!" Drake snarled again.

"Easy," Trace said from his position in the back.

Screw easy. "I have to get to her." He could feel Trace's eyes on him. Drake turned his head to meet Trace's stare. "If she's dead, so is Case."

Noah whistled. "Man, calm down. The FBI is already there. Your woman is safe."

Your woman. He knew that was exactly what Jasmine was. Had he really thought he might be able to give her up?

Noah's sister. Shit. They'd find a way to work all of that out. Maybe he'd let Noah take some swings at him. But Drake wasn't walking away from her. The fear in his gut told him that he *couldn't* walk away.

"Faster," Drake whispered.

Yeah, he should have driven...but the way his hands were shaking, he was afraid he would've wrecked the car and never gotten to Jasmine.

***

"Drake won't care what happens to me," Jasmine said softly. Her throat ached. Her jaw ached. And she couldn't hear the jazz music any longer. "I'm not—"

"Anna Jean? No, you're not. Not even close. You're a whore from a trailer park. A woman with a few useful talents."

Her eyes narrowed. "And you're a psychotic dick who gets off on blowing things up and killing people. So in comparison, I think I'm the one with more *talent*."

He backed up a step. "You didn't just call me—"

"I did." Holy crap, she had. "You're going to kill me, so what does it matter? I see you for exactly what you are. You're a monster, Maxwell. A monster hiding in the clothes of a man."

"And Drake?" Spittle flew from his mouth. "What is he?"

It broke her heart but she said, "I thought Drake was my hero." She'd wanted him to be. "But...but I guess that wasn't in the cards. He didn't care about me. I was a woman he took to his bed. By the time my body is found, he probably won't even remember my name." *Keep talking. Don't let Maxwell think he can use you against Drake.* Because she wasn't about to let Drake try to trade his life for hers.

Maxwell's furious expression told her that he believed every word she said. Good. She twisted her hands once more against the ropes. If she could have broken free from those ropes, perhaps she would've had a fighting chance.

But maybe she'd never had that.

"Uh, boss..."

Her head turned at Saxon's measured voice. He stood near the lone window.

"There's some action out there."

Maxwell waved that away. "Drunks. The homeless on the streets. It's after midnight and they always—"

Saxon stiffened. "They're armed! I count five—six? I can see them moving across the street!" He spun toward his boss. "They're coming!"

"No! No, that's not possible!" Maxwell stormed toward the window. He stared outside. "Fuck, *no!*"

And then Jasmine started to laugh.

Maxwell whirled to face her.

"I guess my talents are pretty useful."

He shook his head and stalked toward her.

"Boss..." Saxon began.

Jasmine raised her voice, drowning out Saxon as she said, "There's no slowing them down. There's no escape." Her heart raced. "The Feds are coming for you, and you're going away for a long time. You're not going to burn anything. You're not going to break anyone. And you're not going to get your precious payback for Anna Jean."

He was still shaking his head.

"I've got you," Jasmine confessed, and she stopped struggling against her bonds. She wanted to remember this moment. To savor it, as she'd savored few things.

"What?"

"You didn't even search me when they brought me in. Just tied me up...and talked your mouth off."

He lunged toward her. Grabbed her shirt. The buttons popped and flew as he ripped her shirt open.

His gaze dropped to her breasts. To the bra and the small, black wire there.

"Surprise," Jasmine whispered.

"No!" Rage exploded in his eyes. She thought he'd hurt her. Attack hard and fast. But he jumped back. "No, this *isn't* how it ends for me!" He pointed to Saxon even as he rushed for the door.

Trying to protect yourself? That's the way it—

"Shoot her!" Maxwell bellowed. "Right in the heart. Kill her and then get your ass out of here."

After giving that order, Maxwell paused at the threshold of the room. *He wants to watch me die. He won't run, not until I'm dead.*

She heaved against the ropes. "Saxon, Saxon, *don't...*"

He had out his gun. "I'm sorry, Jazz."

"Don't!"

He fired.

***

"You need to stay out here," Victor told Drake as the FBI agents swarmed the warehouse. "Civilians aren't clear to hit a crime scene."

Trace and Noah were at Drake's side. They were all watching silently, waiting, as the teams entered the building.

"How do you even know she's still alive?" Drake asked, frantic. "Who's monitoring the surveillance feed?"

"My best agents are listening to every word. Relax. We've got this shit covered."

The blonde from the police station rushed up to them. "Sir, we lost the feed."

No.

A gunshot blasted. Drake's blood froze. He didn't even realize he'd started running toward that warehouse, not until three agents grabbed him. "She's in there!" Drake snarled at them. They must've heard the gunfire. "*He's hurting her!*"

Not Jasmine. She'd been hurt enough...

Scars on perfect skin. Wounds that she never should've had.

"Let me get to her!" But they were hauling him back. "Noah, Trace, *help me!*"

And even though it would probably get their asses arrested, his friends swarmed. They knocked those FBI agents on their asses.

Victor tried to block Drake's path. Like a guy on crutches was going to stop him. "I'm getting her," Drake promised.

"It's too dangerous! A civilian can't go into that scene. My agents......they'll get her," Victor promised. Did the guy even hear the doubt in his voice? Because Drake did.

Drake shoved the man aside.

Victor shouted his name. Drake didn't stop. He didn't have a weapon, the Feds had made sure of that, but he didn't care. He wasn't sitting on the sidelines.

Noah and Trace were running with him. The fools that tried to get in their way got thrown to the side—badges or no badges.

Then Drake saw the other FBI agents running *out* of that building. They were hauling ass. *What?*

"Bomb!" One yelled. "Clear the area. Clear—"

The explosion sent Drake flying off his feet. He hurtled through the air and slammed down inches away from a light post.

Heat lanced over his skin, and, for a moment, he lay there, stunned.

Then his eyes took in the inferno before him. The warehouse wasn't just smoking. It was blazing. Fire shot from the windows even as part of the right wall collapsed.

He staggered to his feet. He could feel blood sliding down the side of his face—he vaguely remembered slamming into the pavement.

"Pull back!" Victor shouted. "Pull back!"

Another explosion had fire streaking into the sky.

"Jasmine?" Drake said her name once, barely recognizing the lost sound of his own voice. Then as he ran toward the fire, he roared her name.

The flames were raging so hot and high. Burning brightly. Destroying everything.

Destroying...her?

Not Jasmine. Not her. Not...her!

"Stop, man! Stop!" Noah was there, fighting to pull Drake away from the fire, but he just wanted to get closer.

"I have to get her out!"

Another window exploded. Glass hit the pavement. Flames crackled.

Noah tightened his hold on Drake. Drake swung at him, connecting with a hard punch, but Noah didn't let go.

And then Trace was there. They were holding him too tightly, hauling him away from the flames.

"I have to get her out!" The fire was stinging his eyes. Burning his throat.

Ripping a hole in his chest.

Trace's grip was like iron around him. "She is out, buddy. She's...she's gone."

No. The fuck, no. "*Jasmine!*" He fought them both. He'd get free. Get through the fire. Get her out of that building.

"Clear the road!" Victor was screaming orders.

And Trace and Noah weren't letting Drake go.

"I have to get to her..." He punched at them, drove his fist hard and fast, not caring that they were his friends. That he was hurting them. "She could still be alive!"

Noah shook him. Slammed his own fist into Drake's face. "The building is a total loss! There's no way she's still alive in there—"

He was going to give up? On her? "She's your sister!" Drake shouted at him. "We can't let her burn!"

Noah's face went slack with shock. Drake pulled from his hold. "We can't," he whispered and then he ran into that building. He'd just cleared what was left of the entrance when the ceiling collapsed.

**

"Mr. Archer?"

Drake cracked open one eye. "Jas...mine..."

"Mr. Archer, you're all right. We got you out."

He cracked open the other eye. Saw an EMT staring down at him, shining a light right at his face. Drake swatted the light away.

"Sir, sir, I'm going to have to insist that you stay calm and remain still. I think you've got a concussion—"

He remembered the rush of fire. Something heavy hitting him. And—

Drake grabbed the EMT and twisted the man's shirt in his fist. "Did she get out, too?"

"Sh-she?" The man's Adam's apple bobbed.

"Jasmine!"

"I-I...you were the only one recovered."

No. Drake shoved him away. He was in the back of an ambulance. How the hell had that happened? The last thing he remembered was the fire.

"Sir, you have to stay—"

Drake jumped out of the ambulance. He would've fallen right on his face then, if Trace hadn't appeared and grabbed his arms.

"Dragged you out of a fire once already," Trace groused. "Don't make me do it again." He put himself in front of Drake—and Drake could see the flames still reaching for the sky behind his friend.

"She's in there," Drake said, voice rough.

"The firefighters said the flames were too hot. No one in that building has survived." Brutal words, but said softly, sadly.

Drake shook his head. "She was...she was alive. She was with me just hours ago."

I've never loved anyone, Drake, but I think...I really think I came close with you.

Trace's expression was grim. "I'm sorry."

Drake tilted his head back. Stared at the flames. They'd consumed the building.

"You're lucky you aren't dead, too. Those boards that hit you were on fire."

Drake realized that a big, thick bandage covered his arm. He lifted his hand. Another covered the side of his head.

"I dragged you out. Noah and I...we pulled you out of there."

"You two are always saving my ass." He couldn't pull his gaze off the fire. "But maybe this time, you should've just left me in there."

His chest didn't burn. It didn't ache. He just felt numb. Drake could barely even feel his heart beating. He looked at that fire, and he just saw Jasmine.

Curling her finger at me in the club...inviting me down to her.

Laughing in New Orleans...licking away powdered sugar as she savored her beignet.

Crying out my name in an elevator...holding me so tightly...so tightly that I never wanted to leave her.

"Was she..." The gruff voice came from Drake's right. It was Noah's voice. "Was she really my sister?"

Please, Drake. I don't want him to know. There's no point in it. Drake didn't speak.

"Was she?" Noah pressed.

Drake stayed silent.

Noah grabbed him. "Did my sister just burn alive in that place? *Did she?*"

"Noah..." Trace hauled him back.

"I wanted my family." Noah's words shot out fast and hard, like bullets. "I always wanted to know—and *you* knew. You knew she was mine and you didn't say a word..."

The firefighters were closing in now. Because the flames were finally dying down? Cops were all over the scene. FBI agents.

"She wasn't yours," Drake heard himself say. That numbness was spreading. Consuming him. "She was mine."

And she was gone.

Something deep inside of Drake splintered.

I could have loved you, too, Jasmine. Fuck...I did love you.

I did.

CHAPTER THIRTEEN

"There's no point in this exercise," Victor announced as he marched into the small office in the New Orleans Police Department. An office that Trace had commandeered with the guy's army of contacts.

Drake stood near the room's lone window. Noah and Trace were already seated, but he couldn't sit. His body was too tight with tension. With fury.

Grief clawed at him every time he closed his eyes. So for the last three days—and it had been three long, wrenching days since he'd lost Jasmine—Drake hadn't slept.

He knew he'd have new nightmares when he slept. Anna Jean wouldn't haunt him any longer. Jasmine would.

She would always haunt him.

"I get that you've done a few favors for the FBI," Victor said as he shoved a laptop case onto the table. "But I don't see why a civilian should get access to classified—"

"Screw the civilian crap. Play the tapes," Drake snapped.

Victor opened his laptop. Booted it up. "This is material that will be used in an ongoing investigation. This could compromise my case—"

Drake stalked toward him. "You mean because Maxwell wasn't in that building when it blew to hell?"

Victor jerked back a bit.

"Yeah, I know," Drake snarled at him. "We can get our own intel. Word is that the coroner recovered the remains of two people in that warehouse. A man and a woman...and according to leaks in *your* office..." Leaks that Trace had exploited with his Weston Securities contacts. "You think the dead man was one of Maxwell's men, a guy named Saxon. *Not Maxwell.*" Just an underling.

Victor's gaze slid to the closed door, then back to Drake. "Yes," he said softly. "We do believe that Maxwell Case escaped from that blaze. He set the bomb—the fire as a distraction so that we'd be thrown off...but we *know* he got away, and we've launched a search for him."

"The guy might not even be in the country anymore," Noah muttered. Like Drake, Noah had been...different since the fire. Quieter. Harder.

"His assets are frozen. Thanks to our...inside man...we were able to learn about all of his off-shore accounts. Maxwell Case is running on his own. He's desperate, he's broke, and we *will* take him into custody. It's just a matter of time." Victor seemed so confident.

Jerk. This confident prick had been the one who was so sure Jasmine would be all right. "It's your fault," Drake accused.

Victor blinked.

"You left her in there too long." He wanted to punish the bastard. He *would* punish him. "You knew where he was holding her. You should have gotten her *out—*"

"Easy." Trace. Trying to be the voice of reason as he carefully positioned himself between Drake and the FBI agent. Trace just didn't get it. There was no "easy" for Drake anymore. There was just darkness. A void. A fire had taken Jasmine—heat and an inferno, and now, all he felt was...cold.

Victor leaned forward and tapped a code into his laptop.

Drake's hands fisted. "You're going to pay," Drake told him.

Victor glanced up, his eyes narrowed. "You think you can threaten me?"

"I'm promising you. You're going to lose everything that matters."

Victor's laugh was bitter. "Now you sound like Maxwell Case. Maybe there's not so much difference between you guys—"

Even Trace couldn't slow Drake down when he lunged for the bastard. "*I'm nothing like him!*" He slammed Victor into the nearest wall. His crutches fell to the floor.

The agent didn't fight back. He just stared at Drake. "Aren't you?"

"You don't have to hunt Case," Drake managed to force out from between his clenched teeth. "The FBI is done with him. The guy's a dead man walking." Even before he'd gotten confirmation from Victor, Trace's intel had told them that the SOB had escaped. Trace and Drake were already hunting the man. When they found him, there would be nothing left for the FBI.

But Victor's jaw hardened. "My man inside gathered enough information to put Case away for life. Case is going down, and it's going to be handled the *right* way."

The idiot didn't get it. "There is no right way. He killed my Jasmine. He's going to suffer."

Victor's brows rose. "She wasn't yours. She was just a woman you picked up for a night—I'm sure you pick up plenty of women and forget them the next day."

Drake leaned in close to him. "She's not the others. Do you understand? There is no forgetting her." There was no moving on for him. She was *inside* of him, where his heart should have been.

Drake had known the risks. He'd seen what love could do to a man. Trace and Noah had both fallen hard. Gotten in too deep. There was a danger in loving too much. When you loved too much, you had too much to lose.

I lost everything.

"Let him play the recording, Drake." Noah's flat voice. "I want to hear what went down."

Because they'd finally gotten access to the last moments of Jasmine's life. The FBI's "inside man" had been wired, and they'd applied every bit of pressure they could to get this access.

Drake stepped away from Victor. Trace handed the agent his crutches. Then Victor shuffled toward the table. "There's no point in this," he said again, but he tapped on the keyboard once more.

And...

"*I expected more from you.*" Drake tensed when he heard that mocking voice.

"Maxwell Case," Victor said. "Asshole extraordinaire."

"*Sorry to disappoint.*" Jasmine's voice—and her voice hit Drake like a punch to the gut.

Noah inhaled sharply.

"*It was a simple job.*" Maxwell was speaking again. "*Get close to Archer. Use him. Help me to wreck him.*"

He was wrecked without her. *She didn't use me. She never did.* Jasmine's voice trembled when she replied, "*You-you shouldn't have set those bombs at the Arrow. Innocent people could've died—*"

Maxwell's voice cut through her words. "*Do you think I give a shit about those people?*"

A beat of silence, then, "*I don't think you care about anyone.*"

"*You screwed that up for me. The Arrow should've burned—the place was meant to blow—*"

"*Because of you.*" Jasmine sounded both terrified and furious. He hated her fear and as for the fury...it was just driving up Drake's own rage. *I should have saved her.* But he hadn't. She'd burned.

"*Because of me.*" Maxwell was gloating.

"*How many others have you attacked?*" Jasmine asked him. "*With your bombs...with fire?*"

Trace shifted, moving closer to the computer. "What the hell? It sounds like she's interrogating him."

Yes, yes, it did.

Maxwell laughed. *"Oh, Jazz, I don't always need those tactics. Destroying a man's life is easy these days. A matter of business. I use tools. Tools like you. I hack into accounts. I learn secrets. I use them."*

Victor paused the recording. "As you see, he was incriminating himself. My man did his job perfectly and—"

"Jasmine is dead." Drake's heart was pounding. Her voice *hurt* him. "He fucked up his job." *I fucked up.*

Victor's eyes glinted. "You feel guilty, I get that. Jasmine...she was different. Maybe it was her eyes or those damn dimples. Whatever it was, she had a way of getting beneath your skin."

Drake caught Trace studying the agent with a thoughtful expression. "Did she get beneath your skin?" Trace asked him.

Victor's head tilted as he continued to study Drake. "This whole bit is about you getting closure, isn't it? Here. Listen to this, okay? Jasmine didn't blame you, not for anything." He typed again and Maxwell's voice filled the small room once more.

"Does Archer care about you?"

Drake stopped breathing when he heard that question. Then Jasmine replied and his whole body shuddered.

"No."

Had she truly believed that? *It's not just fucking to me.* Her words. They should have been his. They should have been *his.*

Maxwell asked, "*Will he come for you, try to save you?*"

No hesitation as she replied, "*No.*"

Maxwell cursed and demanded, "*Then what good are you to me?*"

"*I'm not.*"

Drake shook his head, helplessly. *No, no, no!*

"As you just heard, Jasmine didn't expect you to rush in, guns blazing, and save her. There's no need for you to feel guilty at all." Victor leaned forward to close the laptop.

Drake caught his hand. "Who was the inside man?"

"I'm not at liberty to say—"

"He's in the room, but he's not speaking. That means he's one of Case's flunkies."

"He speaks...but you aren't going to hear him. Revealing his identity would just compromise other cases that the man worked for us—"

"So this guy," Trace broke in, "he made a habit of working undercover for the FBI? For you?"

Victor's chin shot up. "I think we're done now."

Hell, no, they weren't. "Play the rest."

"I don't—"

"I want to hear it all."

But Victor shook his head. "There's no point."

"There is to me!"

"Why? *Why?*" Anger cracked in Victor's voice. "Do you want to hear her when she begs them not to shoot her? When Maxwell ordered her to be shot in the heart—and she *was?* Look, the fire didn't kill her. She was—she was dead when we heard the first shot."

Noah staggered a bit and crashed into the table. The laptop fell, hitting the floor hard. Victor dove down to retrieve it, but Trace beat him. He lifted the device. Handed it back to the agent.

Drake couldn't move. He remembered the sound of the gunshot that had blasted moments before the warehouse went up in flames.

"This is the end," Victor said. He gave a firm nod. "She's gone, and you have to just...just move on. I'm sure she'll be easy to replace."

He wanted to rip the guy apart. "No, she won't be."

Victor juggled his laptop and the crutches. "Yes, well...I think we're done here. I certainly hope our paths never cross again." Then, without another word, he turned and exited the room.

The men didn't speak until he was gone.

"*That's* one of the FBI's lead agents?" Noah was disbelieving. "I don't like that bastard! 'Easy to replace...' We're talking about a woman's life!'"

"Sometimes," Trace's voice was thoughtful, "there's more to a man than meets the eye."

Screw all that. Drake marched closer to Trace. "Did you get it?"

Trace opened his right hand. "Copied all the files...good job distracting him, though I was worried you were about to slug Victor...crutches or no."

Drake grunted. "I *was* about to slug him...crutches or no."

"Let's get out of here," Noah said, shoving back his shoulders. "I don't want any cops breathing down our necks. Not with what's coming."

What's coming...*their attack*. They weren't going to let Case get away. It was personal for Drake. Personal for Noah. As for Trace...

Hell, maybe he was just in it for fun.

No, he's in this fight because we're friends. Brothers. Not of blood, but from a bond that went deeper than that.

When they left the station, they passed Victor. The agent threw a glare Drake's way right before Victor headed into Detective Taggert's little office.

Drake knew he wore a glare of his own. *Your time will come, too.*

Because he wasn't done with that agent.

***

"Are you...are you sure you want to hear this?" Trace asked softly when they were back in Drake's apartment above his casino. "Maybe I should just review things. I mean, if the shooting is on here—"

"You sound like Victor. Just play the damn thing." Drake downed his second glass of whiskey. Noah was already on his third.

Trace tapped a few keys on the computer.

"This is the last sixty seconds of the recording. We should go back and hear it all to see—"

"*Play it.*"

Trace exhaled and hit another key.

"*The Feds are coming for you, and you're going away for a long time.*" Jasmine's voice. Only she didn't sound scared. She sounded...satisfied. "*You're not going to burn anything. You're not going to break anyone. And you're not going to get your precious payback for Anna Jean."*

"A ghost," Noah said, voice rough, "still trying to drag us all into her hell."

Not anymore, she wasn't.

"I've got you." Jasmine's voice had dropped.

"What?" That snarl was Maxwell's.

"You didn't even search me when they brought me in. Just tied me up...and talked your mouth off."

Drake stiffened as he started to realize what was happening.

There was a gasp, the sound of something tearing—*what the hell?*—then...

"Surprise," Jasmine said.

Drake couldn't move.

Trace's lips curved the faintest bit. "I'll be damned. I thought it might be her...inside man..."

"No!" Rage thundered in Maxwell's voice. *"No, this isn't how it ends for me! Shoot her...Right in the heart. Kill her and then get your ass out of here."*

Drake took a step toward the computer. "Who is he giving that order to?"

In the next instant, Drake had his answer as Jasmine said, *"Saxon, Saxon, don't..."*

Then the man replied, softly, sadly, *"I'm sorry, Jazz."*

The gunshot made Drake jerk.

"Right to the heart." Saxon's voice. Flat. Cold.

"Good...now let's get the hell out of here! Come on!" Maxwell's footsteps thundered away.

Only...it sounded as if he were the only one to leave.

Silence.

Then... *"Jazz?"* That was Saxon's whisper.

Drake's gaze flew to Trace.

"Jazz, we don't have much time. You okay?"

Drake couldn't breathe. Couldn't move.

"I'll be fine...once you get me out of these ropes."

"Sweet hell," Noah whispered. "The bullet didn't kill her!"

The recording stopped.

"Did the fire kill her?" Noah wanted to know. "Shit, it did. They found her remains, and—"

Trace shook his head. "That FBI agent is protecting his informant, agent—whatever she is."

Drake sucked in a deep breath. "She's still alive."

Trace held his gaze. "She could be. There's only one person who can tell us if Jasmine got out of that fire..."

FBI Special Agent Victor Monroe.

Hope burned in Drake, melting through the ice. "Let's make him talk."

"If she is alive, he's not just going to give up that information." Trace tapped his fingers against the desk. "We'll have to be careful."

"Screw careful," Drake retorted as his heart thundered in his chest. "I want her *back*."

***

"Will I get a funeral?" Jasmine asked because she was curious about that.

Saxon grunted. "I don't think I had one."

Sighing, she turned to face him. Saxon had been her constant—and only—companion for the last week. He'd hustled her out of New Orleans before she could blink, and now they were holed up in a cabin nestled in the Smoky Mountains.

The view was phenomenal. Almost like touching heaven.

And the ache in her heart? It wouldn't go away.

Her hand lifted to her side. Her stitches were gone now. Everything about her past was supposed to be gone. If only it were easy to shove away the memories.

"Have you been crying again?" Saxon chided, his voice sharp. He always got pissed when she cried.

Ah, Saxon. Friend. Protector...Annoyance.

"Because that dick isn't worth your tears. Archer is a player, not someone you can count on."

She *had* been crying. She cried those stupid tears every night when the lights were out.

A car's engine rumbled in the distance. She looked out of the window and saw the flash of headlights pushing up the mountain toward them. Finally. "Victor's coming." He'd said that he would come for her when it was safe. She and Saxon hadn't been the only ones to escape that blaze.

Of course, Maxwell had known how to get out. It had been his fire, after all.

The headlights came closer. They knew the driver was Victor—and not some lost tourist—because he'd called them moments before. They waited together as his pick-up pulled into the narrow drive.

Saxon headed out to meet Victor, but Jasmine stayed inside. Goosebumps were on her arms. This was it. Victor would tell her about the new life she was slated to begin.

The past was over. Gone.

Forget it...forget him.

Victor had a cast on when he came inside, but he didn't let the cast slow him. He moved easily, fluidly, barely using his one crutch. When the door shut behind him and Saxon, Victor glanced her way and a wide smile curled his lips. "Hey, Jazz...love that new look."

The shorter hair. The *blonde* hair.

He opened his arms and she hurried toward him, giving him a hug because Victor wasn't just her FBI handler.

He was her friend.

He and Saxon were the closest things to family that she had.

She'd met Saxon first, when she was seventeen and so scared. Saxon had been on the streets, too. But he'd made his living fighting— brutal and hard bouts in boxing rings that shouldn't have existed. No rules...just blood. Victor had been his opponent in one of those fights. They'd both wound up nearly broken, nearly *dead* in that battle. And Jasmine had been the one to patch them both up.

No one else had cared when the fight was over. Folks had collected their winnings and left the two broken warriors behind.

She'd stitched them both up. Taken care of them.

Over the years, they'd taken care of her, too.

Victor had gone into law enforcement. That move had stunned the hell out of her. And then Saxon...he'd followed the guy. Only while Victor played the straight and narrow, Saxon had sought the undercover missions. He'd wanted an up-close dose of danger and adrenaline.

He'd gotten those doses. With interest.

And...somehow...Jasmine had found herself following them. Working odd jobs for the government. Getting pulled into their web.

Until she'd been in so deep that there hadn't been any chance of going back.

Victor hugged her so tightly that the breath nearly left her body. "You've got some serious explaining to do," he growled the words against her ear. Victor's body was rock hard against her.

He was a big guy. Strong and tough, and she'd once even had a crush on him. Back when she'd been eighteen.

Now...now all she could think about was Drake.

Victor eased away from her a bit. "You had a brother you never told us about?"

"*What?*" Saxon half-shouted.

Jasmine shook her head.

Victor curled his hand under her chin. "And before you even get the urge to lie, let me stop you. I heard it from Archer. When that building started blazing, the man went crazy. Told Noah York that they had to get you out...cause you were the guy's sister."

Saxon pulled her away from Victor. "Is that true? You've got a brother?"

This hurt so badly. "Jasmine Bennett had a brother. One that her mom put up for adoption. I'm not Jasmine. She's dead, remember? I heard she died in a New Orleans fire." Her breath rushed out. "I'm Elizabeth. Elizabeth Farrow." That was the name on the ID she'd been given by Saxon. New name. New life.

"Why didn't you tell me?" Victor asked her.

"Uh, you mean why didn't she tell...*us*?" Saxon threw out. "Dammit, Jazz, you're supposed to share shit like this!"

They acted as if it were easy. "You've spent the last five years undercover, Saxon. In and out of nightmares. And, you, Victor...you do things that I don't...I don't always even want to know about." The monsters he hunted terrified her.

"Jazz..." Saxon began, his deep voice close to a growl.

"Elizabeth," she correctly softly.

"Drop the BS," Victor ordered her. Of the two men, Victor was the one usually snapping orders. Saxon was the one who usually went off and did whatever the hell he wanted. "Why didn't you really tell us? If that guy was your brother, I would've—"

"Done everything to put us together." Fine. She'd say the truth. They knew all her secrets, anyway. "I didn't want him to know about me, all right? He had his own life. He didn't need me and the tangled mess that I carry."

Victor's gaze held hers. "I like your mess."

"So do I," Saxon immediately added.

"Yes, well..." Dammit, she was getting teary again. "That's behind me now. Elizabeth is a good girl—"

Saxon coughed.

"She's a programmer. She has no criminal past. She doesn't have killers chasing her—"

Victor glanced away. *Oh, no.*

"She *doesn't* have killers chasing her," Jasmine said again.

He sighed. "We haven't found him yet. Maxwell's gone to ground, and I don't know how the hell he's managing to avoid our agents."

She backed away from him.

"We're going to find him," he rushed to reassure her. "It's just a matter of time."

Jasmine nodded even as fear twisted inside of her. She headed back toward the window. Stars were shining overhead. So many stars.

"But Maxwell Case isn't our only problem," Victor's voice flowed behind her. "Drake Archer is proving to be difficult."

"Like I didn't see that one coming," Saxon muttered.

Jasmine rubbed her chilled arms and stared out into the night. They were isolated out there. No other cars were on the long, winding road leading to their cabin. They had the perfect vantage point to watch and guard their position.

"The guy's acting obsessed. What the hell did you do to him Jasmine?"

She bristled. "Nothing."

"Really? Cause I've got my bosses breathing down my neck about you. Archer is demanding to see your remains. Your remains! I don't think he's buying your death, and the more he pokes around, the harder this situation is to contain."

A light appeared in the distance. Jasmine's eyes narrowed.

"You had to go and sleep with him." Victor was annoyed then. "*Him*. You couldn't just find some safe, boring accountant-type—"

"I told her not to sleep with anyone," Saxon had to add his two cents. "I knew trouble like this would come."

"It's her eyes." Victor was quick to jump on this bandwagon.

Jasmine narrowed said eyes even more.

"They make her look all vulnerable. Like she needs protecting. She pulled Archer in, and he is all twisted up because he thinks—"

"Someone's coming," Jasmine told them.

"*What?*" Saxon hurried to her side. "Shit." He pulled her away from the window. "You were followed," Saxon accused Victor.

"No way!" Victor denied immediately, sounding affronted. "I covered my ass. Took every possible precaution." Now he was at the window, too. "That's just some lost tourist."

But he didn't sound convinced, and he was already reaching for his weapon, the gun he kept holstered under his left arm.

"Go upstairs, Jazz," Victor said. "Lock the door and stay in the bedroom until Saxon or I come up there."

Saxon pulled out a gun from the nearby desk. "Keep this with you."

Her mouth had gone bone dry. "Because of a lost tourist?"

Saxon held her stare. "If someone comes up there and it's not me or Vic...*shoot*."

She could hear the growl of a car's engine. Getting closer and closer. Since when did tourists race up a mountain, in the dark? Jasmine turned and hurried up the stairs.

CHAPTER FOURTEEN

Jasmine carefully shut the bedroom door behind her. She clicked the lock into place. Killed the lights. Then backed up, moving until—

She backed *into* something. Not the soft edge of the bed that she'd expected to hit.

A person. Big. Warm. Hard.

Jasmine opened her mouth to scream, but a hand covered her lips, choking back the sound. She twisted and squirmed, determined to bring up her weapon.

"Now why would you want to use that..." A deep voice rumbled in her ear as the gun was taken from her. "On me?"

Her heart stopped. *Drake.*

"I'm going to move my hand away from your mouth, and you aren't going to scream."

She nodded.

"Because if you scream, those two jerks downstairs will run up here, and right now, I just want to deal with you." The words were angry. Hard.

She didn't care.

Drake was there.

His hand lifted. She turned in his arms. "Drake, I—"

His mouth crashed down on hers. It was a hard, desperate, almost brutal kiss, and Jasmine loved it. She strained to get closer to him. She'd missed him so much. It had felt as if someone had sliced right into her heart. No, as if someone had taken her heart.

His tongue thrust into her mouth. She rose onto her toes as she arched against him. One kiss, and the desire had ignited within her like a maelstrom. She couldn't get close enough. Couldn't touch him enough. Couldn't—

His mouth tore away from hers. They were surrounded by darkness and the harsh sound of his breathing filled her ears.

"If I planned to...punish you for every lie you told me..." That voice was a rasp against her ear. "What do you think I'll do...since you let me think you were *dead*?"

"I'm sorry. The plans were in motion long before we met." Jasmine Bennett had been ordered to go into Maxwell's organization—she'd been assigned the task of gathering intel on him. Of bringing him down. He'd been her last job. She'd already gotten too close to being caught before. Her "death" had been bound to happen, no matter what. "And I...I didn't think it would matter so much to you."

His hold tightened on her. "It mattered."

"D-Drake?"

Footsteps pounded up the stairs. The doorknob rattled. "Archer!" Victor snarled. "I know you're in there."

Drake didn't move. "It's Jasmine's bedroom." His voice drawled out. "Where else would I be?"

Victor shouted and *kicked* in the door. With a broken leg, the man seriously kicked in the door. Jasmine whirled around in shock as light flooded the room. "Victor, no! You have to be careful!" She tried to go to him.

But Drake hauled her back to his side. "What have you done to your hair?"

He'd noticed that?

"You can't be here!" Victor strode toward them. She didn't know where his crutch was, and his cast thunked a bit with each angry step that he took. "Do you know how much danger you're putting her in? You and those two idiots downstairs!"

"One of those idiots is her brother." Drake's voice snapped with anger.

"*I'm* her brother! Me and Sax! We're the ones who've always been there for her—"

Drake pushed Jasmine behind him. "You're the two that used her. That put her life at risk again and again, and that shit is stopping. She's not going to be in danger any longer. That won't happen. She's not—"

"Stop it!" Jasmine yelled.

And, wonder of wonders, they did.

Both men whirled to face her. Jasmine straightened her shoulders. "I'm the one who did it."

A frown hardened Drake's face. His face...how many times had she closed her eyes and seen him in the last week? But he looked different now. The faint lines on his face were deeper, sharper. His eyes blazed with a bright fire and there seemed to be a wildness clinging to him, pulsing just beneath the skin.

"I made the choices. I wanted to right the wrongs. I did it all. Me, not them." If Drake wanted someone to direct his fury at, he could stop looking at Victor.

He needed to look at her.

"You have to get out of here, Archer," she heard Victor snap. "It's not safe for you to be here. We worked hard to make Jazz vanish. You're about to destroy everything!"

But Drake didn't move. "I'm not leaving without her."

"You don't have a choice." Victor was adamant. "We've got too much riding on this case. Jasmine is dead, and you need to move the hell on."

Drake didn't look at Victor. His gaze pinned Jasmine in place. "I thought that I'd watched you burn."

"Drake..." She had to fight to keep her breathing steady. "Why did you come after me?" She'd never thought that he would. She'd already pictured him with someone else, and Jasmine had hated that other woman.

His jaw locked.

That wasn't going to do for her. "Tell me."

"You shouldn't have left me." The words were rough, bitten off. "You let me think you were dead." A muscle jerked in his clenched jaw. "Do you know what that did to me?"

"I'm sorry." She was. More sorry than she could ever say. "I didn't want—"

"I'm the one who told her she couldn't have contact with you." *Thunk. Thunk. Thunk.* Victor caught her hand and pulled her away from Drake. "Because you're dangerous, Archer, and I knew you'd make this whole thing blow up around us. You're pissed? Be pissed at me. I'm the one who made her leave you. I'm the one who did it all."

And Drake most definitely *was* pissed.

Drake glared at Victor.

Victor glared back even as he tugged on Jasmine's hand. "Let's get back downstairs before Saxon starts swinging...if he hasn't already."

Jasmine let him pull her away from Drake and back down the stairs. Victor didn't so much as flinch as he headed down all those steps, even though she knew his leg had to be hurting him. But that was Victor. Pushing through the pain, just like he'd done in their early days.

Drake followed closely behind her, and her body was so attuned to him that every muscle was taut. He'd come after her. That had to mean something, didn't it? If she'd just been another lover in the dark to him, then Drake never would have bothered searching for her.

It has to mean something.

And maybe, just maybe, it could mean everything.

***

Drake hated Victor. The smug FBI agent was begging for an ass kicking, and if Jasmine hadn't been standing between him and that jerk, Drake would be obliging him.

"How the hell did these guys get here?" The one called Saxon demanded. Big, blond, and with go-to-hell eyes, Drake remembered that fellow all too well.

So he was another one who'd been in on the FBI's game all along. "You could've said something," Drake snarled at him. "Instead of taking her away from my cabin and leaving me running after her in that swamp!"

Saxon lifted a brow. "Was I supposed to say something before or after you started shooting at me?"

Drake lunged forward.

"Try it," Saxon invited. He didn't back away. He stepped toe-to-toe with Drake. And he was smiling. A hard flash of teeth. "You think you're so tough because you and your boys spent some time pulling Black Ops? You're not the only one who knows how to dish out some hell." His hands were fisted, and Drake could see the line of scars that ran across Saxon's knuckles.

"No one is trying anything!" Jasmine's voice rose as she shoved her way between them. The light glinted off her hair. Blonde and shorter than before. Still sexy. Hell, the woman would always be sexy to him, but he missed that deep red of her hair. He wanted her back the way she'd been. He wanted her...*just the way she was before.*

Her secrets. Her lies. He just wanted her.

The floor creaked as Noah stepped forward. Noah, who'd been far too quiet on this whole mission. "Is it true?" Noah asked, his eyes locked on Jasmine. "Are you my sister?"

Her lips parted in surprise then her gaze flew right to Drake. He saw pain in her stare. Betrayal? No, hell, *no,* he hadn't betrayed her. "I thought you were dead! I wasn't really thinking of controlling my mouth." Sonofabitch. He'd only thought of her. Drake made himself take a few steps back. He had to get his control—and hold onto it.

She didn't understand just how much things had changed for him. For them. She would.

"Is it true?" Noah was less than a foot away from Jasmine.

Her open mouth closed. She shrugged. A careless move, even as her chin lifted a bit into the air. "I don't know what you're talking about."

Trace stood near the fireplace. The unlit fireplace. "A DNA test will answer your question quick enough, Noah."

Noah nodded. "Yes, it will."

Jasmine backed up a bit. When she retreated, Drake noticed that both Victor and Saxon advanced, as if they'd protect her.

What had Victor snarled at him earlier?

I'm her brother! Me and Sax! We're the ones who've always been there for her!

"Is that why you all followed me?" Jasmine's voice was muted. Hurt. "Because you wanted to test my DNA and see if I was a match for Noah?"

Noah's eyes flashed. "I want to know if you're my family."

"You have a family," Jasmine said softly. "I saw your wedding picture. A beautiful wife who loves you. You don't...you don't need me."

"Let me be the judge of what I need." Noah's voice was gruff and his eyes glinted with emotion. "*Are you my sister?*"

Almost miserably, Jasmine nodded.

He crept closer to her. "H-how?"

Jasmine's lips quirked. Her dimples flashed, and Drake could tell by the expression on Noah's face that her smile had just gotten to him.

The way it got me?

"The usual way babies are made." Her smile slipped away. "Our mother had you first. She was sixteen then, and she gave you up. I-I have a picture of you as a baby. It's upstairs. In my room. It's you and the people who adopted you." Her voice lowered. "That's how I found you. That picture."

Noah's face whitened. So much emotion blazed in his eyes. "She kept you?"

There was an odd note in Noah's voice. Confusion. Pain. And as much as Drake wanted to rush forward and grab Jasmine, to hold her tight, he knew that Noah needed this time.

So did Jasmine.

Even Saxon and Victor had retreated, though they still glowered suspiciously at Drake. And as for Trace...he was at the window, keeping guard. Always on alert.

"She kept me," Jasmine said with a slow nod. "I think maybe...at first...she had plans for us. Dreams. Because she regretted letting you go. She used to cry about that. About you."

Noah's face was a tense mask.

"It was better...for you not to be there." Jasmine's voice was so careful, and Drake knew that she wasn't going to tell Noah the full truth about her mother. *She doesn't want to hurt him.* "Life wasn't easy then. The parents you had—they loved you, and they gave you a good life. You shouldn't...you shouldn't—"

"I already know," Noah said softly, cutting through her words.

Her lashes flickered.

"Weston Securities," Noah murmured. "You think I didn't find out everything I could about you...and her...as soon as Drake told me?"

Now Saxon and Victor stepped forward once more, their protective instincts obviously aroused. *I'm her brother! Me and Sax!*

Noah waved them back, not looking even a bit intimidated. "I wish I'd known about you. I would have *come* for you."

Her gaze fell to the floor. "Maybe you should do that DNA test. Make sure I'm who you think—"

Noah caught her chin and tipped her head back. "I would have come for you."

A tear slid down Jasmine's cheek. "I didn't want to put you at risk." Her attention shifted to Drake. "I didn't want to put any of you at risk."

"Yeah, well..." Victor's voice had roughened. "Looks like they put *themselves* at risk. And now they've got you right back in the crossfire, too." His furious stare was directed at Drake. "Maxwell Case thought she was dead. Everyone was supposed to think she'd burned in that fire. But now you're here, and you could've tipped off Case!"

"We were careful." It was Trace who replied. Drake was too busy staring at Jasmine. She'd just hurriedly wiped away the tear on her cheek. He hated to see her cry. "No one followed us."

"You sure about that? Cause I'm not buying that story!" Victor started to pace. "We need to move her to a new safe house. Get her out of here so we can be sure this place wasn't compromised." He nodded toward Saxon. "Let's get her bag and start moving her out of here."

Victor really thought Drake was just going to let her vanish again? "It's not happening," Drake said simply.

"Did you just give me an order?" Victor glowered at him. "Cause it sounded like you tried to order *me* around."

"I told you a fact. Jasmine isn't going to vanish again."

"Since when do you get to decide her life?"

Since she became my life. He didn't tell the jerk that. What he felt for Jasmine...that was between him and her. They needed to be alone for any more revelations.

"I want to...know you." Noah's voice was halting as he spoke to Jasmine. "I found out you were my sister in the same moment I found out you were dead—or, I thought you were dead." He exhaled. "I *want to know you.*"

And Drake just wanted her.

So he stared at Jasmine. "You don't have to run." Slowly, he advanced toward her. His hand lifted. Touched the blonde hair. "You don't have to be someone else. You don't have to start a new life in a different place. You don't always have to be looking over your shoulder." That was exactly what she'd do, as long as Case was out there.

"So what is she supposed to do then?" Victor wanted to know.

Drake didn't look away from Jasmine. "Stay with me. I can keep you safe. I can protect you. I can stop him."

Her lips trembled.

"Stay with me," he told her again, and the words were as close to a plea as he'd ever come.

"No, no way." Victor *thunked* closer with his cast. "You are in way over your head, Archer. You can't keep her safe. You can just get her dead."

"You underestimate me," Drake said softly.

"No, I just know what you are." Red stained his cheeks. "I mean, big deal, so you once pulled some missions when you were playing soldier."

Playing soldier? Oh, that jerk was pushing him too far.

"But now you spend your days drinking in casinos and flirting with women. You are in so far over your head because you're—"

Trace's laughter stopped him.

Drake let his own lips curl. "You shouldn't believe everything you read in your FBI files. Jasmine isn't the only one good at pretending to be someone else." He let his hand fall away from Jasmine's hair. "Maxwell is already after me anyway," Drake told him. "So I'll put myself up as bait. I'll draw him out. I'll stop him because the FBI sure as shit isn't having any luck."

Victor snarled at him. Yeah, the agent reminded him of an angry wolf.

"I'll stop him," Drake said again. "And you won't have to run."

But Jasmine shook her head. "He's not the only enemy I've made."

He leaned in close to her. "Do you think I'm afraid?"

She searched his eyes. Shook her head once more.

"Then *stay* with me."

Silence. Tension stretched, filling that room, and...Jasmine nodded.

"No!" Victor was furious. "This is a huge mistake! Jasmine, you can't trust this guy—"

"But I do!"

"You're his current addiction. He wants you, and Drake is used to taking what he wants. But what happens when he gets tired of you? When he gets bored? He'll toss you aside, and the lions will close in."

Tired of Jasmine? "Not going to happen." He was being patient with the FBI prick, mostly because he knew Jasmine had ties with the guy and since those ties were familial and not sexual, he was giving the man a bit of leeway.

That leeway was going to end.

"We have a helicopter waiting to take us out of the mountains," Drake told Jasmine.

"Because your last escape flight went so well?" Victor's face had darkened. "This isn't happening! Jasmine, you're going with me and Saxon. We'll keep you safe. The way we always have. You can count on us. You know it and—"

"I want Drake."

Victor stopped talking.

"I love you, Vic, and Saxon, you'll always be my champion, but I...I need more." Her voice broke. "I don't want to start over again. I don't want to run anymore. I want to have a real life, and I want to stop pretending."

Victor's face had gone slack with shock.

But Saxon...he just nodded.

Her hand curled around Drake's. "I'll get my bag, and I'll go with you."

Fuck, yes.

"But you have to promise me one thing."

He'd promise her the whole world. And he'd give it to her.

I will never feel that agony again—I will never lose her again.

"Promise me that Maxwell won't hurt you. That we will stop him."

Easy enough. "I promise. Princess, I've got resources that you can't even imagine." And all of those resources were in play then.

He'd found her. He'd get Maxwell. End the nightmare.

Jasmine gave him a smile. Not the one that made her dimples wink, but one that still had his heart aching. Then she looked toward Noah. Tentatively, hopefully, her gaze flickered over him as she backed toward the stairs.

No one spoke as she turned and climbed those stairs. When she disappeared at the top, Drake wasn't surprised to see both Saxon and Victor head toward him.

"What in the hell..." Victor grated, voice low because Drake knew the guy didn't want Jasmine overhearing this, "are you doing? You screwed her, and now you think you can take over her life?"

"She took my life." He faced off against the two men and knew that both Noah and Trace had closed in behind him. They always had his back. "And I will protect her with every bit of power that I have. She doesn't need to be afraid any longer—"

"Because she has you?" Saxon cut in. "I didn't see you doing a whole lot of protecting back at that cabin—"

Drake drove his fist into Saxon's gut. Saxon grunted.

"For the cabin," Drake murmured. "Because it was my grandfather's, and I loved that place. You should've found another way inside."

Saxon's eyes glinted. Not with the rage Drake had expected. Almost with...humor? "I thought you'd hit harder."

"If you hadn't gotten her out of that warehouse, I would've."

Saxon nodded.

"This is bullshit!" Victor wasn't softening at all. "Jasmine is under federal protection. You can't just take her out of here! I won't let you!"

"Your federal protection didn't stop me from finding her. It won't stop him." Flat. True. "You need more power than the Feds are giving you. Work with me. We'll take out Case, and then you'll know that Jasmine is safe."

Victor's face twisted. "I don't like you, dammit!"

"Because I'm the asshole who—"

"*You aren't good enough for her.*" Victor's words fired out. "You're too dangerous and you're unstable. You lack control, and you live on the edge too much. Jasmine needs someone different. Someone safe."

Drake knew he would never be safe. And the edge—that was the only place he knew. He also knew one more thing. "You're right. I'm not good enough."

Surprise rippled across Victor's face.

"And I'm dangerous and uncontrolled, just like you said. But maybe that's what she needs. Maybe she needs someone who isn't afraid to kill in order to protect her."

"I'm a federal agent, you can't tell me—"

"I would break any law, I would do anything, to keep her safe. No one will hurt her, not ever again, because I'll be with her."

Beside Victor, Saxon gave another grim nod. "That's what a man should do. Kick the ass of anyone who threatens his woman."

"Jasmine *isn't* his." Victor was still furious. "They just met. She's something different for him. She's—"

"She is different, and she made me...different, too."

Then he heard the faint sound of Jasmine's footsteps. Coming back.

"You'll throw her away when you're done." Victor's eyes blazed. "Throw her to the lions at the door."

Drake shook his head. "No one will take her from me." He paused a beat. "Not Case. Not you. You may be her family, but I'm going to be her future." His low words were a vow.

"I'm ready."

He turned toward her voice. Jasmine was at the base of the stairs, a small, black bag clutched in her left hand. Her right hand was curled around a piece of paper. No, not paper. As she moved toward Noah, Drake saw that Jasmine was actually holding a photograph.

"I thought you might like this. Our...our mother is the one holding you." Her lips hitched up in a half-smile. "And the people behind her—well, you know them, right? The thing I liked most about that picture...you can already see the love in their eyes."

Noah's hand trembled when he took the photo.

Jasmine gave him another of her dazzling smiles. Noah just stared at her, lost.

I know the feeling, buddy.

Then Jasmine hugged Noah. A quick, fast hug. She tried to pull back, but Noah's arms locked around her and he held her tightly. He whispered something to her, but Drake couldn't catch the words. When Jasmine pulled back, her eyes glinted.

She eased toward Drake. "What's the plan?"

She had tears in her eyes. But Jasmine quickly blinked them away.

He frowned at Noah. "The plan is that Noah and Trace will stay here, keeping guard and making sure we aren't followed. You and I are heading for the helicopter. We're getting out of here, *now*." Because his intel told him that this place had been compromised.

That's how I found it. The location had already been compromised. I was just lucky enough to beat the bastard here.

Victor shook his head. "Jasmine, you don't have to leave with him. We can protect you."

The guy needed to let it go. Drake glowered.

"I *do* have to go. Because when I left without him before, it ripped my heart out."

Drake's gaze flew toward her.

She was staring at him. "I want to see what can happen."

I've never been in love, Drake, but I think...I really think I came close with you.

He took the bag from her. Twined the fingers of his left hand with hers. He didn't head for the front door. His motorcycle was back behind the cabin. Hidden in the trees.

Noah crossed his path. "Keep her safe."

Always.

Then Noah leaned toward him. "I love you like a brother, man, but if you do anything to hurt her, *ever,* I will bury you."

Drake nodded. Fair enough. It looked as if Saxon and Victor weren't the only angry big brothers he'd be facing.

But for Jasmine, he was realizing that he'd face anyone. Anytime.

He slipped from the cabin with Jasmine at his side.

***

Saxon crossed his arms over his chest and studied Trace Weston and Noah York. "So what happens now?"

"Now...we spring our trap."

Victor was wobbling on his cast. Victor liked to pace when he was angry, and Saxon knew that cast was seriously cramping his buddy's style.

"And if that trap backfires?" Victor wanted to know. "What if Drake winds up getting Jasmine killed?" Victor stopped wobbling and pointed at Noah. "If she's really your sister, you should be scared as all hell. Drake Archer doesn't have the kind of history you can trust. He's a playboy and an adrenaline junkie!"

"He loves her," Noah said simply.

Saxon nodded. He'd already figured that out for himself.

Victor's mouth hung open. "What? There's no way. He doesn't love anyone or anything—"

"You saw him when that warehouse exploded." Trace Weston's voice was low. "You already know how he feels, but you don't want to admit it because you don't want to lose her."

Victor swallowed.

"Now we have plans to put in place. Because according to *our* intel, Maxwell is already on his way here."

"*What?*"

"We didn't tell Jasmine because if she'd known...Drake didn't think she'd leave the two of you behind."

Drake had been right. Saxon rocked forward onto the balls of his feet. "That intel of yours had better not be wrong."

"It isn't." Trace seemed certain. "We found your location because it had already been leaked. We just managed to beat Maxwell here, but he *is* coming. And we have to be ready for him."

Saxon had been waiting for his chance at Maxwell. Ever since the sonofabitch had punched Jasmine. *Right in front of me.* He hadn't seen the blow coming. And it had wrecked him.

I'm so sorry, Jazz.

"We wait," Trace said, "and when he gets close enough, the bastard is ours."

CHAPTER FIFTEEN

The motorcycle roared to a stop in what looked like the middle of nowhere.

Jasmine tightened her hold on Drake even as he braked the bike. What were they doing? She didn't see a helicopter there.

He rose, and she followed him, ditching the helmet that he'd given to her. "Drake? Drake, why are we stopping here?" The stars—looked like a million of them—glinted down on her.

"Because I can't go anymore...I need you too much."

It couldn't be as much as she needed him.

"Jasmine...we *have* to talk. There were things I couldn't say with those two guards of yours listening to our every word."

Her guards—Victor and Saxon? She turned away from him and nervously rubbed her arms. She felt chilled out there.

He wrapped his arms around her and pulled her back against his chest. "Do you know what it was like for me?"

"I—" No, she didn't. Jasmine didn't have a clue.

His mouth pressed to her neck, scorching her with his kiss.

She trembled. They were surrounded by the woods. He'd pulled off the narrow road, and they were far away from prying eyes.

It's just us.

"When I saw the fire...when I saw that place explode, do you know what it was like for me?"

Helplessly, Jasmine shook her head.

He kissed her neck again.

"I was ready to burn with you."

Her heart slammed into her chest. She never wanted Drake to suffer because of her.

"I didn't plan on you." He seemed to surround all of her. Jasmine could feel the heat of his arousal pressing against her. Only fair considering that she'd just nearly melted with the light caress of his lips against her throat. "I knew better than to trust a beautiful face."

Because of Anna Jean. Would that woman's ghost never stop haunting her?

"You risked your life for me."

He nipped her with his teeth. A gentle punishment that had her aching even more.

"You stared at danger. You fucking made me *laugh*, and you caught me. You slipped beneath my guard when I should have been watching..."

One hand rose and slid up her side, resting just beneath her breast. In that wilderness, they seemed totally isolated. Just her. Just Drake. Just the faint howl of the wind through the trees.

His hand curled around her breast. Her nipple was already tight and hard with arousal, and she gasped at the electric contact.

"You lied to me." His mouth was on the spot where her shoulder and neck met, that curve that she'd never realized was so incredibly sensitive.

He kissed her there even as his hand fondled her breast. The wind seemed to kick up around her, and her long skirt blew back against her legs.

"I-I had to lie..."

"You deserve your punishments."

Both of his hands were on her now. Strong, rough hands. Her hips squirmed, pushing back against him.

"I knew you lied...and I didn't care."

Once more, she felt the nip of his teeth. Jasmine was pretty sure her panties were soaked. *I missed him so much.*

One of his hands slid down her stomach. He caught her billowing skirt and slid under it. She pushed up onto her toes and tried to widen her legs a bit more.

"I heard the recording they made of you. You told Case that I wouldn't come after you. That I didn't care."

His fingers brushed over her panties. Her eyes closed as a moan built in her throat.

"You were supposed to lie to him, but those words didn't sound like a lie."

Helplessly, Jasmine shook her head.

His fingers pulled the panties to the side, and then he was touching her. Stroking her with his slightly callused fingers—sliding two fingers *into* her.

"You weren't lying to him. You thought you didn't matter to me."

Faster, harder, he worked her sex with one hand while his other stroked her breast. Jasmine's whole body was bow tight. A release was coming. Just seconds away—

He spun her around. "You thought wrong, princess." He jerked open his jeans. His cock sprang out. Before she could suck in a deep breath, he'd lifted her up—she *loved* that man's strength—and he was inside of her. Surging deep and hard, filling her so much that she ached, and the ache felt *good.* "You." Thrust. "Were." *Hard* thrust. "Wrong."

His hands were steel bands around her waist as he lifted her into each thrust. Strong and hard and wild. She couldn't slow down his rhythm. She didn't want to. Jasmine just held onto him, squeezing him with her sex, and when the pleasure burst through her, she kissed him as she tried to give him back some of that blazing euphoria.

The pleasure lashed her whole body. Inside. Out. Pulsed through her with a sensual energy that ignited her.

Her hands sank into his hair. She kept kissing him, deep, sensually, and with all the passion that she had.

She felt him come inside of her. Long, hot jets that just made her tremble all the more.

He didn't ease his hold on her. She didn't let him go. They were still in the night. She wished that they could just stay there, alone, and forget the rest of the world. Forget the danger and the fear.

But his hands were slowly sliding down her body. He eased her back to her feet. Her knees shook and he held her when she trembled.

He pressed a faint kiss to her forehead. It was...tender. Jasmine had to swallow the lump in her throat. "Where is that helicopter going to take us?" Jasmine whispered.

"Any place you want to go."

She just wanted to be with him.

He straightened her clothes, again with movements that were strangely tender. She'd thought he was furious with her, but he didn't act like a man enraged as he settled her back on the motorcycle. He handed her the helmet. Hesitated. "Go back to red."

She blinked at him and tried to catch her breath.

"I miss the red hair."

Her lips curled. "And here I thought blondes had more fun."

"You're beautiful any way, and I'll take you..." His voice roughened. "Any way I can get you."

That was how she'd take him, too. Did that make her desperate? Lost? Jasmine didn't really care.

His hand curled around her thigh and seemed to scorch her right through that fabric. "You matter to me." The words were growled, heavy with arousal. "I would have walked through that fire for you. You *matter*."

Her breath caught in her throat. "You matter to me, too," she said softly. But those weren't the words she wanted to say. Fear held them back.

"I don't even know when it happened, but I do know this...when that warehouse caught on fire, I knew my life was over, if you weren't in it."

She didn't want to cry. Not again. She'd done plenty of that in the last week so she quickly blinked away the tears that wanted to fill her eyes.

"Stay with me. Now...and for the days that are coming. See what we can be for each other."

Didn't he realize what she'd done? She'd already made that choice. When she'd left Victor and the safety of the FBI, she'd been choosing the life she might have with him. The life she wanted. "I'm not going anywhere without you." Because she'd finally found the home that she'd sought for so long.

And that home—it was wherever Drake was.

He gave a grim nod, then climbed onto the bike. The motorcycle's engine snarled to life once more, and soon they were whipping through the night. Her arms curled around him as the darkness passed in a blur, and she held him so tightly.

I love you. Those were the words she'd wanted to give him. Too fast. Too soon. That didn't matter to her. Drake was in her heart, and when the moment was right, she *would* tell him.

Fear wouldn't hold her back forever.

***

Drake didn't stop again, not until they reached a small strip of pavement in the darkness. A landing pad. The lights on the helicopter were shining and the blades were already whirling.

Drake had told the pilot to start up as soon as he saw them coming.

He tossed aside his helmet and reached for Jasmine's hand. "Come on!" The wind from the helicopter blew against him. The sooner they got on that bird, the better.

"Wait, my bag!" Jasmine bent to retrieve the small bag that he'd stuffed into the motorcycle's saddlebag.

The pilot was inside the chopper. The helicopter's lights were blazing, so Drake couldn't see inside to the guy, but he knew Quincy Cole would follow orders. He'd made special arrangements to have Quincy come with him to the mountains because the fellow was one of the few Drake trusted completely. The guy was good in a—

Gunfire rang out. The blast hit Drake in the shoulder and he stumbled back.

"Drake!" Jasmine grabbed for him.

Another shot rang out. Only this time, that shot hit *her*. It slammed into Jasmine even as Drake tried to twist his body and protect her.

But he wasn't fast enough.

"No!" Drake roared as he pulled her tightly against him. He could feel her blood, pulsing from a wound on her stomach. This wasn't happening. This *wasn't*.

"Did you really think you'd be a step ahead of me? There was no way I'd let you beat me to Jasmine," a familiar voice called out. *Not Quincy. Not Quincy...* "I was just waiting until I could get you both together. It's fitting for you to go out this way!"

Drake turned his head. The pilot had come out of the chopper, only it definitely wasn't Quincy. This man was taller, bigger, and even though the light was behind him and Drake couldn't see his face, he knew the man.

"Maxwell."

Laughter. "Thanks for arranging my getaway ride for me. After I kill you two, it will be nice to fly away. Anna Jean was the one to teach me to fly, you see. That woman loved the sky."

"D-Drake...?" Jasmine's voice broke on his name.

"It's all right." *I promised to protect her.* "It's just a graze, princess. You're okay."

"No, you're not, Jasmine," Maxwell told her, his words gleeful. "You're bleeding out. That's a gut shot. One designed to give you maximum pain, because I felt that was what I owed you. If you don't get medical attention immediately, you'll die." That laughter again. "And you won't be rising from the dead this time."

Carefully, so carefully, Drake lowered Jasmine to the ground. "I didn't find you...just to lose you again." He *wouldn't* lose her. "Don't be afraid...of what I do." Because he was going to do exactly what *had* to be done.

Maxwell wasn't lying. It *was* a gut shot. And Drake was getting Jasmine that immediate medical attention because she would not be dying on him.

She nodded, her head barely moving against the ground. Her breath was choking out.

I'm so sorry, princess.

He'd failed her, again, and she was about to see just what he truly was.

He slipped the knife from his boot. He always had a weapon on him. Did Jasmine realize that? Probably not. Because she didn't know all his secrets.

"I want you to stay right there!" Maxwell ordered him. He could hear the man's footsteps coming closer. "I want you to watch while she dies in front of you. I mean, you watched my Anna Jean die, didn't you? So it's only fitting that you watch that treacherous bitch Jazz die, too!"

"I'm...c-cold..." Jasmine whispered.

"I'll warm you."

Her gaze flickered to him. "You...already did."

Drake swallowed and kept the knife concealed. He just needed a few precious seconds to attack his prey.

But Jasmine didn't have seconds.

The gun shoved into the back of Drake's head. "Watch her. Stare right at that bitch as she chokes on her blood and you have to—"

Drake lunged up and twisted around in a flash. He knocked the gun out of the bastard's hand. Then he drove his knife right into Maxwell Case's heart. "Don't ever call her a bitch."

Maxwell's breath heaved out. His hands clamped around Drake's arms.

Drake twisted the knife and he smiled. "You should have stayed the hell away from me...and what was mine."

Then he shoved that bastard to the ground. The knife was still in Maxwell's heart. Exactly where it belonged.

Drake whirled back to Jasmine. "I've got you, princess." He lifted her. Carried her to the chopper. He strapped her in and used those straps to put as much pressure on the wound as he could. She cried out in pain, and the sound wrenched through him.

Then he jumped forward to grab the controls.

"I don't...want to die..." Her weak voice.

"You're not." He flipped the switches. Called out on his radio. He wanted help. He'd get help. "I'm not losing you."

He'd already thought she left him once. He couldn't survive that kind of pain again. He wouldn't.

The helicopter's blades whirled and the bird lifted into the dark sky.

***

"You were supposed to have a plan!" Victor stormed into the hospital's emergency room with his crutch pounding frantically onto the linoleum floor. "You bastard! This is your fault!"

He lunged toward Drake, then stopped short when he saw the blood that covered him. "J-Jasmine's?"

"Most of it." He met Victor's gaze head on. "Maxwell shot her."

"I heard." Victor's voice had lowered. Saxon was beside him. Looking just as furious and scared. "What happened to your shoulder?"

The paramedics had insisted on taking out the bullet. "Nothing."

Saxon narrowed his eyes on him. "And what happened to that bastard Maxwell?"

"He was waiting for us at the helicopter."

"You said she'd be safe with you," Victor gritted. The man's face was chalk white. His eyes blazed with emotion. "I trusted you with her life! Look what you did!" He dropped the crutch and attacked.

Drake let him take his swings. He knew he had them coming. Them and more.

He didn't quite expect Victor to have such a strong punch, though. That first hit damn near broke his jaw.

He took the second hit.

The third.

"Fuck man," Victor snarled. "You won't even *fight* me."

No, he wouldn't. He looked up at Victor. "Jasmine loves you." He knew that with certainty. He'd heard it in her voice.

At Drake's words, Victor's body shuddered. He whirled away. Nearly fell when his broken leg hit a chair, but then he stumbled away.

The emergency room doors swung open again. This time, Trace and Noah rushed inside. Noah, Christ, he looked terrible.

Probably the same way I look.

"I was supposed to save her." He'd promised her that.

He'd never wanted to break a promise to Jasmine.

Drake waited for Noah to kick his ass. He deserved his pound of flesh, just like Victor.

Instead, Noah just asked, in a voice heavy with pain, "Is she going to live?"

Drake's hands fisted. "She has to."

"Where is Maxwell Case?" Saxon snapped.

"Where he fell." Drake's jaw locked. "With my knife in his heart."

Victor stood in the corner. Talking fiercely into his phone. Probably checking with his FBI buddies. They'd find Case's body. Drake hadn't missed his mark.

He swallowed and just tasted his own sick fear. "He was at the launch pad. I thought we'd beat him to the mountains, but he made it here ahead of us."

Noah just watched him with an unblinking stare.

"That bastard...he killed Quincy." He'd seen the man's body near the chopper. "And he just waited for me." He forced himself to keep looking into Noah's eyes. "I led her straight to him." He'd been so certain he could keep her safe.

So wrong.

"I fucked up."

Noah clamped a hand over his shoulder.

Drake tried to choke down his fear. "I don't want to lose her."

Noah's hold tightened. "Me, either, man. Me, either."

Helpless, lost, Drake could only stand there...and wait.

***

Jasmine opened her eyes. "I want...Drake."

Machines beeped around her. Her body *hurt*. And she remembered everything that had happened to her. Well, everything up until the moment she'd passed out in the helicopter.

"He's gone, baby."

Victor's voice. Her head turned. Victor was beside her bed. Holding her hand. Looking as if he'd been to hell and back.

"Gone?" Fear whipped through her and the machines around Jasmine began to beep frantically.

"Dammit, look what you did." Saxon stepped closer to the bed. "He's not dead, Jazz. Maxwell didn't get him." He gave a low whistle. "Your boyfriend pretty much carved that guy's heart out. You don't have to worry about any threats from Maxwell ever again."

She pulled in a deep breath.

"As for Drake...Vic here got the guy taken into custody. Some BS about obstructing a federal investigation." Anger hummed in Saxon's words. "He had your man dragged out of here in handcuffs."

Jasmine tried to sit up—and failed. "You...didn't."

Victor's hold tightened on her hand. "I think I went a little crazy," his confession was hushed, "when I saw you in the OR."

"You went into the operating room?"

He gave a slow nod. "I thought you were dying on the table. I was so furious—"

"Scared," Saxon tossed out.

"It was Drake's fault." Victor's gaze slowly lifted to meet her stare. "He took you out of the safe house. He's dangerous. A threat that I couldn't allow to stand near you anymore."

She could only shake her head. "Let him go."

Saxon rocked forward onto the balls of his feet. "I told you, Vic, you were losing your mind." A pause. "What little you had left of it."

"Drake saved me!" Her throat hurt. Burned. Had they put a tube down her throat? Oh, jeez, she hated those tubes. And...what about her stomach? The gunshot? She didn't want to look at the damage to the rest of her body. "Let him...go!"

Victor rose to his feet. "You're...going back to him?"

Always.

But then Victor gave a hard shake of his head. "You can't."

He wasn't going to stop her.

"It's not safe. You had other cases, Jazz. Other enemies. We have to make sure that all the threats facing you have been eliminated."

Once more, she tried to rise in the bed. Moving hurt like a bitch, so she didn't get very far. Maybe a precious inch.

"You're not getting out of this hospital any time soon," Victor's voice dropped. "And I can't let you go to him. I can't put you in the line of fire again."

"Victor..."

Saxon cut his stare toward his friend. "Get her lover out of FBI custody. Do it now, so that Drake can have time to cool down and not want to kick your ass."

Oh, Jasmine was pretty sure Drake wouldn't forget an ass kicking.

And he won't forget me.

"He gave you some free hits," Saxon continued, voice flat, "but you know that shit will be over."

What free hits? Jasmine shook her head. "I think I love him."

Victor stumbled back as his mouth gaped. "Him? *Him?* No! We talked about this! You were supposed to fall for an accountant, a doctor. Someone—"

"Safe."

He nodded.

"Get him out of custody," Jasmine ordered—or tried to order. Talking seemed to be such an effort, and her eyelids wanted to sag closed. Stupid drugs. She hated them. "Let him know...I'm all right."

"I will." It was Saxon who gave that promise.

"But you can't go to him." Victor was adamant. "Not until it's safe." His voice roughened. "Because I can't handle seeing you hurt like this, baby. I can't."

She struggled to keep her eyes open and on him.

"We might not be blood, but you're my family," Victor said. "And I won't let anyone ever hurt you again. No matter what rules I have to break...or who I have to destroy."

He sounded so fierce. And so like Drake. "You have..." Her words were slurring because sleep was calling her again. "A lot...in common with him..."

Silence. Then, gruffly, "That's what scares me."

It didn't scare her. She knew Victor was a good man. Deep down. Beneath that dangerous exterior. As for Drake...

I know he's my man. She'd find her way back to him. Because she wasn't going to let her chance at happiness slip away. Not now.

***

When Jasmine's eyes sagged closed, Victor didn't let go of her hand. She looked too pale against those crisp sheets. Too fragile.

"You won't be able to keep her away from him," Saxon warned.

Victor glanced up at the only man he considered his friend. His family. For so long, it had been him, Saxon, and Jazz against the world.

"You sure as hell won't be able to keep him away from *her*," Saxon added, his eyes watchful.

"He got her shot!"

One brow rose. "He flew the chopper that got her to this hospital. He stopped her bleeding. He saved her life." A pause. "And he carved out the heart of the asshole who hurt her. In my book, that makes him—"

"What?" Victor's hold tightened on Jasmine's hand. "Okay? One of the family?"

"If he's with her, then he is family, whether you like it or not." His gaze slid toward the closed hospital room door. "So is that other poor bastard out there. The one who won't stop pacing the hallway."

Noah York.

"Why didn't she tell us about him?" He'd thought Jasmine was as alone in the world as they had been. He could still remember the first time he'd met her. His hands had been broken. His ribs cracked. He'd been spitting up blood in that rundown boxing ring. No one else had so much as given him a second glance.

Then her soft hands had been on his shoulders. She'd promised him that everything would be all right.

He'd thought of her as his angel. An angel who'd gotten caught in hell with him. "I wanted more for her." That was why he'd worked so hard to get her *out* of those undercover operations, but Jasmine had kept pushing herself right back in them.

"She likes the danger, just as much as we do." Now Saxon was looking at Jasmine once more. "Why do you think she was so drawn to Archer?"

Victor had to bite back a snarl. "I don't like him."

"You don't have to like him," Saxon murmured as a smile tugged at his lips. "You do have to get his ass out of FBI holding, or else Jazz will rip you a new one when she finally gets out of this hospital bed."

She wasn't getting out of that bed anytime soon. He'd read the reports. Felt as if *he'd* been the one gutted. So much pain. Too much, for her.

"And you know Archer isn't going to just stay there, anyway. You're lucky he hasn't called in some of those high-powered contacts of his and had your ass demoted at the Bureau."

Victor had wondered about that part himself. "Why didn't he?" He forced himself to let go of Jazz. *She's going to be okay.*

"You blamed him for what happened to her." Saxon shrugged. "It was obvious the man blamed himself, too."

And the guy was just staying locked up? "Doesn't make sense."

But Saxon had turned away. "It does...if he loves her."

Victor's spine snapped up at that. "Archer doesn't love his women."

Saxon's hand was on the door. "I don't think he has any women any longer. I think he just has...her."

Victor shook his head. Saxon hadn't seen the background reports on Archer. He didn't know about the man's past. Archer wasn't going to get heavily involved with someone. He was just—

"Because she loves him, it doesn't mean we lose her. Blood or no blood, do you think Jasmine would ever turn her back on us?"

Victor didn't answer.

"So you need to go make peace with Archer. Cause if you don't, the holidays are going to be shit-ass awkward." Saxon exhaled heavily. "Now I've got to talk with the *brother* because if I don't, that guy is gonna tear down this hospital."

Victor glanced back at Jasmine. "Fuck."

***

Drake didn't move when the door opened and Victor walked inside the small office. He stared up at the FBI Agent as his gut clenched. "Jasmine?"

"She's awake."

Drake's heart raced in his chest.

"The doctors expect a full recovery."

Beneath the table, his hands fisted.

Victor paced toward him. The lower part of his right leg was in a black boot, and there was no sign of his crutch. "Why the hell are you still here?"

She's awake. A full recovery. "I'm in custody, where else would I be?"

"Don't feed me that BS. You're *letting* the FBI hold you. Why? Why haven't you used one of your high priced lawyers or pulled one of those puppet strings that you and your pal Weston control—why haven't you gotten out? Why have you been letting the FBI play guard dog around you?"

Drake inclined his head toward him. "You know why."

Victor's hands slammed down on the table. "Jasmine? You expect me to believe you stayed prisoner for her?"

Drake didn't reply.

"You nearly got her killed. You said you'd keep her safe." Victor's words rushed out in a furious barrage. "I let you take her, and then...then the next time I saw her, they had her cut open on an operating room table."

Drake's jaw locked.

"When her eyes opened, you were the first thing that she asked about. *You.*"

His chest ached.

"How many enemies do you have out there, Archer? Do you even know? How many of them would love to hurt you...by going after Jasmine? By going after the woman you love?"

"Too many to count." Did the agent think he hadn't realized this? He didn't want Jasmine hurt. That was why he'd stayed with the FBI guards. Why he hadn't gone back to the hospital, when every cell in his body was screaming for her.

He never wanted to see her bloody and in pain again.

"Shit. You didn't deny it." Victor shoved away from the table. "You were supposed to deny it!" His hands flew into the air.

Drake rose to his feet. "I won't put her at risk again." He'd been selfish. He could see that now. And though he felt like he was cutting out his own heart, Drake made himself say, "I won't pull her back into my life." He couldn't—because he couldn't put her at risk ever again.

He was more than obsessed. He was lost in her. And if he didn't stay away, while he could, he knew that Jasmine would never be free of him.

Victor pointed at him. "You didn't deny it!"

No, of course not. "It's my fault she was hurt—"

"Loving her, you dick," he gritted out. "You didn't deny loving her."

Why lie?

Victor swung away. Marched toward a wall. Banged his head against it.

What the hell?

"The holidays are gonna be a bitch," Victor muttered as his shoulders slumped.

Weren't they always? Especially since Drake spent them alone. "You're sure she's going to recover?"

"Yeah, yeah, I'm sure. Jazz is a fighter, always has been." He pushed away from the wall. "But you can't see her now. The cases she was working, they aren't closed, and I need her out of the public eye. I need her safe."

He didn't want to just see her. He wanted to hold her. To never let go.

"I thought I'd be able to protect her," Drake said slowly. "I was wrong. I won't be making that mistake again."

Victor laughed. "Hell, yeah, you will. It just won't be today." He waved toward the door. "You're free to go."

Drake blinked. "Just like that?"

"Just like that. Sorry for the inconvenience for the last—um, forty-eight hours."

Drake paced toward him.

Victor held up his hands. "She wouldn't like it if you kicked my ass."

Drake was so tempted...but Victor was right. "Make sure she has a good life."

"Uh..."

"A perfect life, got it? No worries, no fears, not ever. You give her *everything* that she could possibly want because if I find out her life isn't perfect, I will be back to kick the ever loving hell out of you." He held Victor's gaze to make sure that message was received, then he swung on his heel and headed for the door.

"I think she loves you, too."

The thunder of Drake's heartbeat filled his ears. "I'm not a good man to love. She's better off without me." For once, *once,* he'd put someone else first in his life. She deserved more than a damaged guy like him.

"I think so, too..." Victor's murmur followed him from the room. "But I don't know if Jasmine will buy that."

Drake glanced back.

"Maybe we are alike," Victor added, his expression turning thoughtful.

What?

"And if it were me, I wouldn't be able to walk away from the woman I wanted more than life. Not without it ripping me apart."

Drake glared at him. *How the hell do you think I'm feeling right now?*

"So let's see how long this lasts...I'm betting when Jazz is free and clear, you'll run her down and never let her go."

"I want her *happy.*"

"Yeah, me, too. That's why I'm telling you...treat her well, asshole, or you'll find a knife at your back when you least expect it."

That didn't sound like a warning from an FBI Agent. Instead of leaving, Drake headed back into the little room. He waited until he was a foot away from Victor. Then he growled, "Keep her safe or that knife will wind up in your throat."

Instead of looking intimidated, Victor laughed. "Damn straight."

Drake glared at the fool. Then he left and with every step he took, he thought of Jasmine.

He had a feeling that she would always be in his mind. Always.

CHAPTER SIXTEEN

Drake wasn't looking for trouble. He wanted oblivion. He grabbed his glass and downed the whiskey in one gulp. Below him, the crowd at his club was a writhing mass. Too many bodies. Heat. Lust. Laughter.

Once upon a time, he would have looked down there and found a woman to seduce. He'd have taken the pleasure to push away the numbness that seemed to fill his life.

Only he wasn't numb any longer. He ached, he hurt, every minute of the day. Because she was gone.

He should have been able to move on. He'd done the right thing, the *good* thing, for once. Shouldn't that have meant something?

Two months. Two long, hellish months had passed. He hadn't touched another woman in that time. Drake didn't want anyone else. Only her.

He didn't even know where Jasmine was. Had the FBI given her a new life somewhere else? Was she still a blonde or was she back to that sexy red?

Did she ever think of him? Because sleeping or awake, she seemed to consume him. Dreams of her were driving him to the brink of sanity. It was getting so bad that he was actually starting to imagine he saw her...

His gaze raked the crowd and locked on the figure of a slim redhead. Her back was to him, and all he could see was the soft fall of her hair—and the black of her clothing. A form-fitting turtle neck and black pants.

And fuck-me heels.

His hands rose and pressed against the glass.

Can't be her. Can't be. I've seen other redheads. Thought they were her...see her everywhere...Can't. Be. Her.

The woman got a drink from the bar, then, taking her time, she turned in her seat.

All of the breath left Drake's lungs.

She tilted back her head. Lifted her left hand. And crooked her finger up at him.

Jasmine.

She shouldn't be there. He'd made the sacrifice. He'd let her go once. There was no way that he'd let her go again. She had to know that.

She smiled up at him. He couldn't see her dimples, not from that far away.

How did she know that he was even there? The glass was tinted—just as it had been the first time he saw her in his club—but she still seemed to stare right at him.

Trouble.

Everything he wanted.

Drake whirled away from the viewing window and rushed down to the club. He couldn't move fast enough. Couldn't get to her soon enough. And when he burst into the club and the pounding music reached his ears, he couldn't see her over the mass of bodies. He wanted those people out of his way. He wanted the only one who mattered to him.

"Hey, boss," one of his waiters called. "What are you doing on the floor?"

Because he never came down there. Not anymore.

Not—

Jasmine.

She was still at the bar. One high-heeled foot swayed softly to the music.

He shoved some drunk guys out of his way, ignored their swearing, and closed in on her. At the last moment, she turned toward him. Her eyes widened—deep, dark eyes.

"Hello, Drake."

His hands closed around her arms. He yanked her off that barstool and up against him even as his mouth crashed down on hers.

She tasted just like he remembered. Like every dream he'd ever had. Like everything he wanted but didn't deserve.

She was soft and lush against him. Fitting him perfectly. His hands snaked around her, and he held her even tighter. His tongue drove into her mouth and when she moaned and kissed him back just as frantically, he was pretty sure he'd lost his mind.

"You can't be here," he managed. *You're safe. You're far away.*

"I am here," Jasmine whispered as her lips pulled from his. "This is exactly where I want to be."

His breath heaved out of him. The music was pounding so loudly he wasn't sure he'd even heard her correctly. He kept her hand in his—*won't let go*—and he pulled her from that bar. Took her to his private elevator. When the doors closed, he yanked her against him again.

Desire churned within him. Too hot and hard to restrain. He should be careful. He should back away from her.

Yet he just kept pulling her closer.

The elevator dinged, and he hurried them to his room. His grip on her hand remained unbreakable. The door closed behind her, sealing them inside.

"Drake—"

He took her mouth. Needed to. His hands flattened on either side of her head, and he tasted her. *Not a dream. She's real. She's with me again.*

Her hands were on his chest. Warm and soft.

He wanted to be naked.

Wanted everything with her.

He heard her moan, and it was music to his ears. She wanted him. She'd come back to him.

Hanging tight to his control—because he knew it would be breaking soon—Drake managed to pull back, but he couldn't let her go. "You shouldn't...be here." He hated the rough, ragged sound of his own voice.

"You're here." Her dark eyes stared up at him. "That means here is the only place I want to be."

Christ. She was *breaking* him. "I tried to do the right thing with you." His hand slid down her body. Carefully, so very carefully, and he remembered her blood pumping between his fingers. "I wanted to keep you safe before, but I'm the one who took you straight to Maxwell."

"No, Drake. You're the one who saved me."

How could she believe that? How could she look up at him with those eyes that seemed to see straight through him? She should see him for what he was—and then run screaming.

But I can't let her go now.

"I walked away once, how am I supposed to do it again?" Victor should have kept her away.

Jasmine shook her head, sending her red hair brushing over her cheeks. "You don't walk away again. Neither do I. My cases are closed, and I'm free." She licked her lips and arousal knifed through him. "I want to be with you. And I-I hope you still want me."

"Only every damn minute."

Her lips trembled into a smile.

"But you have to be careful," Drake warned her. "You have to know...I can't have you again and let you go." That wasn't the way he worked. "You shouldn't have come back."

Her hands rose. Curled around his neck. "And you shouldn't have stayed away for so long. I'm not afraid of you, Drake Archer."

Why not? He'd nearly cut out a man's *heart* in front of her.

"I'm not afraid of you. Not of any enemies that you have. What I am afraid of...I'm afraid of being without you. Because that's not how I want to live. That's not how I can live. I need you. I love you."

Her words rocked right to his core.

And sealed her fate.

"It's done," Drake managed to say, the words gravel-rough and final.

She blinked at him.

"I tried to be good, but, now, princess, it's too late." He lifted her up, using so much care, and he sat her on the edge of his desk.

"Drake?"

He stripped her. Tossed her clothes away. Kept that stranglehold on his lust.

"Too late," Drake said again as his fingers trailed up her bare thigh. "I can't ever let you go now. You came back...that was your mistake..."

"Not a mistake. Not...ah...*I missed you...*"

His fingers were between her legs. He was going to use care with her, even if it killed him, but he *had* to get inside of her. Because then maybe the terrible ache he felt would end.

Maybe.

Or maybe it never would vanish because Drake would never forget the fear he'd felt when he thought that he'd lost her.

She was already wet for him.

He was burning alive for her.

Drake pulled her to the edge of the desk. Her legs rose around him. She smiled.

He was lost.

He damn near ripped his clothes away, then Drake pushed into her, locking all of his muscles because he wanted to drive deep and take and take and take.

But he didn't. Slowly, inch by inch, he filled her. Sweat broke out on his brow as he held to his control. Then he was sheathed fully inside of her. As close to heaven as he'd ever get.

He pulled back. Thrust again, slowly, so slowly.

"Drake!"

She tried to push against him. He curled his fingers around her hips and held her there. He'd give her pleasure. As much as she could handle. And she'd never leave him.

Never.

He kept one hand on her hip, and his other slid between their bodies. Her eyes were on his. Her face flushed. Her breath panting.

Wet. Tight. Hot.

He strummed her clit. Worked her with slow touches and took her with long thrusts. Her breath panted out even faster. She choked out his name.

When she came, he felt the contraction of her delicate muscles all along his cock. That silken caress drove him over the edge and his own release pounded through him. He grabbed for the desk in that frantic moment, because he didn't want to hold her too fiercely. He nearly broke the desk as the climax churned through his body. Hot. Intense. The fucking best release of his life. The pleasure left him shuddering.

But not sated. Not done. He could never be done with her. They were just getting started.

"Drake, let me stay with you."

Let her stay? His head lifted. He could taste her. "I told you, princess, you made a mistake. My life's not worth living without you. I can't let you go again."

He kissed her once more.

"And even if I have to fight Noah, Saxon and that jerk Victor, I want you at my side. Always." He'd fight every enemy that he had—anyone who tried to keep him from her.

Her lips lifted in the smile that had first twisted his heart. "You don't have to worry about Noah. He's the one who told me where you were."

Well, well...*thanks, buddy.*

"As for Saxon and Victor, they are my family, but they know *you* are, too."

He was?

"No one will stand between us," she promised him. "There will never be anything between us again."

His chest wasn't aching anymore. He didn't hurt. But... "I don't want to hurt you." That was his fear.

"Then love me, Drake. Love me forever and you never will."

So easy. "I already do." He loved her more than life. "And I always will."

Her dimples flashed, and her smile was the most beautiful sight he'd ever seen.

Trouble.

Yes, he'd found it—and he was so glad that he had.

THE END

A NOTE FROM THE AUTHOR

Thank you so much for taking the time to read MINE TO CRAVE. I hope you enjoyed Drake and Jasmine's tale. The "Mine" books are such fun to write—dark tales of love and obsession.

If you'd like to stay updated on my releases and sales, please join my newsletter list.

https://cynthiaeden.com/newsletter/

Again, thank you for reading MINE TO CRAVE.

Best,
Cynthia Eden
cynthiaeden.com

ABOUT THE AUTHOR

Cynthia Eden is a *New York Times*, *USA Today*, *Digital Book World*, and *IndieReader* best-seller.

Cynthia writes sexy tales of contemporary romance, romantic suspense, and paranormal romance. Since she began writing full-time in 2005, Cynthia has written over one hundred novels and novellas.

Cynthia lives along the Alabama Gulf Coast. She loves romance novels, horror movies, and chocolate.

For More Information
- *cynthiaeden.com*
- *facebook.com/cynthiaedenfanpage*

HER OTHER WORKS

Trouble For Hire

- No Escape From War (Book 1)
- Don't Play With Odin (Book 2)
- Jinx, You're It (Book 3)

Death and Moonlight Mystery

- Step Into My Web (Book 1)
- Save Me From The Dark (Book 2)

Wilde Ways

- Protecting Piper (Book 1)
- Guarding Gwen (Book 2)
- Before Ben (Book 3)
- The Heart You Break (Book 4)
- Fighting For Her (Book 5)
- Ghost Of A Chance (Book 6)
- Crossing The Line (Book 7)
- Counting On Cole (Book 8)
- Chase After Me (Book 9)
- Say I Do (Book 10)
- Roman Will Fall (Book 11)
- The One Who Got Away (Book 12)

Dark Sins

- Don't Trust A Killer (Book 1)

- Don't Love A Liar (Book 2)

Lazarus Rising

- Never Let Go (Book One)
- Keep Me Close (Book Two)
- Stay With Me (Book Three)
- Run To Me (Book Four)
- Lie Close To Me (Book Five)
- Hold On Tight (Book Six)
- Lazarus Rising Volume One (Books 1 to 3)
- Lazarus Rising Volume Two (Books 4 to 6)

Dark Obsession Series

- Watch Me (Book 1)
- Want Me (Book 2)
- Need Me (Book 3)
- Beware Of Me (Book 4)
- Only For Me (Books 1 to 4)

Mine Series

- Mine To Take (Book 1)
- Mine To Keep (Book 2)
- Mine To Hold (Book 3)
- Mine To Crave (Book 4)
- Mine To Have (Book 5)
- Mine To Protect (Book 6)
- Mine Box Set Volume 1 (Books 1-3)
- Mine Box Set Volume 2 (Books 4-6)

Bad Things

- The Devil In Disguise (Book 1)
- On The Prowl (Book 2)

- Undead Or Alive (Book 3)
- Broken Angel (Book 4)
- Heart Of Stone (Book 5)
- Tempted By Fate (Book 6)
- Wicked And Wild (Book 7)
- Saint Or Sinner (Book 8)
- Bad Things Volume One (Books 1 to 3)
- Bad Things Volume Two (Books 4 to 6)
- Bad Things Deluxe Box Set (Books 1 to 6)

Bite Series

- Forbidden Bite (Bite Book 1)
- Mating Bite (Bite Book 2)

Blood and Moonlight Series

- Bite The Dust (Book 1)
- Better Off Undead (Book 2)
- Bitter Blood (Book 3)
- Blood and Moonlight (The Complete Series)

Purgatory Series

- The Wolf Within (Book 1)
- Marked By The Vampire (Book 2)
- Charming The Beast (Book 3)
- Deal with the Devil (Book 4)
- The Beasts Inside (Books 1 to 4)

Bound Series

- Bound By Blood (Book 1)
- Bound In Darkness (Book 2)
- Bound In Sin (Book 3)
- Bound By The Night (Book 4)

- Bound in Death (Book 5)
- Forever Bound (Books 1 to 4)

Stand-Alone Romantic Suspense

- Never Gonna Happen
- One Hot Holiday
- Secret Admirer
- First Taste of Darkness
- Sinful Secrets
- Until Death
- Christmas With A Spy

Made in the USA
Coppell, TX
14 October 2024

38651932R00184